D1825782

Love Interrupted

by

Jade Winters

Love Interrupted

by Jade Winters

Published by Wicked Winters Books

WICKEDWINTERS

Copyright © 2015 Jade Winters

www.jade-winters.com

ISBN: 978-1-518-67509-6

Other titles by Jade Winters

Novels

143
A Walk Into Darkness
Everything To Lose
Caught By Love
Guilty Hearts
Say Something
Faking It
Second Thoughts
Secrets
In It Together

Novellas

Talk Me Down From The Edge

Short Stories

The Makeover
The Love Letter
Love On The Cards
A Story Of You

Chapter One

Dylan grabbed a bottle of Jack Daniels from the kitchen worktop and took a hearty swig. Kicking off her heels and dropping her bag on the grey porcelain tiled floor, she hurried along the hallway to run a bath. She felt momentary disgust with herself. Of course, she had known what kind of man Mr Michaels was, yet she had helped him keep his fortune while the mother of his children lived a life of poverty. He was pond scum. No, even that was too good for him. He was Satan incarnate. So what did that make her? *A very good divorce solicitor!*

She grabbed a fresh towel from the airing cupboard, and her mind turned to her prize—the reward she would receive for being a traitor to her sex. It was a dirty job denying people a financial settlement they thought they were entitled to, but someone had to do it, so why not her? After all, she'd been groomed for the position ever since she had begun studying law ten years ago. Dylan smiled inadvertently at the thought of the hefty bonus and pay rise that was in store for her. The only thing that put a dampener on her spectacular win was there was no mention of the elusive partnership she so desperately wanted.

Dylan stripped naked and unceremoniously threw her clothes to the other side of the room before sinking into the soothing warm water, breathing in the bath oils she'd mixed. Bottle of Jack still in hand, she closed her eyes, turning her thoughts to the evening ahead. Dylan realised with dismay she hadn't had sex in over three months, which was a lifetime for her. Her latest case overwhelmed her to the point of working as many as sixteen hours a day. She barely had the time to sleep, let alone anything else.

'Sex or sleep? Sex or sleep?' she said aloud, lifting the bottle's neck to her lips. The burning liquid assaulted her throat and tongue, sliding down her gullet and warming her insides. Dylan hated to admit it, but she missed having a woman in her life. Not only for the sex but the companionship. Unfortunately, her work schedule allowed insufficient time to build a strong foundation for a relationship. When it came down to choosing between love or work, she always chose the latter, and she couldn't see that changing anytime soon.

'Oh, sod it, I can sleep when I'm dead,' she said, finally making up her mind to cruise the bars in search of someone she could connect with for a few hours. It would help to recharge her batteries for her next case. After all, it could be the one that finally propelled her onto the next step of the partnership ladder.

Chapter Two

Harper only realised it was after nine when the sound of her mobile phone broke her attention. She glanced down at the caller ID. *Oh crap, now I'm really in for it.* She cleared her throat and put the phone to her ear

'Hey, sweetheart. Now, before you say a word, hear me out ...'

'I'm all ears.' The voice on the other end of the line was cold and impersonal.

'I was meant to meet you earlier, right?' It was as clear as day that Harper was fishing. In all honesty, she couldn't actually remember their arrangements.

'Kaboom. She's suddenly regained her memory. Harper, I sat by myself in that damn restaurant for over an hour. The looks of pity were an embarrassment. Even the waiter knew I'd been stood up. I felt like a right prat. And to do this to me on my birthday of all days. How fucking humiliating is that?'

'Stella, God! I'm so sorry. Shit. I totally forgot.' Harper jumped to her feet and began clearing her desk. 'Twenty minutes. I'll be there in twenty.' *I need to get her a card, dammit! I hope Tesco is open. If I show up empty-handed, my life won't be worth jack shit.*

'Don't bother,' Stella mumbled. 'You're everywhere but where I need you ... always.'

'Come on now. That's so not true.' Harper scrambled for an example to prove her point, grabbing the first one that came to mind. 'Ha! I came to your nan's for tea last week,' she said triumphantly.

'And left after an hour!'

'Only 'cause there was an emergency at work.'

'Exactly. Work, work, work. It's all you bloody think about. Well, I hope it's worth it, 'cause I'm done with you and your shit. Go and play superhero on someone else's time.'

Harper dropped onto her seat. 'What the hell's that supposed to mean?'

'I'll make this really simple for you, shall I? We. Are. History.'

The line went dead. Harper stared down at her phone. *Is she for real? Dumping me over a missed date. What's the world coming to?* Okay, so she knew it wasn't just any date; it was the poor woman's birthday, but Stella hadn't even given her a chance to explain the importance of the case she was reviewing. If she had, she'd have known the blame for her absence lay at the door of the hot-shot divorce solicitor who had literally run circles around her colleague earlier today. Harper was all for trying to win the best outcome for a client, but some of the underhanded tactics played by the opposing solicitor to get the right deal for her own client, were outrageous. It seemed the rumours about Dylan Blue being cold-blooded and ruthless were true. *I bet she'd go as far as selling her own mother if it helped her win a case.* Harper closed the file she had been reading, opened her desk drawer, dropped it in, and slammed it shut. It was true she wanted to save the world. She wanted to be a beacon of light and stand up for those who had no voice.

Like me, once upon a time.

Harper grabbed a pile of work files from her desk and headed for the door. The one saving grace was that it wasn't her who had to tell the client that after being a housewife for forty years and rearing two sons, she was going to get nothing—at sixty-five the woman was now penniless.

Damn Dylan Blue—if Harper ever had the misfortune of crossing paths with that woman, she'd look her straight in the eye and tell her exactly what she thought of her.

Chapter Three

Robyn paced the living room floor, a pinched, tension-filled expression on her inflamed face. 'Why the hell should I have to pay maintenance for your baby?'

Abi blinked rapidly. 'Oh my God, I can't believe this. My ... *my* baby? Have you heard yourself? You're talking as if I planned for our baby by myself.'

'Rephrase that, Abi,' Robyn scowled.

'There's no "our". That's what I've been trying to drum into your thick skull for the past year.'

Abi cocked her head. Her heart pounded against her chest, but she fought to keep her voice steady. 'So what're you saying? That you're just gonna walk away like you've got no responsibility towards our child? 'Cause if you do, think again. I don't care what you say, Robyn, Jake's your son, and you're as much responsible for him as I am.'

Abi's estranged wife's illogical behaviour astonished her. Just over a year ago, Robyn was excited about trying for a child. Fast forward to today, and it felt like seven lifetimes ago.

'No, that's where you're wrong.' Robyn stopped near the dining table and pounded her fist on it, causing the contents to fly in the air. 'You think I'm going to let you and your greedy demands fuck up my life because you can't bear for me to be finally happy?'

'Finally happy?' Abi folded her arms over her

stomach. She tried to maintain eye contact with Robyn but bottled it, not able to bear the hate and anger in her eyes. Instead, her gaze dropped to the floor. 'So what was our time together then? All doom and gloom?'

Robyn took a few jerky steps towards her, then stopped abruptly. Sneering, she threw her hands in the air. 'I give up. Seriously, we're just going round in circles. From now on, I'm just letting my solicitor deal with you.' Brushing past Abi, she stormed towards the front door, kicking a packet of nappies lying in the hallway to the side. 'Look at the fucking state of this place. It's a shithole.' Roughly pulling up a folded buggy that had fallen in front of the door, she reached for the door handle and wrenched it open.

Abi did a quick run-walk behind her, glancing through the crack of Jake's bedroom door as she passed by. 'That'll be about right. Run away. Why did I expect anything different from you?' Abi called out as Robyn started towards the communal stairs. The stench of piss in the air was overpowering. Abi nearly laughed out hysterically when she saw Robyn's face crease in disgust. *Imagine having to frigging live here.*

Robyn stopped a couple of steps down and glared at Abi through a space in the railings. Her eyes burned into Abi's with mock pity. 'You've brought this all on yourself, not me.'

Abi slapped a hand on her forehead. 'Are you crazy? You're punishing me because I want you to be part of Jake's life. Despite the fact that you cheated on me. No mention of that in the divorce petition was there?' She stooped slightly, bending to hold the rail. Her trembling hands gripped the cold steel tightly. 'And now you don't wanna help raise him or pay maintenance. What kind of a mother are you?' she demanded, her eyes wide and wet with the sting of betrayal.

'A reluctant one,' Robyn said, raking her hands through her hair. 'And I'll tell you what's crazy. Expecting me to pay for a child that isn't even blood-related, that's crazy. If you want an easy ride, go and find yourself a rich sugar daddy.'

'You actually think I want the money for me?' Abi quickly scanned her immediate surroundings to see if any of her neighbours' doors were ajar, eavesdropping on their conversation. Satisfied they weren't, she continued, 'This isn't about us. My only concern is Jake and what he needs to make sure he has a decent upbringing.'

Robyn fixed her with a stony stare. 'No, what I think is that you're jealous that I've found someone else.' She spat the words through gritted teeth. 'It burns you that I've got someone younger, doesn't it?'

Abi said nothing. Instead, she watched as Robyn broke into a run, taking two steps at a time. Seconds later, she heard the entrance door slam shut with finality. Despite the warm air, she involuntarily shivered and wrapped her arms around her chest. Defeated, she slowly returned to her flat. She had neither her youth nor beauty with which to retaliate.

She was just a single mother, working two jobs, trying to make ends meet. Robyn was right about one thing, though. Her life was a mess, and she had no one to blame but herself.

She had given up her dreams and aspirations for love and look where it had landed her.

Chapter Four

Adrenaline coursed through Robyn's body as she jumped into the driver's seat and slammed the door behind her. She dropped her forehead onto the steering wheel with a muffled thud. 'That bloody woman infuriates me.' Mimicking a growling dog, she then added, 'How did I let this happen to me, Tiffany? How?'

'Calm yourself down and tell me what happened,' Tiffany chastised, rummaging through the Subway bag sat on her lap.

'Abi's still going on at me about wanting money for the baby.'

When Robyn initiated divorce proceedings a week ago, she had stupidly assumed the process would be a quick one. She hadn't considered for a second that Abi would be so hard to get rid of. She was refusing to get divorced until Robyn agreed to pay for her baby's upbringing. *Like that's ever going to happen.*

Tiffany unwrapped her sandwich and took a large bite from it, chomping away with her mouth open. 'You're gonna have to sort this out pretty sharpish 'cause you're gettin' seriously borin'. All you ever yap on about is that bloody baby and her mother.'

Robyn tilted her head to the side and grimaced. 'Weren't you taught not to speak with your mouth full?'

'Hey, don't start gettin' arsey with me,' she said firmly. 'I ain't the one tryin' to fuck you over.'

Robyn closed her eyes and groaned.

'You're right. My bitch of an ex is.'

'Anyway, maybe you should take your dad's offer of gettin' you a new solicitor? The one you've got at the moment is an idiot.'

'You've got that right. Seriously, what solicitor in their right mind would think handing over fourteen hundred quid a month for a baby that isn't mine, is "reasonable"? It's daylight robbery. I'd rather go on benefits than have to pay it.'

Robyn sank back in her seat and wiped the thin film of perspiration from her forehead with the back of her hand. Just when she thought her life was on the up and up, a big black cloud appeared, pelting fat raindrops down on her dreams.

She had spent months fantasising about making love with Tiffany in Venice while the gondolas hovered on the water, their fire-lit lamps reflecting on the rippling waves of the lazy canals. The two of them sipping red wine in the vineyards of Tuscany at sunset, enjoying the good life. Abi's stubbornness had soon put a stop to that. Until her divorce was finalised, the plans for Robyn's work promotion and transfer to Italy were on hold.

Tiffany devoured the remaining piece of her sandwich, only speaking once her mouth was empty. 'So whatcha gonna do then? Something's gotta give.'

Robyn huffed. 'The one saving grace is Abi can't

afford a solicitor. So, yeah, I think I will let Daddy hire me someone new. Someone who can put the fear of God into her. There's no fucking way I'm letting some over-the-hill has-been ruin my life.'

In the cold light of day, Robyn saw Jake as just another burden, the same as his mother, and Robyn wanted nothing to do with either of them.

Tiffany flipped down the mirror and messed with her hair. 'So that's sorted then. Let's go and get pissed. All this drama between you two is depressin' the fuck out of me.'

'It's quite frightening.'

Tiffany pulled a face. 'What is? Goin' out for a drink?'

'No. To see how much Abi has changed. She looks like shit.'

Robyn's mind sourced hazy images from a time when Abi looked so hot; just one glance from her ocean-blue eyes was enough to seduce Robyn on the spot. How she used to love running her fingers through Abi's thick, long, glossy hair. *That was before she became pregnant with that parasite.* Ever since she gave birth, Abi had been a shadow of her former self. Dark shadows under her eyes and a pale complexion seemed to be her permanent features nowadays. Robyn glanced over at Tiffany as she ran liner carefully along the curvature of her lips. Licking her lips to moisten them, she applied her lipstick and rounded it off with strawberry gloss. Tiffany was just what she liked, her fresh skin still unblemished and smooth. Robyn loved young women. They were so impressionable. They had no idea what life was really about, how cruel it could be, or how easy they were for men and women to feed on.

So young and sexy and, most importantly, childless. Tiffany's presence only served to remind Robyn what a lucky escape she had made. What on earth had possessed her into thinking she wanted to commit to family life? *I'm way too young to be sitting at home every night with a dribbling sprog.*

Robyn fired up the engine, glanced out the window at the decaying block of flats Abi was holed up in, and pressed her foot down hard on the accelerator, causing the car tyres to screech as the car took off along the road. She would stop at nothing to get Abi and Jake out of her life for good—nothing!

Chapter Five

'Ted, I couldn't get the potatoes, so I didn't make bangers and mash,' June explained, her hands fanned out in front of her defensively. Ted moved threateningly towards her under the cruel brightness of the kitchen bulb that hung from its electrical cord. Outside, the weather was as wild as Ted's eyes, teeming with fury.

Still nursing a stomach ache from this afternoon's vomiting spell, June prepared herself for the impact. Before she could brace herself adequately, Ted's drunken frame planted a hefty wallop across her face, taking her clean off her feet. The small woman fell with her forehead hitting the table, sending a chair clattering down with her and skidding across the floor.

'I told you I don't eat rice!' Ted bellowed through a foaming mouth reeking of brandy. At sixty-five, Ted was out of shape, his jawline concealed under layers of unshaven fat, and his belly jiggled over the belt of his trousers.

'You will make me some proper bloody dinner woman, or I swear to God you'll be sorry. I take care of this house; I pay for everything ... yes, even the goddamn cigarettes you suck into your lungs every day. All I ask is a proper fucking meal, and you give me this shit.'

He picked up the plate of rice and pork sausages,

flinging it across the kitchen where it connected with the wall with a mighty crash. The whole floor was covered in food; food June spent half an hour preparing. Now on her knees on the floor, she had no way of shielding herself against his kick burying itself in her ribcage, making her screech like a tortured kitten. Her face contorted in pain, and she felt the sickness of earlier take her once more. Ted stood over her as she spat bile and convulsed on the floor, choking and coughing.

'Am I supposed to feel sorry for you now? Christ, get your act together, June,' he ranted.

The empty bottle of Hennessey had fallen on the table when June's body slammed into it, spilling the last tumbler of alcohol. Ted set it upright before examining the remains of his dinner. June's head pulsed with dead pain that spread over her skull like a helmet, and her eye ached in the socket as she spat the last of the sour water from her gullet. She dared not look up yet as she heard the clinking of bottles inside the fridge door. They rattled under the force of Ted's inebriated tug while he violently pulled the door wide open. He belched out loud, took a beer and slammed the door carelessly before walking towards the living room.

'I'm hungry, June. Make it snappy,' he said nonchalantly as he left the kitchen.

June wanted to cry, but she physically couldn't. The abdominal pain she had been suffering for the past few months was only growing worse, and she found that she could hardly stand up straight anymore, let alone spend hours cooking the right food for her abusive husband's ever-changing preferences. He always ate rice. Now he refused simply because she could not get potatoes for mash. This had been a regular occurrence soon after he'd put a ring on her finger; he'd begun manipulating her actions and using the most ludicrous things as excuses to hurt her. June corrected her posture as best she could and crawled to the cupboard under the sink to get a bucket and cloth for the mess she inadvertently made on the kitchen floor. She could hear him knocking things over in the living room, but she would never go in there now, not for complaint or assistance. June was certain Ted would kill her in a fit of rage eventually. Sometimes she wished he would, if only to rid her of the excruciating abdominal pain she had to endure in silence so as not to set him off.

After she cleaned up the puke and washed her hands, June started to cook pasta, hoping it would appease her unstable husband. The rain came down just as darkness started to fall, making the sky eerily purple behind the grey clouds that ushered in the darkness over Dorchester. It was a metaphor June did not need to entertain right now, the coming of the night over the land, just like whatever demon ate her entrails was slowly consuming her body.

June had made the biggest mistake of her life the day she married him. *A sweet charmer hiding behind a dark facade.* She thought she was doing the right thing, giving her ten-year-old daughter a father that she'd never had. Instead, she'd lost her. In the end, June had no choice but to force her only child out of the family home. It was the only way she could protect her before Ted turned his attention towards her. Somehow, June had managed to hide the domestic abuse. Coming out with plausible stories for a bruise here, a black eye there. The broken ribs were well hidden beneath her clothes. She couldn't let her know what kind of man she'd brought into their lives. Knowing her strong-willed daughter, she would have tried to make June leave. That would have cost them both of their lives, June was sure. *If he's going to kill me, I pray to God I get to see Harper again before he does.*

Chapter Six

'Cathy,' Dylan said to her personal assistant, handing her the notes for a statement. 'On my desk. Two o'clock.'

Cathy slumped. 'Eek! Can I finish after lunch? I was supposed to meet my mum.'

Dylan froze in her tracks. Her eyes narrowed. 'Two o'clock, Cathy. No later. See your mother on your time—not mine.'

'If you insist,' Cathy conceded, reaching for her mobile phone.

Dylan could feel Cathy's eyes burning into her back until she kicked the door of her office shut behind her. She no doubt thought Dylan was the Wicked Witch of the East, but she was unapologetic about her demands. That was how she did things. If it had to be done, it had to be done yesterday. It had to be flawless, and no matter what sacrifice was needed, she would lay it on the line. All or nothing, that was Dylan's approach to her career, and she did not mind cracking skulls to achieve it.

Dylan's phone rang and, noting the caller, she picked it up immediately.

'Dylan. My office, please,' Gregory Maynard requested in his calm authoritarian tone.

'I'll be right there.' Dylan replaced the phone on its receiver. She grabbed her notebook and pen from her desk before hurrying out of her office and down the hallway.

'Good afternoon.' Dylan smiled as she entered his lavish office. 'I didn't see you this morning. Big case?'

'Is there any other kind at this practice?' he asked, closing the door behind her. 'Please, sit.'

Dylan sat on the leather seat in front of his desk while Gregory positioned himself on the edge of the desk, propping himself against it and folding his hands in front of him.

'We have a new case,' he began. 'A good friend of mine has a daughter who wants a quickie divorce.' He rubbed his hand through his greying hair, bringing it down to his chin. 'We "have" to make this happen, Dylan. He's placing his faith in this firm and me.' He got up and walked over to the window, staring down from the 8th-floor office, overlooking Temple, London's legal district.

'Is the father anyone I know?' she asked, shifting uncomfortably in her seat.

'Max Massey. The CEO of Magenta.'

'The investment company in the Docklands?'

He turned to face her and raised his dark eyebrows. They conflicted with the short brush of straight grey hair overhanging his forehead. 'You've heard of them?'

'I have, yes, from my time at law school.' A ripple of self-satisfaction ran through her. 'So he wants his daughter's case to be handled as discreetly as possible?'

'Now, see, that is exactly why I know I can rely

on you.' He strode back to his desk. 'Here's the file,' he said, passing her a thin case file she was almost disappointed with. 'This case needs to be cut and dried. It can't go to court. A baby is involved, and it just might ruffle a few feathers with the more moral citizens. I don't want the media getting wind of it.'

'Consider it done,' she answered, perusing the first few pages.

Gregory resumed his position, propping himself on the corner of his desk. 'You know what a favourable outcome for our client will mean?' he said, his steely look demanding attention.

'We scratch his back, and he'll scratch ours.'

'Correct. So I want you to impress the client. I want her to report only good things back to her father,' he explained, his usual tranquil tone making him sound more like a professor of theology than a deadly advocate.

'I'll take care of it,' she reassured him.

'Good.' He nodded. 'And don't forget, look into everything.'

'Of course.'

Gregory continued, 'We can never afford to be lenient or ignorant, not for a minute, you see?' His clear blue eyes that belied his age bored into hers. 'Even the strongest armies have to keep stock of their enemies' positions. You never know who we might come up against.' He folded his hands around his bent knee.

Dylan couldn't help but smile. On his wedding

finger, a single gold band shimmered, confronting the irony of a man who made a living from broken marriages and spousal abuse, bitter custody battles and heartbreak, while he lived in blissful harmony with his wife.

'Understood. I'll take a look at the file and contact his daughter to set up an appointment,' Dylan said. She stood up, straightened her skirt, and walked towards the door.

'One more thing, Dylan,' he said quickly.

She turned to face him, her eyes remaining fixed and unwavering. 'Yes?'

'If you get the desired outcome, you'll be up for Junior Partner.' He broke out into a grin. 'That's how confident I am in your abilities.'

Dylan beamed, fighting the feelings of dread that flooded her at the same time. Those were the words she had longed for since she started working for the firm. For now, she avoided the immense pressure of Maynard's expectations and enjoyed the moment.

'Thank you. You know I won't disappoint you,' she asserted with a slight bow of her head.

'I know, Dylan, I know. You are my daughter after all.'

***

In her spacious office, Dylan sat at her glass desk and flicked through Robyn Massey's file. 'Let's see what we've got here, then?' she said as she scanned the pages. The case looked simple enough to Dylan. Ms Massey and her soon-to-be ex-wife had been married for five years. A quick glance at Ms Massey's income showed she was a high earner. *One hundred and fifty grand a year.* Dylan let out a low whistle. *Not bad for working for Daddy.* The child in question was three months old. Robyn Massey wasn't the biological mother although her name was on the birth certificate. Dylan scanned the rest of the pages, checking to see who was representing Robyn's wife.

That's strange. No solicitor. Open and shut for sure. Why on earth would it be handed to me? Not that she cared. The quicker the win, the faster she moved up the work ladder. She continued reading, noting quickly that Robyn Massey's previous solicitor had only filed a divorce petition. There was one problem concerning maintenance for the baby. Her new client wanted to absolve herself of any responsibility.

Dylan cupped a hand to her chin. 'Hmm, this could be interesting after all.' Before she could plan her strategy, she would need full disclosure on the arrangements the couple made regarding the pregnancy—before and after. As well as any affairs or transgressions, something Dylan knew most people were reluctant to share, to the detriment of the case outcome.

She put her feet up on the desk and read carefully. Piece by piece, she picked apart the circumstances of the case, as she always did. This way, she could find discrepancies more easily and reshuffle the facts. This was called *spinning*—twisting the facts to serve the purpose of the spinner's intentions, and Dylan was a master of it.

A knock on the door revealed Cathy. In her hand, she held a folder with the statement she had completed during her lunch break.

'Ah! Thanks, Cathy,' Dylan said curtly. 'This one will have to wait now. We have a new client that gets preference over Mr Wallow.'

Cathy's mouth fell open when Dylan took the folder and tossed it into the 'To Do' tray for later attention.

Looking at Cathy with one eyebrow slightly raised, Dylan asked, 'What?'

Cathy's cheeks turned scarlet. 'Nothing. Nothing. I'll have a quick snack in the kitchen, if you don't mind, having missed lunch to finish your urgent work.'

Dylan answered very cordially, 'Of course, Cathy. Take all the time you need. You deserve it.'

Cathy's eyes widened, but she remained silent as she turned on her heel and left.

Dylan sank back in her chair, smiling at her personal assistant's futile exasperation, before returning her attention to the file.

Chapter Seven

Abi crept into Jake's bedroom. The baby slept like a rock, unmoved, apart from the tiniest light snore. He didn't seem bothered by the small, cramped space into which she'd managed to squeeze his wooden cot. Nor the drab pine furnishings that surrounded him. In an attempt to brighten the place, Abi had painted the walls in a soothing pastel colour and hung animated pictures of animals and teddy bears. It wasn't perfect, but for now, it would have to do.

Abi tucked Jake's blue blanket under his chin and rested the palm of her hand against his cheek. Her heart squeezed painfully at the thought of leaving him. 'Don't worry, little one, Auntie Tia's here.' She spoke softly as she leant into the cot and kissed his forehead. 'She'll take care of you while Mummy's at work.'

It was hard to believe that at one stage a baby was the last thing Abi wanted. Until the age of thirty-eight, she was the sole carer for her elderly parents. When they both died within six months of each other, despite her grief, she was relieved her caring days were over and was looking forward to only having herself to think about. It would have remained the case had she not met Robyn.

She heard a creak behind her, and the door opened. Abi's sister edged into the room and stood beside her. Tia was slightly taller than Abi with a mass of frizzy blonde hair trailing halfway down her back.

'Why don't you let him sleep a bit longer? I'll look after him here today. He looks so peaceful and angelic.'

Abi tilted her head and sighed. 'I know. And to think if it wasn't for Robyn's insistence on us having a child, he wouldn't even be here.' She snorted. 'I thought I'd finally made it, Tia, despite all the odds. Instead, I'm working two dead-end jobs, I've got bills coming out my arse I can't afford to pay, and all the responsibility of being a single mum. Some fairy tale ending, aye?'

Tia bumped her shoulder. 'Come on. Don't be so hard on yourself. You weren't to know that Robyn would turn out to be the lowest of the low.' Tia glanced down at Jake, then whispered, 'All that matters is something good came out of the whole sorry mess.'

Abi nodded her head in agreement. *Yes, I have Jake, if nothing else.* 'Do you think I'll ever figure Robyn out?'

'Why do you need to?'

'I dunno. I mean, it's fair enough if she doesn't want anything to do with me, but what's Jake done?'

Tia gripped Abi's hand. 'Maybe Robyn's just an arsehole. Who knows and, to be honest, who cares? Some people can't cope when kids come into the picture. But do you know what? That's her problem, not yours.'

'I didn't tell you this before, but as soon as I became pregnant, Robyn wanted me to have an abortion. That's despite it being her idea. Explain that one if you can.' Abi sighed. 'Apparently I pressured her into parenthood.'

Abi still couldn't believe the juvenile capacity by which Robyn, a normally intelligent person, could determine such a thing.

Tia's expression faltered just a fraction. 'What a bitch. And there I was thinking her cheating on you with that slut was as low as she'd go.'

Abi's jaw tensed at the mention of Robyn's unfaithfulness. The thought of Robyn and her young lover made her feel physically sick. She fought to keep the bitterness out of her voice when she spoke. 'It's a pity Robyn doesn't share your morals.'

'Let's hope karma bites her in her fat arse. If it's true what I heard about her girlfriend, it will, tenfold.'

A breath hitched in Abi's throat as she envisioned the two of them. Happy and in love, with not a care in the world. There was no worse feeling than the sting of realising that your wife was loving someone else, and you had now become invisible. A close second was being left alone to deal with all the responsibilities because you and your child simply became inconvenient. The irony amazed her sometimes; how the very thing she never wanted, the perceived bane of her existence, became the one thing that kept her going—the one thing that inspired her and would love her unconditionally.

'Like you keep telling me, I just need to take one day at a time and stop thinking so far ahead.'

Tia placed a hand on her shoulder. 'That's right, so no more moping about, alright? Get some fire in your belly. Let that bitch know you're not gonna be her doormat anymore. I know the old Abi's in there dying to get out.'

'Please, less of the old. My creaking joints are the only proof I need to know I'm no spring chicken.'

'Young, old, it doesn't matter. You'll meet someone one day. In the meantime, you need to get Robyn out of your head.'

Abi raised a smile, but there was no humour in it. 'That's easier said than done, believe me.'

Despite what her head told her, Abi still missed Robyn—*her Robyn*. She missed being loved, the companionship, and the feeling of being important to someone. But she knew in her heart Robyn wouldn't be coming back to her. It was over. Their once sweet love had gone sour, no matter how she wished it was otherwise.

'Nothing lasts forever, Abi. Not even heartache.'

Abi leant into the cot and pecked Jake's chubby cheek, then pushed herself back to a standing position. 'Anyway, enough of this. I'd better go and get ready for work.' She made for the doorway, turning to face Tia before stepping out into the dank, dark hallway. 'You're the only one that's been there for me. I don't know what I'd do without you.'

Tia smiled. 'Well, it's a good thing you and Jakey aren't going to have to, isn't it? I'm not going anywhere.'

If I could at least afford to pay her for looking after Jake, I wouldn't feel so guilty. Abi had been forced back to work only a few weeks after Jake's birth. Robyn had kicked them out of their home, with no thought to what they would live on or where they would go. Luckily, Abi had managed to find a small flat that she could just about afford. Thinking of money, Abi's heart sank when she realised she still had four days until payday with only five pounds left to her name. After paying the rent, food bills, and all the stuff Jake needed, she was barely keeping her head above water. Abi refused to go on benefits. Why should she when she had a wife who should be contributing to their son's upbringing?

Against her better judgement, Abi found her mobile in her bedroom and sat down on the bed, squeezing it between her hands. She took a minute to gather her thoughts. The message had to be quick and to the point. She knew how Robyn hated time wasters. Abi turned the phone upwards and typed out a text message with great reluctance.

> *Hi, Robyn. I was wondering if you can help Jakey and me with some money for food, please. Have not been able to make ends meet this week. Thanks in advance.*

When she pressed the send button, her fingers left behind a residue of vapour, her heart pounding from the unpleasant rush of having to engage with Robyn at all.

Her heart stopped as her phone buzzed.

'Please don't make me regret texting you Robyn,' she said, anxious inside.

Her sweaty fingers opened the message. It was a simple reply, but it carried chapters of psychology within it.

No, I won't give you any money. Not now, not ever. That's what you have a job for.

Chapter Eight

Still reeling from Robyn's text message, Abi gave up trying to hide the fact that she was crying. By some sort of grace from God, she found herself walking to work in heavy rainfall. Like her tears, the water came unrelenting. Rapidly darting like phantoms, the people who passed her by shimmered in and out of her line of sight. A blast of wind blew back her hood as she hastened through the sheets of rain, wetting her hair and spoiling the meagre make-up she'd applied. She roughly pulled her hood back on top of her head. The more she thought of Robyn, the angrier she got— denying her money for food was the final straw. *How can she be so cruel? So uncaring? All I ever did was love her, and this is how she repays me. By shitting on me from a great height.* Up until now, Abi had played by the rules. But no more. She was going to have to stop feeling sorry for herself if she was going to pull her shit together.

All great wars have begun with one foot, not a foot advancing towards the enemy, but a foot put down. For Abi, that war had just begun. That revitalizing thought made her raise her head. Across the street, under the turmoil of the darkening sky, she noticed a brown building. It was an old, weather-torn lump of bricks that had been beautifully restored. *Am I going blind? How could I have not seen it before? I walk down this street every day?*

Yet there it was, larger than life in its quiet authority. She crossed the road and stood in front of the towering building. A small plaque in marble had black chiselled lettering on it that convinced Abi that all things did happen for a reason:

Syner & Associates—Solicitors

Did it have to rain for me to finally see what has been right in front of me all this time? Abi's mum had always told her that 'some solutions could only be seen through tears'. A faint smile played on her lips as she added her own thoughts. *Just as some restored old buildings can only be seen through veils of rain.* With little regard for the hour, Abi veered from her usual timed course to work and entered the building.

Inside the lobby, the heavy glass door slammed behind her with a clamour. Abi flinched, waiting for the glass to shatter and then let out a sigh of relief when it remained intact. She eyed her immediate surroundings with interest. Two large curtain-less windows stretched from the high ceiling to the floor where huge potted plants obscured their bottom windowsills. Only black wrought iron bars adorned the windows as if the renovators wished it to be a prison. The polished wooden floor was covered by a large Persian rug.

Above the only entrance to a wide corridor, Abi admired a painting that held a tinge of menace to it. Sharp and contrasted, the oils on the canvas depicted a stunning redheaded goddess, standing before two giant doors. Under her flowing red hair was a beautiful pale body and face, but her eyes were positively striking. Bright blue, narrowed eyes pierced Abi's as if she were being watched by a depiction from centuries before.

'Who are you?' she asked the painting inadvertently, and almost immediately she felt utterly stupid.

'Her name is Syn.' The words came from behind her, silky and smooth.

'Oh my God.' Abi slammed her hand on her chest and turned to face a woman just escaping the chaos of the rain. Despite the weather conditions, the woman's sleek blonde hair remained perfectly unruffled.

'I'm sorry. Did I scare you?' The woman smiled as she closed the front door and wiped her feet on the mat carefully.

'Um, uh ...' Abi awkwardly shook her head. 'Actually, no. I just feel silly for talking to a painting.'

The newcomer shook her head. 'Not at all. In churches, people speak to statues and pray to unseen spirits, so to speak. There is power in faith, no matter what the medium, I say.' The woman's grey-green eyes sparkled with mischief. 'Harper Anderson.'

Abi took an instant liking to her warm nature. 'Nice to meet you. I'm Abi.' Abi smiled and briefly shook the woman's elegant hand. 'What did you say her name was?' She pointed at the painting of the stern deity.

'S-y-n, pronounced as "sign". She's the Norse

goddess of ... well, a few things, one of which is justice. But there's a special twist because this handmaiden presides over unfair cases—those where people have been wronged unjustly, and they need an advocate to vindicate them in a court of law,' Harper explained to Abi in a dreamy voice while admiring the painting. It was clear that she was a fan of the goddess. She looked at Abi and, in a rather playful, almost adolescent voice, she said, 'Cool, huh?'

Abi laughed and looked up at Syn's firm expression, and deep inside she felt a sense of belonging, a sort of protection settling over her that she could not pinpoint.

'In that case,' she looked at Harper, 'I've come to the right place.'

'Are you here to see Charles ... or Martha, perhaps?' Harper asked.

'Oh, no. No. Actually, I don't really know who I came to see. I just ...' Abi lowered her eyes to the ground and sought the right words. She could feel the unfairness scratch at her sense of justice again, a slithering demon of emotions causing her eyes to suddenly brim with tears.

'Abi?'

Harper's voice floated in the air and, in Abi's troubled mind, the image of Syn came together with that sweet sound of compassion that soothed her and made her feel safe from the hurt scratching at her composure.

'I need help.' Her voice was high pitched as she

tried to cram the past year of her suffering into a few sentences. 'I haven't got enough money to live on … my baby will be the one to suffer … my wife doesn't want to support him … I can't go on like this anymore!'

Abi finally buckled under the emotional stress of reality and her preordained doom that she was convinced nobody in Britain's cruel judicial system would ever care to change. Here she was, pathetic and beaten, imploring a stranger just to listen, hoping that by some miracle it would seep through somewhere in karma's conduits.

'Abi. If I can help you with your problem, I will. Don't fret, okay?'

Immediately she felt stupid. 'I'm so sorry,' Abi said, fussing with her hair.

'You have nothing to apologise for. You're clearly under a lot of stress,' Harper said. 'Listen, I have half an hour free before my first client is due. If you've got the time, come to my office and tell me what this is all about.'

'But you don't understand,' she muttered. 'I can't afford to pay solicitors' fees, and my soon-to-be ex-wife knows it.' Abi sighed in defeat as she looked around the prestigious room, then at Harper dressed in an expensive grey suit. 'I doubt I could even afford a minute of your time.'

Harper looked at her quizzically and raised her eyebrows. 'You're in the middle of a divorce? Well, in that case, you really have come to the right place. And don't worry, you won't have to pay for my services.' There was a strong determination in Harper's voice as she led Abi towards her office. 'Your wife will, out of the settlement you're going to win.'

Chapter Nine

The cup of coffee warming Dylan's hands provided the much-needed caffeine boost her body was craving. She glanced at the oversized clock on the wall. Robyn Massey was due for their first appointment any minute. Putting the cup on her desk, she quickly checked the documents she needed Robyn to sign were all in place.

'Ms Blue,' Cathy said, suddenly appearing in the doorway.

'Christ, Cathy! You trying to give me a heart attack?' she cried with a gasp.

Cathy covered her mouth with her hand, but Dylan could see a glint of satisfaction in her eyes from making her jump. 'Ms Massey called. She's not coming. She wants you to meet her at her office, instead.'

'Excuse me?' Dylan snapped, slipping her stylish black framed glasses a little down her nose to look at Cathy.

'She said, I quote, "I don't have time to drive all the way there for such a minor matter, it would be better for me if she met me at my office at five-thirty".' Cathy looked at her notepad where she had written down the address given by Robyn.

Dylan sat, stunned. Her pen dropped to her lap while she kept her eyes fixed on Cathy.

'You're messing with me, aren't you?' So Robyn Massey was playing true to form, wanting everyone at her beck and call. She sounded exactly like the arsehole her prior solicitor said she was.

'No, I'm not.' Cathy shook her head contritely.

'You're telling me, not only is she late for her appointment, but she now wants me to go halfway across the city in the rush hour because she deems our meeting unimportant?'

'Hey, don't shoot the messenger. If you leave now, it should only take ...' Cathy looked at her wristwatch. 'Around two hours,' Cathy finished gleefully.

'Jesus Christ! What a bitch!' Dylan raved just loud enough to rant and just soft enough not to be heard by any of her colleagues in the hallway. She slammed the folder shut on her desk and gestured for Cathy to bring her the jotted address.

'It's times like this I wish I had a clone to deal with clients,' she said as she perused the location.

'Two of you? How would the world cope?' Cathy said sarcastically.

Dylan narrowed her eyes but ignored her comment. 'God, I hate humans.'

'I hope you don't hate all of us, Dylan,' Gregory said, poking his head around the door and shocking Dylan back to reality as Cathy returned to her desk, tittering.

'No, of course not, just one at the moment,' Dylan said reflexively, waving her hand demonstratively across Robyn Massey's file. *Just this pain in the arse.*

'You know most, if not all, of our clientele, are

bona fide pricks.'

'Do I ever.'

He raised his eyebrows. 'Well-paying pricks at that.'

'I know.'

'And we have to accommodate their arrogance as far as humanly possible.'

'It's very unfortunate, though, isn't it?' she said, looking up at the ceiling thoughtfully.

'I totally agree with you.' He smiled, tapping his lean, gold-adorned wedding finger against the doorway's aluminium. 'But then again, we chose this profession because no matter how cordial we are, we know that evil pays. We don't condone it. We just make sure that those who do, make us rich in the process.'

'With respect,' Dylan smiled in obvious admiration, 'you're slicker than the Devil.'

'That's what you keep telling me.' He grinned. 'And I'm pleased to see you're exactly like me.'

Before Dylan could reply, he turned and walked off with a self-assured gait.

'The Devil would be nothing without his sinners, would he?' she said to herself as she gathered up her files, signed off from her laptop, and placed it in the black leather Samsonite sling bag she always carried with her. *Robyn's lucky this case is important to my dad otherwise I'd tell her to shove it where the sun don't shine.*

When she walked past Cathy's desk, she tossed a deposition in Cathy's 'In' tray and said, 'Needs

Maynard's signature after you re-draft it. Thanks.'

Dylan rushed to the lift and disappeared behind the silver sliding doors. But not before she heard Cathy say, 'Get knotted, Ms Blue.'

***

Dylan arrived at the specified address as directed by her sat-nav. While driving like a maniac through traffic, she'd repeatedly tried to call Robyn on her mobile to tell her that she would be at least another twenty minutes, which was a miracle in itself considering the time of day. Not that Dylan really cared. It wasn't her fault that Robyn had pissed her about—so if by being late she was inconvenienced, tough shit.

As she turned the corner of the front facade of the building, where the 'Reception' sign was hidden behind a giant Yucca bush, she saw a tall, slender woman with short spiky hair unlocking her Lexus. Trusting her gut instinct that this was her new client, Dylan pulled up to the car and lowered her window.

'Ms Massey?'

The woman turned to face her, nodding her head irately. 'Is this the service I'm paying for? You're late, I was just about to leave,' she barked, hands set on her waist.

Dylan was taken aback by the aggressiveness of the woman. Though attractive, her features were stern and her grey eyes steely cold—vacant, even.

Dylan smiled as she exited her car, taking her

time to move to the rear door and gather her belongings. Only after locking her car did she finally speak.

'May I remind you, Ms Massey that my services are paid for by your father. Therefore, I would appreciate you refraining from confusing me with the hired help. Also, I would kindly advise you to address me with respect.' She smiled to lighten the obligatory blow she had to deliver to circumcise Robyn's attitude. 'This advice is free—remember it and we're going to get on swimmingly.'

She watched as Robyn swallowed her attitude quickly with a sheepish smile. 'Sorry. I'm tired, it's been a long day.'

'Obviously. Shall we go inside to your office … unless you want to discuss your case out here?'

'No, inside,' Robyn said, gesturing to the door of the reception area. 'I'm sure you could do with a drink after your long drive over.'

If there was any malice behind Robyn's words, Dylan missed it. All she saw was a woman who seemed in shock that someone hadn't crumbled beneath her rudeness.

'I just need to go through the basics with you and get your signature on a few things. I won't keep you long.'

'No worries, take as long as you want, Ms Blue. I'm the one who's inconvenienced you, after all,' Robyn said, leading the way along the narrow path to the building.

'Yes, you did,' Dylan said haughtily as she remembered her evening plans had been interrupted because of this ill-mannered woman. Dylan strode into the air conditioned building with purpose and mentally pushed any grievances to the back of her mind. *Let the games commence.*

Chapter Ten

Harper's office smelt like the perfume counter at Boots. It was a well-known fact that Shay, her assistant, stopped by there daily before she bought her lunch from the sandwich shop next door. Although she hadn't been in Harper's office for a few hours, the fresh citrusy scent still remained. Harper stood by the window overlooking a busy main road. She liked to people watch and imagine the kind of lives they led, who they went home to—or not. Now that the working day had officially come to an end, she had a decision to make. With her mounting workload, should she take on Abi's case or pass it on to another colleague?

Harper had many single parents come through her door for help, but for some reason none had left the kind of impression Abi had. In a way, she reminded Harper so much of herself. Abi was certainly not ready to admit defeat, no matter how much she'd tried to convince herself that she was weak or inept. Deep down she was a fighter. With the constant blows her wife had laid on her, Harper was surprised that Abi wasn't on her knees already. She knew stronger women who wouldn't have got as far as she had.

A tap on the door broke into her thoughts. Shay, a petite woman with a slight limp and glasses, appeared in the doorway. Her glossy brick red hair fell on her shoulders with soft curls and her pale skin gave away her Irish origins. 'Well, what's it to be? Yay or nay?'

Harper looked at her quizzically.

Shay let out a frustrated sigh. 'You know what I mean. Abi. The woman that came in earlier.'

Harper made a snap decision there and then. 'At the moment, it's looking like a yay.' Somehow, she would have to fit her in. Even if it meant working late. Abi's lack of money wouldn't be a problem. Harper's firm allowed their solicitors to take on clients who couldn't afford to pay but didn't qualify for legal aid, at their discretion. But only if they thought they had a good chance of a settlement.

Shay broke into a grin. 'Fantastic! If a woman ever needed your help, it's her. I don't know how you do your job, listening to all of these people suffering. I heard Martha is thinking about leaving law and studying massage.'

Harper laughed. 'Martha, a masseuse? You've got to be kidding me.'

'Nope. Her assistant told me she's still in pieces after being ripped to shreds by one of the wolves over at Maynard's.'

'She'll be alright once she settles in. All newbies get dragged across hot coals in their first few cases. The memory soon fades after you've been round the block a few times.'

Shay looked doubtful. 'If you say so. But I wouldn't stay here if I were her. I'd rather be happy than miserable, regardless of the money.'

Harper smiled at her sadly. Shay Morgan had been in a serious car accident in which she nearly died. Instead of looking at her survival as a godsend, Shay's then husband turned his back on her. He'd told her she was broken goods because of the injuries she'd sustained and had divorce papers delivered to her hospital bed.

Syner & Associates were assigned to facilitate the divorce proceedings, and that was when Shay's plight compelled Harper to take her under her wing and hire her as an assistant when she was well enough to leave the hospital.

'Do you think you'll get a decent settlement?' Shay asked, scrutinizing Harper through her thin spectacles.

'She has a good case. I'm going to try my very best,' Harper told Shay matter-of-factly. 'I won't be fighting just for her, though. There's an innocent baby involved as well.'

'It's always the children who come off worst.'

'Yes, they do, and that's why I'm going to take great pleasure in hammering Abi's wife. Imagine abandoning a baby just because she decided motherhood didn't suit her.'

Shay gasped. 'Terrible. Absolutely terrible.' She dropped onto a chair opposite Harper and stared up at the ceiling in thought, her mouth agape. 'When I hear how cruel people are to each other, sometimes I wish I'd died in that car crash.'

Harper reached over and squeezed her hand.

'There're a lot of good people in the world, Shay. They're not all bad apples. Even the ones that pass through the doors of solicitors like Maynard's.'

'If you say so,' Shay nodded.

'Anyway, I've told Abi to contact the Child Maintenance Service to sort out support payments straight away. Her wife has just bullied her since they split. Forcing her to leave the family home, withholding money. If this goes to court she won't have a leg to stand on.'

'Is there anyone else involved?'

'Isn't there always?'

Chapter Eleven

Like liquid, metallic crimson, the nail polish poured itself from the tiny hairs of the brush and bled out onto Tiffany's fingernail. With expert precision, she gently spread the red stickiness from her cuticle to the edge of her elongated nail where it ended in a brisk spittle of gel. The smell always intoxicated Robyn. It reminded her of when she was a teenager, and she'd sleepover at her best friend's house. She would watch Melanie groom herself like a grown woman and fantasise about her running her newly-painted nails down her back, screaming out in ecstasy as Robyn fucked her senseless. Unfortunately, that's all it ever remained—a fantasy.

Tiffany blew on her nails. Her thick lashes twitched as she looked Robyn up and down. 'So are you gonna take your solicitor's advice or not?' she purred in her husky voice. It held so much authority, that hoarse porn moan of hers, and she knew it.

Robyn looked at her in mild alarm. 'What? Transfer some of my assets to my parents and give them even more power over me.' She shook her head. 'I don't think so. Besides she was only kidding. It's illegal to do that shit.' *Sometimes I forget she's only twenty-one. It's like dating a teenager. She doesn't understand anything about life.*

'You don't have to tell her. And you don't have

to do it with your parents. Do it with someone else. It makes sense if you don't want Abi gettin' her sticky fingers on your money.'

'In theory yes, but in reality there isn't anyone I trust enough ...' Robyn rubbed her hand over her face when she saw the disappointment on Tiffany's features. She didn't want to risk Tiffany falling into one of her strops. The last time Robyn had upset Tiffany over a trivial matter, Tiffany hadn't spoken to her for two whole days. Instead Robyn had been subjected to a lot of eye rolling, heavy sighs and the refusal to have sex. She was in no rush to get into her bad books again. 'Oh, fuck it. That's not what I meant to say. It's just too risky is what I mean.'

'You could always transfer it to me?' Tiffany said with not a sign present in her expression that she was joking.

'To you? Now, why would I want to do a thing like that?' Robyn asked, running her clammy palms down the sides of her thighs.

Tiffany sighed. ''Cause it's the only way you're gonna get outta this mess. Once your divorce is over, you can have it transferred right back, done and dusted.'

Why couldn't she at least have more than a couple of brain cells in her head? As if I'd hand over my money to the likes of her. If it weren't for the mind blowing sex, Tiffany would have been history months ago.

'Look, let's not spoil our weekend before it's even started,' Robyn said. 'Now help me choose something to wear.'

Robyn opened the wardrobe door and flicked through the clothes, unable to decide.

'Oh, for fuck's sake, Robyn. Just pick anything, will ya? If you take any longer, we're gonna get stuck in traffic,' Tiffany cried in dismay, her voice carrying that distinct force Robyn hated, the tone she took when she was not getting her way.

'Just give me a minute. Don't throw a tantrum like a fuc—' Robyn stopped abruptly when she caught sight of Tiffany's image in the mirror, her pretty young face distorted in what she could only construe as a dare for Robyn to finish her sentence. Robyn's eyes roamed over the perky mounds peeking through Tiffany's stringy top, her lean lines running into long, smooth legs. *If we don't get out of here soon, we'll never leave.* Reluctantly Robyn returned her gaze to her clothes and dressed quickly in a pair of jeans and a T-shirt. 'Come, let's go.'

'Finally!'

'I don't want to hear any moaning from you about the place when we get there either. I had to kiss my colleague's arse to get the keys to his house.' Robyn doubted Tiffany would find fault with the place, though. The pictures Robyn had seen of the lakeside property were stunning.

An hour later, Robyn's Lexus glided along the winding lanes. The Hertfordshire countryside was impressive in the stark contrast the grey sky lent the rolling stretches of green grass and trees.

'How far now?' Tiffany asked, shifting in her seat.

'Why are you so impatient? Can't you tear your eyes away from your bloody phone and look at the nature around you?' Robyn said, staring ahead at the small rusty signs emerging from behind the foliage flanking the road, directing her to the Manning plot.

'It's borin'. Who wants to stare at trees and grass? I'm not a cow, ya know.' Tiffany blew her gum into a bubble and burst it with a loud pop. 'Are you sure you know where we're goin'? I thought this car would have a sat-nav fitted,' she whined, tugging at her top.

Robyn was getting a tad irritated with her childish bitching, but the sight of her small, erect nipples protruding through her top mollified her instantly. *Why does she have such an effect on me?* Since meeting Tiffany she'd felt like a hormonal teenager, not the grown woman she was. *But I'm not complaining.*

'Do I know where I'm going? Of course I do. There we go. See? I told you,' Robyn said suddenly. She smiled like a little girl bragging to her mum for that little bit of praise. Ahead of them, in the cloudy light of day, a rusty overgrown gate slumped.

'Awesome,' Tiffany raved sarcastically.

Robyn stopped the car and got out to unlock the padlock that was hidden under the creepers and spider webs.

'Come on, you fucking piece of shit,' she cussed under her breath, making sure Tiffany could not see her wrestle with something as simple as a lock.

'Are you managing alright?' Tiffany called from

the car.

'Yes, just have to see which of the keys fit in here,' Robyn yelled back, wishing Tiffany would just shut her mouth and do something constructive for once.

Robyn slung the gate aside with great ceremony and wiped her hands on her jeans. The gravel road looked black in the embrace of the bright green long grass and shrubs rocking in the slowly growing breath of the wind. It took no more than a moment for the skies to open and the subsequent downpour to drench her T-shirt. Tiffany's words urging her to hurry to the house came back to annoy her.

'Fucking great,' Robyn complained through pursed lips as she ran for the car and jumped in.

'So are we gonna just sit here in the rain like a pair of muppets?'

'Seriously, Tiffany you need to stop now. You're grating on my nerves.'

'But it's pissin' down.'

'Tiffany, I'm not making it rain,' Robyn snapped as she navigated the slippery mess under the Lexus. *Nag, nag, nag. That's all she's done all fucking day.* Robyn gritted her teeth. She decided the best way to stay sane around Tiffany was to concentrate on the benefits of having her around. That way she wouldn't be at risk of having a heart attack or stroke at the age of thirty-five. 'The house is just around the corner. We can make a fire and fuck to our hearts' delight until the rain stops, alright?' she said with a smirk.

'Ha!' Tiffany exclaimed. 'How're you goin' to make that fire, lover? All the trees are wet, and we didn't buy any logs, did we? God, why do I agree to come out into these rugged spider-infested shit holes with you?'

'Stop complaining, for Christ's sake. I'm sure there will be wood inside,' Robyn said abruptly. So there might not be a fire. Big fucking deal. The fact that she'd brought her to this magnificent house for the weekend should have been enough. Especially as staying in such a place would be a step up for her. Tiffany was brought up on a council estate and if it wasn't for Robyn that's where she'd still be. *Most probably flipping burgers at McDonalds or something.* Robyn realised with a start that Tiffany was exactly like Abi. At the beginning it was all teeth and smiles, but once they had their feet under the table, they turned into ungrateful bitches, who were never pleased no matter what you did for them.

'I knew you'd manage to fuck the day up somehow, I knew it,' Tiffany said, completely ignoring Robyn's request.

'What do you mean?' Robyn's frown fell deep into her forehead as her voice grew louder in discontent. 'Well!'

Tiffany shrunk back in her seat. Robyn's thunderous question obviously sounded a bit too aggressive. A loud clank beneath the undercarriage of the vehicle snapped them both out of their engagement. The car sank to one side.

'What the fuck was that?' Tiffany yelled, gripping the edge of her seat.

'The car's stuck, obviously,' Robyn replied, dropping her foot on the accelerator to push the car forward, but the tyres just spun around aimlessly. Robyn's heart sank at the sound. Now she would never hear the end of it. But surprisingly, Tiffany said nothing. Like a hail of bullets on a tank the rain pelted the windows and body of the stationary car. Tiffany pulled out her mobile phone.

'What are you doing?' Robyn asked.

'Callin' my mate Billy to come and get me. What d'ya think?' Tiffany frowned, quite indifferent to the problem. 'Hey, Billy boy. Tiffany. Listen, do me a favour ...'

Robyn's heart thundered crazily, and a flush rose to her cheeks. 'Tiffany!'

'What?' she asked after she'd disconnected her call. 'You're welcome to come back with us. I just don't see the point of sittin' here in the middle of nowhere, waitin' for the rain to stop. We're stuck, rain or no rain.'

The audacity of the bitch drove Robyn beyond control. 'You shouldn't have done that.'

'Why not? I solve problems. I don't sit around moanin' about the situation,' she said nonchalantly. 'I mean, look at ya. If you have to go to court you're going to lose half of everything. You know you can hide it but you just boo hoo the idea. I'm startin' to think you just love all the drama.'

Robyn's jaw and fists tightened. Tiffany was pushing her over the edge. She didn't know when to back off. Any normal person would have picked up the cues that Robyn was annoyed, but not Tiffany. She existed in a world of her own, where everything and everyone revolved around no one but her and her wants and needs. This was one aspect of their relationship Robyn didn't like. Robyn liked to come first at all times.

'For God's sake, Tiff, not that shit again. Can't you leave it alone? I'll sort something out. Now what am I going to do about my car? I can't just leave it here.'

'Okay, keep your hair on.' Tiffany pulled her lips into a sarcastic smirk. 'I know what. You stay here with your precious car while I get back to civilisation. Call the AA, they'll come and babysit you,' she said with a tone of faux reassurance that bordered on patronisation.

Claustrophobia engulfed Robyn. She wound down the window for some much needed air and inhaled deeply. 'Tiffany, you're not leaving me here,' Robyn said sternly, locking her hand over Tiffany's wrist.

Tiffany gave her a frightened look. 'You're hurtin' me, Robyn.'

Within seconds, an eruption of volcanic anger exploded within Robyn over which she had no control. Robyn had never laid her hand on another person before but this was the closest she'd come. It took all her strength not to punch Tiffany straight in the face with all the force she could muster. Instead her anger came out through her words. 'You will not treat me like something you've just trod on, you little cunt. You might get away with that shit with your pathetic friends, but I will not tolerate your juvenile power plays, you hear me?' Robyn growled at her through the onslaught of the storm outside.

Tiffany's cheeks turned a chalky white. 'I don't know what you're talkin' about. Let me go.' She tried to yank her arm away, but Robyn's grip tightened.

'You're staying here with me. You go where I go. Right?' she said, sinking her nails deep into Tiffany's flesh. *I want to smash the fucking bitches head in.*

Tiffany nodded and smiled weakly. 'Whatever you say, Rob.'

Quivering with rage, Robyn dropped her arm. 'Good. Now get back on the phone to whatever arsehole you just called and tell him we've got it sorted.' She leant in, their faces barely inches apart. 'Don't fuck with me ever again,' Robyn said in a low threatening voice. 'Remember, anyone who gets in my way always lives to regret it.'

Chapter Twelve

'You have mail' pinged in the lower corner of Dylan's computer screen. Absent-mindedly her eyes drifted away from the letter she was reading and she clicked on the message icon. It was an email from Syner and Associates solicitors. Dylan leant back in her seat and smiled. The win remained fresh in her mind, and she still felt on a high. Syner & Associates? She didn't think their firms would cross paths again so soon. Dylan checked to see if the sender was Martha Thomas, the opposing solicitor she had sent cowering in defeat a few days before. It wasn't. It was from another solicitor by the name of Harper Anderson.

Dylan's eyes skimmed the email. One line in particular caught her undivided attention:

I will be representing the respondent Abi Massey ...

Dylan picked up the mug of coffee that had been sitting on her desk for the past ten minutes and pulled her face at the taste of the lukewarm liquid as soon as it made contact with her taste buds. She needed a few seconds to get her head around this new piece of information. *So the wife claiming to be broke and destitute has now gone and found herself a solicitor, and from Syner and Associates, no less.*

She fired back an email straight away:

I thought the Massey case was going to be uncontested?

A curt reply came minutes later:

It was, but not anymore. We shall be filing our own divorce petition.

So much for a cut and dried case. Dylan leant forward, clicked open the browser and typed Syner and Associates into the search engine. Within seconds, their website appeared on the screen. She clicked on the 'Our people' link in the navigation menu and then scrolling down, stopped at Harper's photo. Her immediate impression was favourable. *Hmm very nice. Blonde, just my type.* Not that she would pursue such a woman. The last thing she needed was to be involved with another solicitor who was married to her work as much as she was. No. Viewing the eye candy from afar would be enough.

Fine. I look forward to receiving it, Dylan wrote back and closed down her email. She didn't waste time with opponents who opted to play hardball with her. She was certain she could make Anderson accept her superficially merciful deal rather than make her client face a court case.

I think it's best to do a little background research on Harper Anderson and find out exactly who I'll be up against. On a whim, Dylan decided to blow out the hot date she had planned for that night. *Looks like it's going to have to be a quick drink at the pub and then home.* She would spend the evening going over Robyn's case and working on her strategy. Leisure time would have to sit on the back burner, *again.*

At ten to six, Dylan alighted from the taxi outside Holborn station. Pulling the band from her ponytail, she let her hair fall over her shoulders. Dylan could shed her professional demeanour now. Work time was over, and she could allow herself to relax for an hour or two depending on who was around. The Kings Tap was a watering hole where many of the legal fraternity hung out after work to let down their hair. It was where foes became friends.

Through the bustle of peak time pedestrian traffic, she made her way past the long line of shops and restaurants until reaching her destination. Dylan entered the pub and eased her way into the crowd. All around her, mainly in groups, men and women dressed like clones in tailored business suits, chatted animatedly about work.

A man of about fifty with thin wisps of hair protruding from a shiny bald patch stumbled into Dylan's path and gave her an appreciative whistle. 'Hello, darling. What's your pleasure?'

Dylan frowned. 'Sorry, what?'

'Drink?' He grinned, closing the gap between them, so his stale beer breath assaulted her nostrils.

Dylan stepped back, tossing her hair with an air of indifference. 'I'm meeting someone,' she stated firmly.

The man pulled his mouth into a sarcastic smirk. 'Your loss, babe.'

Dylan's gaze drifted briefly down the length of his body, then returned to his eyes. 'I doubt it.'

'Bitch,' he hissed before roughly pushing past her and moving on.

'Dickhead.' Dylan gritted her teeth. That was what she hated about straight bars. In 2015, a lone woman still couldn't go into one without being accosted. She wouldn't mind if she were out on the pull, but it was obvious from the clientele that it wasn't a pick-up joint. Pushing the encounter to the back of her mind, she started down the floor, squeezing herself between the crowds.

'Over here, Dylan,' she heard from her left. Dylan turned to see Dave, her work colleague.

'Hi there, how's everything?'

'In a word—hectic,' he said in a public schoolboy drawl.

An eager-looking barman appeared behind them. 'What can I getcha?' he asked.

'I'll have a dry white wine, please. Dave?' she looked at him enquiringly.

Dave shook his head. 'Nah, got to get off, the missus is expecting me.'

'One white coming up. Won't be a mo,' the barman said before darting off.

Dave drained the last dregs of his drink and planted it on the bar. 'Catch up with you during the week.' He took off his trilby and ran his fingers through his mane of dark hair before replacing it. Although he was only fifty, he looked a lot older. The dark shadows under his eyes only served to highlight his wan complexion. The relentless hours expected of solicitors didn't suit everybody, especially as people aged. Dave edged his way into the crowd and his tall, thin frame soon disappeared.

The chirpy barman returned minutes later with her wine, giving her a flirtatious smile as he accepted payment. Dylan smiled back politely and turned around to face the crowd, scanning the sea of faces for anyone she knew. Looking towards the back of the pub where it was less busy, she did a double take when she spotted a blonde woman sitting with a group of men. Squinting, Dylan leant forward slightly. *Is that Harper Anderson?* As if sensing she was being watched, the woman turned her head away from the man who was speaking animatedly to the group and looked in Dylan's direction. *It is her.* The combination of her sleek blonde hair and fine-boned features was breathtaking. Harper was undeniably gorgeous, much better looking in person than the picture on her firm's website.

She lost sight of Harper when the men she was sat with stood and put their jackets on, blocking her view. *Oh shit they're leaving.* Without thinking, Dylan took a step forward and squeezed through the throng of people, making her way closer to Harper's table, stopping a few feet away. She didn't know why she had the sudden urge to meet her. *Maybe it's because she's so goddamn hot.* Relief swept through her when she saw Harper still in her seat with her jacket hooked on the back of her chair. Seconds later, the group of laughing men left. Dylan waited until they were out of sight before she made her way to Harper's table.

'Harper Anderson?' she asked by way of introduction.

The woman looked up in surprise at the sound of Dylan's voice. There was no sign of recognition in her eyes.

'Dylan Blue,' Dylan said smiling.

'Oh,' Harper responded, unperturbed by their surprise meeting. She dropped the beer mat she'd been tapping the table with and picked up her drink.

Oh? What kind of a response is that? 'You emailed me this morning about—'

Harper took a sip of wine then placed her glass on the table. 'I know who you are,' she said curtly.

Dylan glanced behind her then back at Harper with a look of puzzlement. 'Have you mistaken me for someone else? 'Cause for someone you've never met before, you're being kind of ... well, frosty.'

'Am I?' the coldness remained in Harper's tone.

A short burst of laughter escaped Dylan's lips when she realised what the problem was. Martha was Harper's work colleague. Most solicitors didn't bare grudges against their opponents. They worked a case, it was won or lost and they moved on, had a drink and got ready for the next bout. Apparently, Harper Anderson didn't play by those rules. 'Oh I see. It's a camaraderie thingy is it? I steamroll your colleague in a case, and I'm the villain? I get it.'

After a moment of awkward silence, Harper leant forward in her seat. 'Not so much the camaraderie thingy as you put it. More like I don't like it when people scrape the barrel to win a case.'

'Then I'd say you must be doing a great disservice to your clients.' Dylan pulled out a chair. 'Do you mind if I sit?' Dylan sat without waiting for Harper to reply. 'So, Harper, I can call you Harper, right? Or would you prefer me to be formal and call you Ms Anderson?'

Harper tucked a strand of wayward hair behind her ear. 'Harper's fine.'

'So I'm in the doghouse for doing my job; is that it?'

For a moment, Harper looked as if she was going to speak, but after a moment's silence, she remained tight-lipped.

'I can see we're not going to hit it off, especially after my client comes out on top,' Dylan continued, determined to get a conversation flowing with Harper. Despite her hostility she liked the sound of Harper's velvet silk voice.

'You're very sure of yourself aren't you?' Harper said, tracing the rim of her glass with her finger.

'That's what I'm paid big bucks for,' Dylan said, her eyes glued to Harper's hands. She couldn't help but wonder what they would feel like caressing her naked body.

'Is that your master? Money?'

It took a few seconds to realise Harper was speaking to her. Dylan shuffled her chair closer to the table and gave her a fixed stare. 'No. I'm sure my master is the same as yours.'

'I doubt it?' Harper's upper body visibly tensed.

Dylan opened her mouth to fire off an equally rude retort, and then promptly closed it. If she was going to have to work with this very attractive but uptight woman, the last thing she wanted to do was get her back up. 'Look shall I just leave? Or can we act like a pair of adults and respect the fact that we don't have to see eye to eye on everything to get along?' She gave Harper one of her winning smiles that had melted some of the biggest icebergs she'd come across in her line of work. Harper's face remained expressionless. For a second, Dylan thought Harper had been immune to her charm, then slowly her face broke into a slight smile.

'Fair enough. We are working the same case after all.'

Phew! I thought I was losing my touch. 'Exactly,' Dylan readily agreed. 'You had me worried there for a moment.'

'You don't strike me as someone who's easily worried.' Harper's features softened, which made her even more attractive to Dylan.

'That all depends.'

'On?' Harper asked.

Dylan's eyes dropped to Harper's sensuous

mouth. 'On who's causing me to worry.'

Harper shifted in her seat. 'Is that right? I'll have to keep that in mind.'

'But I'll tell you what is worrying me, though.' Dylan frowned. 'That your client is being difficult by filing her own divorce petition. If she wants a divorce why doesn't she just agree to my client's petition?'

'Because it contains a pack of lies.'

'That's a matter of opinion,' Dylan replied. 'So what exactly does she want?'

'Only what she deserves.'

'Which is?'

'All assets accumulated during the marriage divided down the middle and a fixed amount of maintenance until the child is eighteen,' Harper said.

Dylan threw back her head and let out a short burst of laughter. 'Come again. I think I heard you say something about dividing the assets down the middle?' She nodded towards Harper's glass. 'What else you got in there. 'Cause right about now, I could use some.'

'Just wine. And you heard right.'

'You weren't kidding?' Dylan asked.

'Nope.'

Dylan shook her head slowly. Harper wasn't pulling any punches, and she liked that about her. She was straight forward and to the point, but having attributes she liked didn't mean she was going to get her way. 'You do know that's out of the question don't you?'

'No, what's out of the question is your client

thinking she can walk away without any responsibility whatsoever.'

'Ha! Okay, all jokes aside now. Did someone send you here to wind me up? Has someone planted hidden cameras?'

'No cameras. Just plain old me.'

I don't think there's anything plain about you. 'Do you really think I would advise my client to accept those terms? Considering how much she's worth and how little your client contributed?'

'I think,' Harper leant towards the table giving Dylan a bird's eye view of her cleavage, 'your client will be getting off lightly by agreeing to these terms.'

'Look, Harper. I'll tell you something right now. I don't beat around the bush. If I didn't find you so attractive, I wouldn't still be sitting here right now.'

Harper's eyes widened. 'Wow, okay, I wasn't expecting that.'

'I didn't think you were easily shocked.' Dylan took a sip of wine before continuing. 'I did a little research about you. I know you were the first openly gay solicitor to come out in your firm when you started there five years ago. You're a bleeding-heart liberal, which is the only reason I wasn't personally insulted by the offer you want to put my client's way ... you're from ...'

Harper raised a hand to silence her. 'As much as I'd like to sit here all evening while you wax lyrical about my life, I'm already familiar with it. What's your point? The offer is a generous one as far as I'm concerned.'

'Is that right?'

'Yes, that's right.'

'No way,' Dylan chuckled in her condescending way. 'Your client won't get what she wants. No way.'

'Look, as you just said, your client is worth a lot of money. I'm also sure you know that her father is a very prominent businessman. Would your client really want this case to be dragged through the courts?' Harper said with a grin. 'And the media?'

The gentle offence in her friendly voice was a kick in the jaw to Dylan. For the first time in her life, she was nearly speechless.

'So you want to play it like—' Dylan started aggressively, but Harper cut her off.

'—I can just see the headlines now "Lesbian daughter of millionaire Max Massey, cheats on wife then throws her and their baby out onto the street".' Harper smirked.

Dylan's mouth dropped open. 'You wouldn't.'

'Like I said, Ms Blue. It all depends on whether your client accepts our offer ...'

'Call me, Dylan, please,' Dylan said, trying to buy time. 'I'm going to have to discuss this with my client.'

'Okay, Dylan, I will have our offer typed out in the morning and couriered to your office for your attention,' Harper stated professionally. 'Call me and let me know your client's decision. Fair enough?'

Dylan smiled and nodded, somehow managing to hide the fury within. It was the first time ever that she'd been outwitted like this. 'Can I ask how your client can suddenly afford you after pleading poverty?'

'Because she can,' Harper replied, bringing the glass to her lips and taking a sip.

'What do you mean because she can? You can't possibly be that cheap,' Dylan said inadvertently as the wine began to loosen her tongue in all the wrong ways.

'There are so many replies to that statement.' Harper laughed. 'But since we're talking business, I won't go down that road. No, Dylan, I'm not cheap. Far from it.'

The two solicitors stared one another down—not in war, but in pleasant appeal. Slowly, Dylan started to smile. 'Good, I like my women to present a challenge.'

'Slip of the tongue?' Harper teased.

'Now you're just begging for a dirty remark.' Spirals of delirious excitement shot through Dylan's body as she observed Harper tug her bottom lip between her teeth. 'We should order a bottle of wine,' Dylan said. 'Somehow, I think it's going to be a long night.'

***

Shortly before 2 a.m., a tipsy Dylan followed Harper up a narrow flight of stairs to her flat on the first floor. The evening, which could have gone either way, turned out to be pleasant enough once Dylan calmed herself after being caught off guard. As for Harper? Dylan shook her head, studying her from behind in the dimly lit hallway. There was no way of denying the attraction she felt for her. Who wouldn't be attracted to someone so hot that you felt like melting at their touch? They were so different yet so alike. They both fought for what they believed was right. Yet, in the same breath, their opinion of what was right and wrong were oceans apart. *In work matters anyway.* On a personal level, they had more in common than either had imagined. They shared the same taste in food, foreign films and music.

'Home sweet home,' Harper said, pushing her front door open and gesturing for Dylan to follow. From the outset, Dylan was surprised at the modest building. An old converted Victorian house in disrepair. It was nothing like her own fancy apartment block, with its concierge and expensive fittings in every room. Harper's place was a nondescript building on a nondescript road. *She's obviously not materialistic.* In her inebriation, Dylan savoured Harper's sweet perfume— something by Lenthéric—she forgot the exact one in the haze of amour and alcohol. Dylan followed Harper eagerly into the blue moonlight that flooded the living room.

'Whoa,' Dylan said, looking around the room when Harper switched on the light. 'The colours in here remind me of peacock feathers and their hues.'

'That was my intention,' Harper said.

Dylan flopped down on the sofa and kicked her boots off. 'You do know peacock feathers are the eyes of the Devil, right?' Dylan grabbed Harper's hand as she walked past her, pulling her down onto the sofa beside her.

'We agreed, coffee and nothing else, remember?' Harper said, leaning away from her.

Dylan wiggled her eyebrows. 'One kiss isn't going to hurt, is it?' Dylan urged slipping closer. She had been imagining what it would be like to kiss Harper all night. She closed her eyes briefly, and in her drunken haze saw the two of them locked in a frantic embrace.

Harper got to her feet. 'Maybe not right now, but tomorrow? Who knows?'

'Who cares about tomorrow?' Dylan said dismissively. 'I'm only interested in the here ...' Her voice fell to a whisper, 'and now ... with you.' She tugged at Harper's arm and brought her down with force; this time she landed on top of her.

Dylan felt her flesh tautening with lust, her groin hot as lava as she took Harper's face in her palms and kissed her deeply before she could respond. Dylan groaned at the softness of Harper's lips sinking into hers. Her pulse soared as she slipped her hand inside Harper's shirt, latching her fingers over the hard peaks of her breasts.

'Stop!'

The voice came from far away. It wasn't until Dylan felt Harper's hands planted against her chest, pushing her back against the sofa that she realised Harper was speaking.

'What's wrong?' Dylan asked stroking Harper's arm.

Harper gave her an incredulous stare. 'What's wrong? Do you even need to ask? What we're doing is unethical.'

Dylan blew out a breath. 'Oh God, don't be so dull. Playing by the rules doesn't get you far in life, Harper. If your job has taught you anything, it should have been that.'

Harper raked a hand through her hair. 'Shit will hit the fan if we cross the line, and someone found out.'

Dylan ran her tongue across her top lip suggestively and brought her face closer to Harper's. 'I won't tell if you won't.'

Unpacified, Harper rose to her feet. 'I think you should go.'

'Oh, come on. Don't be a spoilsport.' Dylan cocked her head to the side. 'You know we're going to reach a deal in a matter of days, why prolong the inevitable?'

'Why? Because I have a client that needs my help. I'm her only hope, and I'm not going to ruin her chances for a drunken romp.'

Dylan's jaw tightened. 'A drunken romp? Is that what you thought this was going to be?' To be fair, she hadn't given a thought to after tonight. But a drunken romp? *What the hell is that anyway?*

'Don't play games, Dylan. Are you going to try and make me believe it was the start of a beautiful romance? Women like you don't love or have relationships. You destroy things.'

'Women like me?' Dylan's eyes narrowed as she searched for her boots. Locating them, she held onto the side of the sofa while she tugged them on. This was too much. To be judged on her work persona was one thing, but to have someone she barely knew make personal insults was a step too far. 'Nope, you're right. It was the beginning of nothing. I'm in deep trouble if your perception skills are this good at work.'

'Are you being sarcastic?'

'What do you think?' She gave Harper one last stare and walked towards the door. 'You seem to have completely figured me out in the space of a few hours. I hope the next time we meet, it will be this pleasurable.'

Dylan didn't look back until she was outside Harper's front door. She rested her head against the wall as she fished inside her bag to call an Uber cab. Thankfully, a driver was close. Dropping her phone back into her bag, her reflections took over. *What the hell just happened in there? Why didn't I cut her down for speaking to me like that? Why did I just stand there and take it like a fool? It's because you like her idiot brain.* That had to be why she felt so emotionally connected to Harper. It was nothing to do with wanting sex. Dylan wanted to share a special moment with someone. To bond. To let someone in to see the real her. *A drunken romp?* No matter how hard she tried to put the episode to the back of her mind, she couldn't. A flame burned, but the woman who ignited it wanted nothing to do with her. All that did was make Dylan want Harper even more.

Chapter Thirteen

Harper didn't know which was worse—the pounding of her head, or the hot, dry desert in her mouth. 'Oh God, no. I didn't ... I couldn't have ... did I?' She strained to recall the night before. She could remember Dylan inviting herself in for coffee when the taxi dropped her off. The little tiff that had been blown into more than necessary. Dylan leaving, and then Harper hitting the brandy bottle as if she were an out of control teenager. Then her mobile phone. Who had she been texting? More importantly, what had she been saying? She swung her legs off the bed, ignoring whatever agony might ensue as she frantically searched for her phone amongst the chaotic scene on her bedroom floor. Finally, she located it under the corner chair. Tentatively, she peeked down at the roll of text messages and sighed a breath of relief. 'Message not sent.' For the first time since she moved into her two-bedroom flat, she was grateful for the crappy reception. Too embarrassed to read what her state of mind had been like under the influence, she hit the delete button for all fifteen messages intended for Dylan. One strong coffee and two paracetamol later, Harper hit the shower and was dressed, out the door and on her way to work within an hour.

'I dread to ask how many you downed to look in this state,' Shay said when Harper stepped into the outer office.

Harper subconsciously patted her hair. For Shay to comment on her appearance, it must be serious. 'I look that bad, huh?'

'Sorry to say, but yes. You look as if you've been dragged through a hedge backwards then frontwards then—'

'—Okay, okay, I get the message.' Harper rubbed her face wearily. She couldn't remember the last time she'd binged on alcohol. Feeling as she did now, she fully remembered why. It always amazed her the way some people knew exactly when to stop. That had never been her case, though. She always walked along the edge of the abyss, slipped and fell, then started all over again. After a few glasses, the urge for more never stopped until the booze was finished, or she passed out. Thankfully, these days the episodes were few and far between, but still, she could do without them, especially when she had important work to do.

'Coffee?' Shay said with a look of sympathy.

Harper nodded. 'You're a woman after my own heart. Let's be grateful I don't have any appointments today.'

Shay walked towards the door, picking up her own empty mug in the process. 'You do have one, so I hope the coffee perks you up. You've got a Ms Blue—'

'—Dylan?' Her heart raced. 'What about her?'

Shay froze in her steps and turned to face Harper. 'Calm down, it's nothing serious. She's coming to see you in about—'

'—She's coming here?' Harper said frantically. Images from the night before flickered through her mind: Dylan's soft lips on hers. The confident way her hands claimed her body as if it belonged to her. The great yearning she felt to be at one with her. 'I can't be seen in this state.'

'Ms Blue isn't coming to take you out on a date. She's coming to discuss …' Shay's eyes blinked rapidly behind her glasses. 'Oh, I see,' she said slowly, a smile spreading across her lips.

Harper glanced at her assistant sharply. 'What? What do you see?'

'Oh, um … nothing?' Shay walked behind her desk, pulled open a drawer and withdrew a small bulging bag. 'Here you go.' She dangled her make-up in front of Harper. 'Bit of blusher and lipstick, and you'll look as right as rain.'

'I don't care if Dylan sees me looking as rough as a dog,' Harper said under Shay's wary, doubtful gaze.

'Who said you did?' Shay dropped her hand to her side. 'But if you don't want it …'

'No wait, give it to me … please.'

Shay raised her eyebrows. 'I thought you didn't care.'

'I don't. But I have to look professional, don't I. What will people think if they see me looking like a—'

'A sight for sore eyes,' Dylan finished for her, entering the office in an ebullient mood.

'Dylan,' Harper said, carefully shielding her face with her hand.

'The one and only. I hope you don't mind me
dropping by like this. I thought we'd discuss the case
further in person. Emails can be so impersonal don't
you think?'

Shay glanced at Harper open mouthed. Harper
bowed her head and grabbed the make-up bag from
Shay's hand. 'Can you show Ms Blue into my office,
please? I won't be a minute.'

Harper darted out the office via a pair of double
doors and hurried down the short corridor, straight
into the toilets. Taking a deep breath, she stood in
front of the large mirror. The reflection staring back at
her was worse than Shay had let on. She looked
deathly ill. Pale was an understatement. *You should know
what drinking does to you. You've seen the damage it can do
first-hand.* With trembling fingers, she unzipped the bag
and rummaged through it.

Dylan's done this deliberately! Catching me off guard. She
roughly applied blusher to her pale cheeks, giving them
a healthy glow. *If she thinks she can get under my skin like
this, she's got another think coming.* Harper applied a coat
of red lipstick to her lips. *Oh, God that makes me look like
a cheap slut.* Darting into the cubicle behind her, she
grabbed a handful of tissue. She rubbed the lipstick
off, applied some eyeliner, finger combed her hair and
headed for the door. *Toughen up!* She told herself. *You
didn't get where you are today by being a soft touch.*

Chapter Fourteen

Seconds later, Harper strode into her inner office with an air of confidence she didn't quite feel. The hangover was returning full force. A pneumatic drill pounded her head. She closed the door carefully behind her and let out a soft sigh. The last thing she needed was to be putting on an 'I feel great act' with Dylan of all people.

Dylan turned from the window and smiled at her appreciatively. 'You scrub up nice after a late night.'

'So do you by the looks of it,' Harper said. She made a rapid mental calculation. They must have parted company around two, give or take an hour for Dylan to get home and wake up around eight, which meant Dylan must have only had around five hours sleep. Despite this, she seemed to be firing on all cylinders. Unlike Harper. *I doubt she was drinking until God knows what time this morning.*

'Me. Oh, I'm used to it. I'm a right goer. But you know that already don't you? What with your psychic senses and everything.'

Harper inwardly cringed as she remembered her unfounded accusations hours earlier. What had she been thinking talking to Dylan that way? Just because she thought it, didn't mean she had to say it aloud. Never say something drunk that you wouldn't say sober was her motto. 'Look about last night …' she started.

Dylan raised her hand. 'No need to apologise.'

'As well as saying sorry, I was going to add that it should never have gone that far. We hold—'

'—Oh, please. Spare me the regret talk. It's way too early for me.'

Harper tilted her head to the side. *Why am I so attracted to this abrupt, in your face woman?* She thought back to the previous evening before things had gone tits up. She remembered with full force how spending time with Dylan had changed her perception of her. *She's smart, intelligent, and sexy as hell, and whether I agree with her downright outrageous views on marriage, she has so much passion and conviction for what she does. Just like me.*

'Whatever you say. Just know it wasn't personal,' Harper said trying to sound as sincere as possible.

Had the circumstances been different, she was sure they would still be wrapped up in their own little cocoon. There was no denying that she felt a strong attraction towards Dylan—a very strong one. Unfortunately, in reality, they were in the middle of a divorce case, each representing a client who wanted the best from their solicitor. It wasn't as simple as just sleeping with someone and the next day you switched your feelings off. Harper didn't know about Dylan, but that wasn't her style. If anything was going to happen between them, she wanted it to be with a clear conscience on both sides.

Harper slid onto her seat behind her desk. Somehow she felt safer with a barrier between them. 'So what do you want to talk about?

'Nice office.'

Harper gestured for Dylan to sit. 'I like it.'

Dylan leant forward, eyeing Harper intently. 'You feeling alright?'

'Yes, why?' she said cautiously, hoping Dylan hadn't noticed she couldn't take her eyes from her face.

'Dunno, you suddenly look a bit peaky.'

Harper shrugged. 'I'm naturally fair skinned. If you think I look pale now, you should see me in the winter.' She paused. 'I don't go in for the fake tan craze.'

Dylan's gaze drifted over Harper's face. 'Maybe you should. It would bring out the colour of your amazing eyes.'

Harper's knees began jiggling under the desk. A habit she acquired in her childhood when she became nervous for no apparent reason. 'Really, you don't say?'

'Yes.'

'How fascinating,' Harper said blandly, noting Dylan's faraway look as she gazed at her.

'Sorry, what did you say?' Dylan said.

Harper gripped her hands together tightly. She had to keep Dylan's flirting at bay. It felt as if Dylan's eyes were slowly undressing her. She knew it wouldn't take much to let her in. Right now that was something she just wasn't going to let happen. 'I said how fascinating. Look, can we get on with this meeting?'

'Sure. Anyone would think you couldn't wait for

me to leave.'

Harper sighed. 'Did I say that?'

'No, but it's just a feeling I get.'

'Sorry, I can't help the way you feel,' Harper said a little defensively.

Dylan looked slightly bewildered. 'So you only spread your love seeds on the weak and needy, is that it?'

'Something like that.' Harper was taken aback by the sour note in Dylan's voice.

'Coffee?'

Harper gave Dylan a quizzical look. 'What?'

'Could I get a cup of coffee, please? Black, no sugar.'

Harper shook her head. There was no chance of prolonging Dylan's visit by offering her beverages. 'No coffee, Dylan. Just tell me what you want. We've wasted ten minutes already.'

'I wouldn't say they were wasted. I like being in your company.'

'Are you trying to knock me off my game by doing this?'

'What being nice? What would you prefer, I get my claws out?' Dylan said with no attempt at a smile.

'Anything's preferable to this.'

'Ten grand.'

'What?' Harper said in a slightly louder voice.

'You say "what" a lot, don't you?'

Harper nodded politely. 'Because I don't know what you're talking about half the time.' The truth was

Dylan's presence had her mind in a tizzy, and she was saying 'what' only to get a head start and buy some time.

'Okay, I'll make myself clear,' Dylan said like a tolerant but slightly exasperated mother to a child. 'I've spoken to my client and the offer is ten grand.'

Dylan's mobile phone pinged. Reaching into her pocket, she withdrew it and raised her finger in Harper's direction. 'Hold on a sec.'

'You've spoken to her already? Ten grand! Are you kidding?'

'No, one minute.'

Harper watched with mounting fury as Dylan read her text message with a smile. *No doubt one of the many dogs she has on a lead sniffing her out.*

'Sorry about that.' Dylan looked up at her, stuffing her phone back into her pocket. 'Yes, I called her earlier. She was quite amused by your offer and also your tactics. Anyway, this is the only offer you're going to get. One payment. Once the divorce is settled, my client doesn't have to see yours again. Or the kid.'

'You are aware that your client cheated on her wife? So her unreasonable behaviour will be grounds for divorce in our petition,' Harper said incredulously as she leant back into her seat.

'Hearsay. Where's your proof? My client only started a relationship with Ms Adams once your client left the marital home.' Dylan withdrew a large envelope from her bag and fished inside. Seconds later, she scattered an array of papers on Harper's desk in front of her.

Harper's heart sunk. She dreaded to think what Dylan managed to dig up to put an obstacle in their way. 'What are these?'

'Emails.'

Harper rolled her eyes. 'From?'

'My client to Adams.'

Harper acknowledged the emails with a jerky inclination of her head. 'So? Do I really have to read their smut?'

'Not the romantic type? Thought not.' Dylan cocked her head. 'I must admit, I had you down as a realist the minute I saw you.'

'Dylan get to the point, please.'

'Look at the top of the page,' Dylan replied coolly.

'And what?'

Dylan smiled. 'See, there you go again with your "what".' She nodded at the paper Harper picked up. 'Notice anything?'

'Can we stop going round in circles, please?' Harper could hear the impatience in her own voice. She didn't know what the cause of it was. The fact that Dylan was infuriating her by playing mind games or because of the premonition she had that Dylan had one over her.

'Look at the dates, Harper.'

Harper scanned the emails, making a note of the date and times they were sent. 'What does this prove?'

Dylan's expression changed from slightly bemused

to one of surprise. 'I thought that would've been obvious. They were merely flirting when your client was accusing my client of cheating. Take the affair accusation to a judge, and he'll laugh you out of court. Take the offer to your client, Harper. It's going to drop a grand a day. The longer your client holds out, the less her payment will be.'

Harper looked at Dylan for several seconds, trying to process the implications of this new information. 'And what about the baby?' she said defiantly, flinging the paper back on her desk.

'Trust fund. Eighteen grand. But that's it. No other responsibility.'

Harper fought to clear her head and get the facts of the story right. 'A thousand pounds for every year of his life? You do know your client was the one who wanted the baby, right?'

Dylan shrugged. 'Again, where's the proof. Is there a paper trail? Did Robyn accompany her for the AI, doctors' appointments, scans, antenatal classes or even to register the birth?' When Harper failed to respond, she continued, 'No, I didn't think so. Does that sound like the actions of someone eager to be a parent?'

Harper remained silent for a few moments, trying to figure out if there was a beating heart beneath all that steel armour. Maybe she had Dylan all wrong. She wasn't just a cold-hearted solicitor, she was a cold-hearted bitch as well. How could Dylan, in all seriousness put a deal on the table where a mother and child got basically nothing? Her voice was a little shaky when she finally spoke.

'You know this makes no difference. Your client is the legal parent of the child and is therefore obliged to take financial responsibility.'

'It's a good deal. Advise your client to take it,' Dylan said with finality. 'She'll be the one to suffer at the end of all this. You and me? We'll just move on. Your client will be the one stuck with the consequences.' She leant forward in her seat. 'Bring the media into this and I will bury your client if you force me to, Harper. Sorry to be crass about it, but it's the truth.'

Dylan pushed herself to her feet and gathered the emails together, leaving them in the middle of the desk, stacked in a tidy pile. 'I'll wait to hear from you. Remember, the clock is ticking.'

Dylan turned and left Harper's office without saying another word.

Exhausted, hungover and depressed, Harper rested her forehead on her desk, pressing her hands against her ears in the hope they would block out the torturous voice mocking her in her head. It was telling her she was going to fail the very client who needed her help more than anything.

Chapter Fifteen

Dylan swung open the door and inhaled a deep breath of the morning air. It had taken every ounce of strength and control to keep her composure. Of course it hadn't really been necessary to visit Harper, but Dylan couldn't help herself. Making the offer in person had its benefits. It meant she caught Harper off guard, which made her vulnerable. Dylan smirked. *The shock on her face when I said ten grand.* Dylan was certain Harper's client would reject the offer—she'd be mad to accept it—but starting low would give Dylan the best chance of getting the outcome her client wanted. The case going to court would be disastrous. Dylan knew a judge would take Robyn Massey to the cleaners. No, she wouldn't let that happen, a settlement was the only way to win.

As Dylan strode along the pavement, memories of the previous night flooded her mind. Harper's lips on hers. The feel of Harper's body pressing against her. Dylan had to see her again, there was no doubt about it. But how when Harper was so stubborn?

Dylan didn't know what was worse, Harper fighting her obvious attraction to her or the fact she seemed to think that Dylan was some kind of ogre. They were both upsetting. Dylan preferred things to be straightforward and wasn't in to playing games.

She fancied the pants off Harper, and wasn't

about to pretend otherwise. Harper was a woman who was true to herself and her values. Dylan liked those attributes. It was hard going against the grain, and it took a sense of confidence and commitment, which Dylan rarely saw in the people she was normally surrounded by. On the flip side of the coin, despite her feelings for Harper, Dylan was going to fight her hardest to get her client the best possible settlement, even if it meant ruffling Harper's feathers. It was her job. Just because she was good at it, didn't mean she liked it most of the time. *Cleaners don't like clearing up people's crap every day. They do it because it puts a roof over their head and food on the table.* This wasn't the first time Dylan had met a self-righteous woman with a mission to save the world. She had witnessed the downfall of many of them when they'd reached empathy burnout. Most, but not all, were now drowning in an alcoholic/drug haze, having finally realised they couldn't save the world after all.

Dylan learnt young. Her father taught her a valuable lesson when she was a child by drumming it into her head that the animal kingdom mirrored the world she lived in. 'It's a dog eat dog world out there, Dylan. You walk your own path, and you're responsible for what goes on in your world—nobody else's.'

All of her life, she had seen people do the meanest things to each other, from the bullying at school she witnessed, to the bullying in the workplace. The evidence was all around her that her father was right, but still, she couldn't help but wonder what

Harper had experienced to see things so differently.

Dylan's thoughts returned to their meeting. *How long will it take Harper to realise that Robyn isn't going to cave in to her client's demands?* It was Robyn's father that was apprehensive of the fall out with regards to the case going public, in reality Robyn couldn't give a shit. The woman had the kind of steely determination that went down well in high powered jobs, but not in your normal day to day existence. That was Dylan's opinion anyway. The offer had been put on the table, now it was a matter of waiting to see if Abi took the bait. If Harper was a good solicitor, the offer would be turned down without a second thought.

'Dylan, wait,' Harper's voice called out as Dylan came to a stop outside her car. Turning, Dylan waited for her to catch up. *Maybe I was wrong about her. If this deal is accepted I will be speechless.*

It took Harper a couple of minutes to reach her. Breathless and panting, Harper bent over, rested her hands on her knees and inhaled in short jerky breaths.

Dylan watched her with amusement. For a woman so slender it was only natural to assume Harper would have been slightly fitter than she appeared at that moment.

'I spoke to Abi.' Harper straightened up and took a deep breath.

Dylan leant against her car. *Surely it can't be this easy? Where's the fun in that?* Dylan's mind had already gone to work on the paperwork that would need filing, and the forms that would need signing.

'She said no to your offer,' Harper said, her breath resuming its natural rhythm.

'Come again?' Dylan still had to play the game of being shocked by the refusal. Saying it was what she'd expected would mean the beginning of the mind games. Though it wouldn't bother her normally, in this case the longer things dragged on, the longer it would be before she could get together with Harper. Dylan nearly licked her lips at the thought.

'The answer is no.'

Dylan raised her brows. It was times like this she was grateful her mother pushed her into drama lessons at school. When it came to bluffing, her poker face was priceless. 'I see. You do know what this means?'

Harper nodded. 'That you and your client go back to the drawing board and try and come up with something that's not so insulting.'

Dylan gave a shake of her head. 'I'm starting to think your client is doing this out of spite, rather than anything else.'

'Spite?'

'Yes, spite.' Dylan smiled to herself when Harper's cheeks flushed pink. It amazed her how easy it was to rile her.

'Do you want to know what spite is, Dylan? Really know? Has it ever occurred to you to see beyond your nose and understand the damage divorce cases like this cause to innocent people?'

When Dylan remained silent Harper took a step towards her.

'Have you got to go to work now?'

Perplexed, Dylan checked her watch. Was it wishful thinking that Harper wanted to go back to her place to talk more? Maybe Dylan could even persuade Harper to forget about work for a few hours. After all it was only a matter of time before Harper's resistance started to fade. It only took a few seconds for that dream to be shattered.

'My first appointment isn't until eleven. Why?'

'Good. Open the car door.' Harper strode around to the passenger side and pulled at the door. 'I said open. I want to take you somewhere.'

Dylan rolled her eyes and pressed the button on her key. The car's locks popped up and Harper pulled the door open and jumped in. Dylan looked heavenwards before following suit.

'Where're we going then? I take it it's not to your place or mine,' Dylan said grinning.

'No. Just drive towards Hackney.'

'Excuse me. That's like half an hour away.'

'Just drive.'

Dylan sighed and slipped her seat belt over her chest. 'You're so bossy.' The engine started smoothly with the soft purr of a cat and seconds later they were heading towards east London.

'So are you going to tell me where we're going?' Dylan asked after they had sat in silence for ten minutes.

'A place where I volunteer.'

'Oh goody,' Dylan said sarcastically. 'Can't wait.

And what exactly am I going to see here?'

'The consequences of your actions.'

Goose pimples rose inadvertently on Dylan's arms. *I pray to god it isn't anywhere too depressing.* 'Where's that then?'

'You'll see,' Harper replied.

Dylan glanced over at her and felt a warm fuzzy feeling overcome her. It was nice to have Harper so near, even if it was under these circumstances. The realisation that it would take but a second to let her hand accidentally slip from the gear stick and onto Harper's thigh thrilled her. Not that it was likely. Harper's expression spoke volumes.

Unable to stand the tension in the air, Dylan switched on the radio hoping a bit of Heart FM would melt the ice maiden. It didn't. All it did was induce sarcastic comments from Harper about the sloppy lyrics. Which was a shame because Dylan found some aspects of the words actually rang true when the singer sang of love and attraction. It was exactly what she herself had experienced since meeting Harper the previous day; the head rush, the pounding heart, the silent need to be near her. Eventually, Dylan gave up trying to engage with Harper and switched the radio off. They rode the rest of the journey in silence.

Harper indicated for Dylan to pull into the car park of a large warehouse. A group of women were standing idly outside the entrance.

Dylan ducked under the windscreen to look up at the building reaching high into the sky. 'You volunteer here?'

Harper nodded.

'Do you mind me asking why? Is it some kind of homeless place for divorced women?' Dylan said trying to inject some humour into the air. It failed miserably. Harper's face was still as serious as it had been at the start of the journey.

'It might as well be. It's a food bank.'

What in hell does this have to do with me? Dylan frowned. 'A food bank?'

'Yes. Come on, let's go inside.'

They both got out of the car simultaneously and headed towards the building. As they neared, several women greeted Harper. Dylan was still trying to figure out where she fit into all of this as they entered the staff entrance of the warehouse. A woman holding a box called out from the top of a ladder. Rows and rows of food lined each aisle.

'Alright girl, how ya doin'?' A short, dark haired woman with a protruding belly, descended the metal staircase carrying a large cardboard box.

'I'm fine thanks, Diane,' Harper said, hurrying over to help her. 'Yourself?'

'Just about keeping my head above water, but it's all good.' Diane dropped the box on a table and began rummaging through the contents. 'Is it really rocket science to remember to put sodding milk in these boxes?' Diane glanced at Dylan and smiled. 'The amount of exercise I do running up and down those stairs—I should be a size ten by now,' she said slapping her round belly.

Dylan couldn't help but like the woman straight off the bat. She had a warm, down-to-earth approach about her.

'Who's your friend?'

'Oh this is Dylan, a work colleague.'

'One of the good guys I hope,' Diane teased, but Dylan noted that it wasn't a hundred percent all humour.

This was one of the reasons she kept her profession to herself when socialising outside of the legal world. People were too caught up in their perceptions of the good guys verses the bad guys, when in reality both sides were just doing the job they were getting paid good money for.

Diane trotted back up the ladder, returning with several boxes of dried milk.

'I forgot to tell you, Harps. That advice you gave me for my friend last week, it was wicked!' Diane dropped a carton of milk into the box missing one. 'Had her husband in a right frenzy with all them big words.' Diane let out a roar of laughter.

So Harper gives out free legal advice to women in need while she's handing them food boxes. What a novel idea.

'I'm glad things worked out okay, Di,' Harper said.

'Right, I'd better get this day movin'. I swear the queues are gettin' longer each day. I don't know nothin' about politics, but I do know whatever them hoity-toity politicians are doing ain't helping the poor.

All they think about is scratchin' each other's balls, know what I'm saying?' She winked. 'Might as well be back in the Victorian days, init?'

Dylan stifled a laugh. Diane had just about summed up MPs to a T.

Harper pulled Dylan to the side, leaving her hand resting on her arm as she spoke.

'Are you ready?'

Dylan looked down at Harper's hand, the heat seeping through like a fireball. 'For?'

'Reality.' Harper handed Dylan some boxes and motioned towards a door at the far end of the warehouse.

Reluctantly, Dylan nodded her head and followed as Harper and Diane led the way down one of the aisles. As Harper pushed open the door Dylan braced herself.

The first thing that struck her were how normal the people queuing looked. They weren't dirty, like the homeless people she saw on TV. Just average people. Some even had children with them. Dylan placed the boxes on the counter, as Diane got ready to serve the line of people.

First in was a jowl-faced woman in her thirties, pushing a sleeping child of around three in a buggy. Dylan noted the boy lacked the healthy glow of a 'normal' boy that age and wondered if he was sick. Dylan cocked her head to the side, paying close attention to what was being said between Diane and the woman. For some reason the woman looked familiar to her.

'Alright, Michelle, how are you doin' today?' Diane said

Michelle looked at her. 'What have I got to complain about? There're a lot of people worse off than me. Been watching the news all morning, and those poor refugees. Heart breaking it is, seeing what's happening to them. Being treated like bloody animals. The poor kids. I just wish there was something I could do to help.'

'I know, doll. The world's gone mad. I swear I don't know how we've got the cheek to call ourselves humans sometimes with the things we do to each other.' Diane shook her head. 'Instead of gettin' better, life's gettin' worse.'

Michelle nodded her head in agreement. She dragged the box of food from the counter and balanced it on the back of the buggy. 'I'll see you soon, Di.'

'Take care of yourself.' Diane waited until Michelle was out of earshot, then said to Harper and Dylan, 'Poor woman. She had it all once. I went to school with her, and we all thought she was the one who had it made. Just goes to show you how life can change in an instant, don't it?'

'So what happened to her?' Dylan asked, genuinely interested.

Diane snorted. 'Filthy bastard of a husband traded her in for a younger model. Some scum lawyer managed to hide all his assets. He ran off into the sunset with his child bride, and Michelle ended up in a council flat with nothin' but cancer. I'm sure it was the stress of the divorce that caused it. I know what I'd do if I spent one minute with that lawyer, I'll tell ya.'

Dylan's mind began to race. 'Do you know her surname?'

'Jacob or somethin' like that.'

'And the husband's first name?'

If Diane thought Dylan was being too familiar there was nothing in her expression to suggest it at all.

'Yeah, never forget that bastard. Called himself Rich. Oh, the irony.'

Rich? Short for Richard. It had to be the same case her father had won a few years back. At that moment she had an epiphany. *Is this place the reality of my job?* In all honesty Dylan rarely thought about the after effects of divorce. All she cared about was winning. She settled cases then moved on to the next one so quickly she barely had time to think about anything but the work at hand. *Am I that thick that I didn't realise these were the consequences of my actions?*

Dylan felt something wet drop onto her cheek. Instinctively, she reached up to touch it. A single tear had escaped her eye. She quickly wiped it away with the tip of her finger. *So this was what Harper was talking about.*

'You alright?' Harper asked with a look of concern.

'Uh, yes,' Dylan said glancing away. 'I had something in my eye.'

The sound of Harper's mobile phone rescued the awkward moment. She patted down her jacket, felt her phone and took it out. She glanced down at the caller ID. 'I need to take this. It's work'

'No problem,' Dylan said.

Dylan watched Harper move to a quiet corner of the room then turned her attention to the people coming through the door. Standing there alone with her thoughts Dylan wondered if all the lost souls milling around were there due to the actions of others, *like me*. Fear and guilt tore through her like a tornado. Dylan pictured the forlorn face of the small boy she had seen only minutes ago, and his mother who looked worn to the bone. Was this the kind of legacy Dylan wanted to leave behind? A worse reputation than scrooge himself. Did she want to have Abi's downfall on her hands? No. There had to be a way round this situation. Her mind raced ten to the dozen. *What can I do?* Harper headed back over to her. Just as she reached her Dylan had a lightbulb moment.

'Harper, I've got an idea that might bring a fair settlement for both parties.'

'Oh yeah?'

'I can't say anything yet, but give me a few hours and I'll let you know.' *I only hope I can convince Robyn to go along with it.*

'Can't wait.'

Dylan hesitated for a moment. 'You know you've got it wrong about me.'

'Next, you'll be telling me the Devil has wings.'

Dylan let out a sigh. 'Believe it or not, Harper, it's true.'

Chapter Sixteen

Robyn stopped pacing Dylan's office floor long enough to see if her solicitor was having a laugh at her expense. 'You're deadly serious, aren't you?'

Dylan nodded her head, saying nothing.

Robyn was convinced Dylan had taken leave of her senses. When Dylan had called her the previous day to arrange a meeting, Robyn assumed there had been some kind of breakthrough in the settlement. That Abi had caved in under the pressure and accepted her terms. What she didn't expect was the woman she'd hired to help her get rid of the excess baggage, to suggest actually taking it on board. Robyn was beginning to wonder if Ms Blue was as hot a solicitor as her reputation made her out to be. 'You want me to look after that baby. Why the hell would I want to do that?'

'I thought you were a smart woman, Robyn.'

Robyn followed Dylan's finger as she ran it across her exposed chest. Robyn was sure it was to draw her attention to her cleavage. *If only my hands weren't full with Tiffany.* 'You thought right. Which is exactly why I don't want anything to do with Abi or that kid.'

Dylan stood and walked to the window. When she turned back to face Robyn several seconds later, her white shirt was buttoned up to her neck. 'Just hear me out for a second, will you?'

'I'm listening.'

'Good. Right. You've made an offer that's been turned down, which is making me think that money isn't the object here.'

'So what is?'

Dylan returned to her desk and leant over it as Robyn stared back at her, mesmerised by the steely determination in her eyes. 'She wants to punish you. Don't you see? Anyone in their right mind would have taken the money and ran.'

'So what's me babysitting gonna change?'

Dylan straightened up and crossed her arms over her chest. 'Jake's important to her, isn't he?'

'And?'

'And, what if she was to think you might be interested in sharing custody of him?'

Robyn leapt out of her seat. 'What? Sharing custody?'

'I thought you were going to listen. If she thinks there's any chance that you'll apply for custody it may scare her into being more amenable to a settlement.'

Robyn ran her fingers through her hair. 'I don't know. I mean she said she wants me involved in his life.'

'There's a difference between being involved and actually having custody. How would she feel about you playing happy families with her son and your girlfriend?'

Robyn grinned. *She's right about that, Abi would go mad.*

'Look, you don't want this to drag on, do you? Abi's solicitor isn't going to let this go. I don't think she'll stop until she gets half of everything you own. Is that what you want?'

'How's she affording her?'

'That's irrelevant. The fact is she has a solicitor and a good one.'

'I thought you were good.'

'I am. But there's only so much I can do.'

Robyn sighed in frustration. It looked like she wasn't going to have much choice in the matter. 'I'm not happy about this, Dylan. Not one bit. To top it off I received this today.' She took out a folded letter from her pocket and threw it on Dylan's desk.

'What's this?' Dylan said, picking up the letter and inspecting it closely.

'It's a request for maintenance from the CMS.'

Dylan glanced up at Robyn. 'Look, you have a couple of weeks before you have to respond so let's try and hammer out a settlement in the meantime. I'm going to have to send a list of all the assets you acquired during your marriage over to Abi's solicitor. So if you can get that to me ASAP we can put this settlement to bed.'

'If you say so.' Robyn smiled inwardly. *What assets?*

Dylan leant forward. 'You pay me to get results. You either trust me, or you don't. It's up to you.'

'Okay, but I'm warning you, if this goes tits up, you're fired.'

'I wouldn't expect anything else.'

Robyn gave Dylan a curt nod and moved towards the door. Her mind already on more important things like how she was going to explain all of this to Tiffany. It was one thing giving money for the baby's upkeep, but looking after it was another matter entirely.

Chapter Seventeen

Harper was remorseful. She had got Dylan's character all wrong. Dylan wasn't the callous person Harper thought she was after all. If her latest action was anything to go by she had a kind streak as well. It had been less than an hour ago that she had spoken with Abi, only to be informed that a breakthrough seemed to have been made. Robyn had arranged to take Jake for the weekend. The cynic in Harper couldn't help but wonder what trick Dylan had up her sleeve but in the end Abi's happiness had overcome any doubt. *Maybe I've clumped all the bad guys into one lump.* It was for that reason she had invited Dylan to her office. To hold out the olive branch, so to speak. When Harper was wrong she was the first to admit it. Now was one of those times. Of course there was the added bonus of seeing Dylan again, that in itself was worth her swallowing her pride.

Harper wasn't surprised when there was a knock on the door at 3pm exactly. She had a feeling Dylan was the punctual type.

Shay popped her head around the door. 'Ms Blue is—'

'—It's okay Shay, I'm expecting her.' Harper subconsciously fussed with her hair and corrected her posture.

Shay's eyes widened. 'You are?'

Harper gave her a reassuring smile and said in a hushed voice only Shay could hear, 'It'll be alright, send her in.'

'Okay. Don't forget you have a meeting at three-thirty.'

Seconds later Dylan swung the door open and Harper was again surprised by the intensity of her attraction to the woman. It both excited and worried her. She was in a constant tug of war with herself. The more she saw of Dylan the deeper the attraction became.

'I thought it was unethical for us to see each other.' Dylan announced as she strode into Harper's office. She shrugged her jacket off and threw it on a vacant chair by the window as if it was her own office.

'Good afternoon to you to. And actually I invited you here to talk, nothing else.'

'Well you're in luck that I happen to have a pair of rather large ears and they love nothing more than listening.'

Harper laughed. For the moment she could allow herself to switch off and enjoy Dylan's company, even if it did move into the realms of harmless flirting. 'I think we're both aware that you have the cutest ears ever,' she teased.

Dylan grinned. 'Thanks.' She dug into her bag and withdrew a bottle of champagne. 'Anyway, I thought the positive break in our case was a cause for celebration.'

Dylan obviously had more confidence in the

arrangement between Abi and Robyn than Harper did. That was for certain. There was something about Robyn, Harper just didn't trust. Of course she knew she was being judgemental, but the things Abi had said about her, gave Harper the impression that Robyn wasn't the type of woman who surrendered easily. Despite this, she pushed her doubts aside, for the moment anyway. 'That's nice of you. I can only have one as I have a meeting in a bit.' Harper stood and left the room for a few minutes, returning with two glasses. 'Sorry it's not a champagne flute,' she said handing it to Dylan.

'No worries. Makes no difference what you drink out of, it all goes down the same hole.'

Dylan's fingers clasped over Harper's. Harper was unable to move her hand away as if stuck in a magnetic grip. The tingling sensations coursing through her veins almost made her give in to the desire to reach out and pull Dylan in for a deep long sensual kiss. Dylan gave her a cat-playing-with-a-mouse kind of smile, then released her hand. The cocky way she was eyeing her made Harper think Dylan knew exactly the kind of effect she was having on her.

For some reason Harper didn't care. She thought Dylan's mind was too savvy not to know that the attraction was mutual, and like Dylan had pointed out, the case would be over soon, touch wood, and they would be free to explore their feelings for each other.

Dylan turned her attention to the champagne and popped the cork. Pouring them both a glass she said,

'Cheers,' before taking a sip.

Harper returned to her seat slightly shaken by the physical contact. She glanced up at the clock on the wall. Unfortunately the meeting would have to come to a close soon if she was to meet her client on time.

'Dylan ... I want to thank you—'

'—For what?' Dylan relaxed back in her seat and crossed her legs.

Did she deliberately show off her thighs? Harper wondered as she tried to dislodge the image from her mind. 'I know you had a hand in persuading Robyn to see Jake.'

'Do you now? One minute I'm the devil with horns, the next I'm an angel with wings. My, whatever will you be thinking of me next?'

'Look let's put all the jokes aside for the minute. We both want what's best for our clients and if we can reach an agreement without going to court that would be the most favourable outcome wouldn't it?'

'I'm glad to see you know when you're fighting a losing battle.'

'A ...?' Harper laughed. 'You're way too cocky for your own good.'

Dylan wiggled her eyebrows. 'Am I?'

Harper grinned. She couldn't help but think how natural it seemed for Dylan to be in her office. As much as she angered and frustrated her at times, when she was just being Dylan the person instead of Dylan the cut throat solicitor, Harper fully understood why she was so drawn to her. She checked the time again. *I wish I didn't have to go.*

'I think you're confusing confidence with cockiness,' Dylan continued, unaware of Harper's internal angst. 'Plus I have an extra incentive to bring this case to a satisfactory close.'

'And what's that then?'

'Let's just say it begins with P and ends with R,' Dylan said taking a delicate sip of champagne.

'A partnership?'

Dylan drained her glass and put it on the table. 'Yep. Not a day too soon either.'

Harper was surprised she wasn't a partner already. Dylan had all the qualities that law firms were eager to promote to the top. Power hungry people who didn't care who they trod on to achieve their goal. 'I'm happy for you.'

Dylan must have sensed Harper's comment was half hearted by her next remark. 'Doesn't look that way from where I'm sitting.'

Harper clasped her hands on the table in front of her. *Truth time.* 'Look, if you want me to be honest, this case kind of leaves a funny taste in my mouth. It's just not right what's going on between these women and the fact that you will get promoted because you save Robyn from parting with her assets. It seems totally wrong.'

'Wrong? I busted my arse to get to where I am today. Nobody ever gave me anything.' Dylan pushed herself to her feet and walked over to get her jacket. 'So if you think for one second I'm going to feel guilty for achieving something that is rightfully mine you've got another think coming.'

'I didn't mean…'

Dylan slipped into her jacket and walked back to the desk, leaning over it slightly. Her bottom lip trembled. 'Do you know what kind of people have fucked up the world?' She pointed her finger at Harper. 'Do gooders like you who do nothing to empower people, it's as if you like them to be weak and dependent to make yourself feel needed, wanted—'

'—That's not true—'

'—Isn't it? Why do you think Abi deserves to take half of Robyn's hard earned money? The money she worked seven days, eighteen hours a day for? Can you really say with a clear conscience that Abi is entitled to it? What the fuck did she do to earn it? She wasn't cooking or waiting on Robyn—she basically did fuck all, bar look after a kid.'

Harper jumped to her feet, ready to stand her ground. 'And you think that's easy? Raising a kid by yourself.' Harper gripped the edge of the table to calm herself. *This is not about me.* She kept reminding herself as her own past threatened to overcome her emotions.

'Oh get real, Harper. Before they split she had a round the clock nanny being paid for by my client. You've read the divorce petition. No sex since the baby was conceived. Your holier than thou client expected Robyn to live like a nun at the age of thirty-five—where's the justice in that?'

No, Harper didn't think anyone should be locked

in a sexless marriage but there had been a very good reason for Abi's abstinence. One that she was surprised Dylan, being a woman, didn't understand. 'Dylan, Abi had pre-eclampsia during her pregnancy followed by postnatal depression…'

'Which,' Dylan interrupted. 'Robyn tried to help by getting the best doctors available. But she refused it all. Instead she turned to drink. Some responsible mother aye?'

Harper sank into her chair and shook her head. Abi had failed to mention that bit of information. *If what Dylan's saying is true, why wouldn't Abi have told me these things?* Surely Abi knew they would come to light at some point. 'This is all new to me,' Harper said to Dylan, whose rigid body had suddenly relaxed.

Dylan moved around the desk and perched on the edge. The sweet scent of her perfume sent Harper's senses spinning. 'I'm sorry I lost my temper with you.' Dylan inhaled and exhaled slowly. 'That's why you shouldn't get too close to your clients. They have their own agenda and they don't care who they hurt to achieve it.'

Am I really that gullible? Could I have been that wrong about Abi? She made a mental note to address the issue with Abi the next time she saw her. 'I really thought Abi was on the straight and narrow. I never thought for a minute she would lie to me.'

'She likes to portray herself as a victim and she's a magnet to people like you.' Dylan reached out and brushed back Harper's hair, letting her fingers caress

Harper's cheek.

The gesture sent shockwaves throughout her body. Dylan's touch felt so natural *and so right.*

Dylan continued, 'And talking of magnets and attraction...'

Before Dylan could finish her sentence, there was a knock at the door and Shay appeared in the doorway holding a pile of folders. She eyed them suspiciously when Harper suddenly jerked back in her seat. Harper clasped her hand to the spot where she could still feel the heat from Dylan's hand. *I'm going to go insane if this case isn't over soon.*

'Time to go, Harper. You're gonna be late.'

The brief reprieve gave Harper a moment to gather her senses. 'Okay. Thanks, Shay.'

Shay remained standing in the doorway. Dylan gave a slight shrug of her shoulders and stood up. She pointed at the bottle of champagne. 'We'll have to have another bottle next time—and believe me there will be a next time.'

I damn well hope so! Harper didn't know how much longer she was going to be able to hold out.

Chapter Eighteen

'You promised you'd take me away for the weekend for my birthday.' Tiffany glared at Robyn as she pulled the sheet over her naked breasts.

Robyn reached over and tugged it back down. She got a kick out of knowing the woman with firm breasts and a fit body was hers for the taking whenever she wanted her. It was a buzz like no other.

'I know what I said, but that was last week. A whole lot of shit has come down on me since then.'

'What am I s'posed to do then? Celebrate on me own?'

'What the hell is wrong with you? Didn't you hear me when I said I have no choice in the matter?' Robyn paused, becoming increasingly irritated at Tiffany's inability to grasp what she was trying to explain to her. She was at her wit's end with it all—the divorce, the baby, work and even Tiffany was beginning to grate on her nerves. The last thing Robyn wanted was a whining baby to look after. To make matters worse, Dylan had stipulated that Robyn herself had to look after Jake— no nannies were allowed.

'After everythin' you've told me 'bout her, that bitch needs to be taught a lesson,' Tiffany said in a voice tinged with venom.

Robyn slowly ran the tip of her finger across Tiffany's collarbone. 'How can someone so young be so hard?'

'Says you?' Tiffany narrowed her eyes. 'How can someone who seems so normal have a temper like a nutter?'

'Tiff, I apologised for my behaviour at the weekend. Wasn't me transferring my assets over to you enough to show you how sorry I was? Considering all the tax I had to pay out to do it.' It was something she had done on the spur of the moment, when Tiffany had threatened to leave her after their altercation in the car. Now that she had time to think about it, it did seem a little too hasty.

'Yeah, but what're you gonna give me next time you lose your rag?' Tiffany said carefully.

Robyn jumped up and pinned Tiffany's arms down to the mattress. 'I only lose it when people take the piss out of me. And you took the piss big time.'

'Like you're taking the piss out of me now.' Tiffany pushed Robyn off her, slid out of bed and headed towards the en-suite bathroom. 'I bet that sly bitch orchestrated this whole thing. She's gonna pay for fuckin' up my twenty-first birthday.'

Robyn laughed as Tiffany disappeared behind the door. 'Oh yeah? And what're you gonna do?'

'Somethin'. Don't you worry. I'm not you, just sittin' around bitchin' and doin' nothin',' Tiffany called back.

'Whatever.' The sound of the shower started. Robyn rolled over to Tiffany's spot and sank her face into the sheets, inhaling her sweet scent. Just minutes ago their bodies had been thrashing about in ecstasy. She would have liked it to have gone on all morning, but Abi would be there soon with the snivelling sprog. She let out a groan and thumped the pillow with her fist. *Two whole fucking days of misery.*

The bathroom door opened, and Tiffany walked out wrapped in a towel. 'Now what's wrong with you?'

Robyn rolled onto her back and stared at the ceiling. 'I'm fucked either way I look at it.'

Tiffany let the towel drop to the floor, opened the mirrored wardrobe and selected an outfit. She stared at Robyn through the mirror's reflection. 'You don't have to do anythin' you don't want to do. Isn't that what you're always tellin' me?'

Robyn felt a stirring of desire as her eyes roamed over Tiffany's pert arse. 'Yes, but in this instance if I don't follow my solicitor's advice, I'm going to lose a shitload of money. Is that what you want?'

'Sounds like a line to me,' Tiffany said, pulling on a skirt that barely covered her thighs.

'Jesus Christ! You're all the same! I thought I was getting away from all this depressing shit when I left Abi.' Robyn rolled off the bed and paced the room naked. 'Maybe I should disappear with the goddamn brat—at least it doesn't talk yet. I feel like my ears are going to explode.'

'Hey, don't take it out on me 'cause you can't say no.'

'Tiff, listen to me,' Robyn said. She opened the slatted blinds and shielded her eyes with her hand from the sun's rays. 'I'm not losing my money because you can't deal with one weekend alone. Just remember if I get done over in this divorce, you'll have less money to buy your precious Louis Vuitton with. So back off and let me get through this once and for all. After this divorce is finalised, we can do what the hell we want. I promise.'

'You promise?' Tiffany nibbled her bottom lip.

Robyn figured the term sex on legs had been made just for Tiffany. She had never seen a woman look so erotic by just standing there doing absolutely nothing. 'I swear on my life, Tiff. Just give me some time to get through this nightmare, and I'll buy you anything you want, within reason, of course.'

Tiffany pushed her feet into a pair of high heels, sauntered over to Robyn and wrapped her arms around her waist. Her slender hand slid down Robyn's clammy skin and settled between her legs. Robyn groaned at Tiffany's expert fondling.

'It's a pity I've gotta go before the old crow arrives isn't it?' Tiffany whispered in her ear.

'Don't stop, we've still got half an hour left,' Robyn said, forcing the words out as she became wet.

Tiffany teasingly withdrew her hand, despite Robyn's howls of protest. 'No, it's for the best. I don't wanna bump into her on the doorstep, now do I?'

Robyn frowned, thinking of the sex she would be missing out on for two nights in a row. 'I can't believe you're leaving me when I'm so horny.'

Tiffany nibbled on her ear. 'Once that minger is

outta our lives, I'll make sure you never want for sex or excitement again.'

Chapter Nineteen

Abi said nothing to her sister about the arrangement for Jake. Only because she didn't want an ear bashing from her. Tia would be the first to indicate her foolishness at leaving Jake with Robyn for the weekend after all Robyn had subjected her to. Nevertheless, Abi found herself packing Jake an overnight bag with his best set of clothes and favourite teddy. *The last thing I need is Robyn saying I'm an unfit mother.* The drop off had been pleasant enough. No cross words were spoken. Neither Robyn nor Abi had much to say to one another. Abi had merely handed Jake over, somewhat reluctantly, with a list of dos and don'ts. For a split second, Abi wanted to snatch Jake back and leg it home, but common sense won the day. Abi would do anything if it meant bringing the whole saga to an end. *Even if it means being apart from Jake for two whole days.* She hoped, no prayed that Robyn might see the error of her ways once she realised what an amazing baby Jake was. Truth be told, it disturbed her to think that she was willing to forgive Robyn so easily for all the mayhem she had caused, but she had to put Jake first. His needs trumped hers. The three of them were irrevocably tied together, whether she liked it or not.

'Morning, Abi,' a cheery voice said from the door behind her.

Abi turned to see her supervisor, Jill, a large and jolly woman in her late forties. She had hired Abi as a part-time cashier, despite her lack of previous experience. If it weren't for this second job, Abi would have gone under by now.

'Oh hey, Jill! How was the bowling?' Abi asked.

Jill presented Abi with a mock look of despair, and then chuckled and shook her head. 'We lost, again on account of Oscar and his over-zealous aim. I tell you, that man should play cricket or something instead.' She refilled the kettle in the small sink and switched it on. 'Want a coffee?'

'Thanks, that'd be great. I'm so tired this morning. I can barely keep my eyes open.'

'Is Jakey with Aunty Tia?' Jill asked casually, scooping up a spoon of coffee and roughly chucking it into a cup.

Abi hesitated for a moment. *Should I tell her the truth about Jake's whereabouts or will she think I'm mad letting Robyn have him?* Abi had cried on Jill's shoulder many a time over the past few months, and she had provided some good advice. If she told her Robyn had Jake, Abi dreaded to think of Jill's reaction. Abi shuddered. She couldn't bear the thought of Jill thinking badly of her, so she took the only option available. Beneath the table, she crossed her fingers tightly and said, 'Yes. The poor woman is trying to save the world and me at the same time. I feel so bad asking her to look after Jake so much.' That in itself was the truth. If she could just settle a financial arrangement with Robyn, she could afford to pay someone to look after Jake, and then Tia could get on with her life as a globetrotting charity worker. It troubled Abi to think of Tia giving up so much for her.

Jill looked at her with pity. 'Oh don't fret about those things. Tia wouldn't do it if she didn't love you. Besides, that's what family are for.'

Abi couldn't help but grin. 'Touch wood, my fortunes are about to change.'

'Oh?' Jill looked at her enquiringly.

'I can't say anything yet, but after this weekend, there might be a light at the end of the tunnel.' *Finally.*

Jill poured the hot water into the cups and stirred, her expression frozen in deep contemplation. 'I hope so. In a few months from now, you won't even remember how bad things were. All roads lead somewhere. Even dead-end streets offer the opportunity to turn right around and carry on.'

'That's so true,' Abi said smiling. She loved it when Jill came out with that kind of saying. They may have only been words, but the meaning behind them actually gave her hope for a brighter future.

Jill passed Abi her coffee. 'Get that down you, and I'll go and open up.'

Alone, Abi took small sips of her drink. For the first time in as many months, she felt anxiety free. Her normally clammy hands were dry. The butterflies that were a constant companion were absent, and most importantly, her mind was calm. She smiled to herself. *Today's going to be a good day. I can feel it.*

By eleven o'clock, the shop was bustling with people. Lively children, sauntering teenagers and bored housewives scattered themselves through the various aisles. Abi bent down to slot one of the many books she'd found discarded on the floor back onto the shelf.

'Excuse me ...' Abi heard a chiming feminine voice. She straightened up and turned to face a naturally tanned woman with supermodel features and a body to match.

Great, stand next to me, just to make me feel even paler than I already am.

'Can I help you?' Abi asked, flashing her best smile at the tall young woman.

'I hope so. I'm lookin' for a book called, "Best Without" or somethin' like that. It's about how some successful lesbians prefer childfree women.' She rolled her eyes skyward with impatience. 'Ugh, I'm not really sure who wrote it ...'

Maybe I should read it. It just might explain why Robyn left me. Abi felt a lump form in her throat at the thought. She tried to let her sigh out slowly so the customer wouldn't notice her despondence. She needn't have worried. The woman lolled her head to the side with a grin and waited for Abi to respond.

Abi gestured for the woman to follow her. 'If we have it, it'll be in the non-fiction section ...' she said with a crack in her voice. Just when she thought the splitting hurt of losing Robyn to another woman was finally dwindling, the scab was picked open and left to the seawater.

Like a puppy, the woman in the short skirt and heels followed Abi through the rows. Her heavily made-up eyes looked over all the dazzling colours of books, paints, birthday cards and ribbons as she walked, paying no attention to where Abi was leading her. She reminded Abi of a child filled with wonder while passing through a sweet shop. Abi halted to point out the variety of books on relationships, and the clumsy woman walked right into her. Her purse fell, and its contents spilt all around them as the woman fell to her knees.

'Oh no! I'm so sorry!' Abi said apologetically, even though the collision wasn't her fault.

To Abi's relief, nobody really took notice of the blunder, and she quickly helped the woman gather up her things. Still the woman just kept her childlike smile and shook her head, 'No worries ... uh ... Abi,' she said, reading Abi's name tag. 'I have to learn to watch my feet instead of all the interesting things around me.' The woman chuckled as she stood with her bag clutched under her arm.

'Anyway, here you are. I'm not sure if we stock that exact book, but there are similar subjects here on this shelf about childfree living,' Abi said, composing herself again. She felt awfully stupid, nonetheless.

'Thanks so much,' the woman chimed, starting to check the sexual health books.

Wouldn't mind a bit of sexual health myself. Abi giggled as she strolled away and went back to the counter. It dawned on her that she never thought about sex anymore. For her, it had become a luxury, something only other people got to do; like world travel or figure skating. Other people got to love. Other people got to lock themselves into each other in the throes of passion. Those days were gone for her. It amazed her how sex, something that used to be common place during her week, had now distanced itself from her.

'Abi, can I see you in my office, please?' Jill called ten minutes later.

Next to Jill stood the tall young woman, looking utterly distraught.

'Of course,' Abi replied and followed Jill and the customer to the office. Behind her, she noticed Harry, the security officer, following her. A bolt of ice cold panic coursed through Abi's body. She didn't know why, but their faces, their body language, and the tense silence was a nasty portend that made her nauseous.

Harry closed the door.

'Please take a seat, Abi,' Jill said, barely able to meet her eyes.

Abi felt compelled to lay a hand on her shoulder to comfort her, but she resisted the urge and hoped she could help fix the situation, whatever it was.

'Is everything okay, Jill?'

'Abi, we have received a complaint from this lady. And I will need your permission for Harry to search you,' Jill said plainly.

Abi's legs went numb, and her stomach churned inside her. What an awful feeling. What could she possibly have done?

'Excuse me?' Abi forced out with a quiver in her voice. Maybe they construed her shaky tone as guilt when, in fact, it was born from an impending feeling of strife.

'This customer reported you to me. Allegedly, you lifted her credit card off her when you helped her gather her belongings after her purse fell to the floor. This is a rather serious accusation, and as such, we will have to search you, Abi,' Jill explained in a morose tone that Abi did not ever imagine she possessed.

'That's ludicrous. Why would I do that?' Abi protested defensively.

Jill gave her a long look, and Abi realised that her supervisor knew how short on cash she was. Obviously getting defensive would put her in a worse light than she was already.

'Oh my God, I can't believe this,' she mumbled to herself, casting a glance at Harry. 'Go on then, search me.'

Harry looked miserable. They were not exactly friends, but they had shared a joke or two before and spoke now and then. Reluctantly he began to search her. In front of Abi, the customer sobbed, but not once did she make eye contact with Abi. Jill looked to the floor. Silence smothered the mood in the small office where only the muffled music and chatting from the store felt like another dimension—a happy one—a million light years away from the bubble of discord Abi was caught in.

'Oh, Jesus,' Abi heard Jill utter under her breath as she looked at Harry. Jill shook her head in what looked like regret.

'What?' Abi asked and turned to face Harry. She looked right at the silver MasterCard Harry held up. Abi felt her knees buckle.

'I didn't take that,' she cried out in disbelief as Harry led her, sobbing, away to the security office to wait for the police.

She could hear Jill apologising to the customer again.

'We'll take the appropriate steps from here, and the police will contact you shortly to see if you want to press charges. Just give me your contact details.'

'Of course. Thank you for sorting this out,' the young lady said, sniffling.

'No problem, Miss Adams. I only hope this hasn't marred the reputation of the shop.'

'I'm sure if your employee is dealt with properly, it won't have. The local papers would have a field day with this story, wouldn't they?'

Chapter Twenty

As far as Harper was concerned, the pastry shop on the corner of her street was the best in town. Despite travelling the world, nothing came close to the superior food Bella's served. It was a family run business eking out an existence in a sea of franchises. The quaint shop only had the capacity to fit four small wooden tables and chairs in the seating area. It was a rarity, but that morning Harper was able to claim one.

'So, are you going to tell me what's going on with you and Ms Dreamy eyes?'

Harper laughed at Shay's description of Dylan.

'Absolutely nothing.' *Not yet, anyway.*

'You sure?'

'Positive.'

Shay leant forward in her seat as if she was going to share something confidential with Harper. 'You know, she looked nothing like I expected. The way people talk about her, I thought she'd be stern looking with a small mean mouth and shifty, beady eyes.'

Harper laughed at how far adrift Shay had been with her description of Dylan.

'So you've seen her a few times now, is she as bad as people make out?' Shay asked, blowing on her coffee.

'I think on a professional level the gossip is most probably true, she can be brutal. Not because deep down she's a nasty person, she just takes her job seriously.' Harper stared down at the twisted napkin in her hands; she unravelled it as she continued, 'I think she would be the same in whatever profession she worked in. It's just unfortunate that when she wins, in most cases, someone gets hurt.'

'Yeah, I suppose if you look at it that way she ain't that bad.'

'I mean, like this thing with Robyn having Jake for the weekend. Dylan won't admit it, but I'm sure she instigated it. She thinks showing her vulnerable side makes her look weak, I suppose.'

'In some people's eyes, it would, but in yours, it makes her look strong, yes?'

Harper nodded. *Oh my God, since when did I become Dylan's cheerleader?* It shocked Harper to find herself defending Dylan. *Isn't that what you do when you're falling for someone? Make up all kinds of excuses for behaviour you wouldn't normally tolerate?*

A waitress stopped by their table and placed a tray with coffees and cakes before them. Both women thanked her in unison. She gave them a brief smile then moved on to the next table.

Harper reluctantly pushed thoughts of Dylan aside. 'Oh, God, I've been dreaming about this all week.' Harper licked her lips. 'This is what life's about.' She hungrily dug a spoon into the thick slab of warm chocolate cake and was about to raise it to her open mouth when her mobile phone rang. Harper shook her head in disbelief.

'Why would it ring right this second?' she said as Shay burst out laughing.

'I told you to turn it off, but you wouldn't listen.'

Harper rolled her eyes. 'Why spoil a habit of a lifetime.' She dug the phone out of her jacket. 'This better be an emergency,' she said, pressing the phone to her ear, 'Harper Anderson.'

Harper dropped her spoon on the plate with a clang. She couldn't believe what Abi was telling her. She'd been arrested. *This is not good.*

'Listen, I'll be there as soon as I can. Just stay calm,' Harper said. 'I'll sort this out, and then see if I can get ... yes ... no, don't worry. Just hang in there. I'll see you soon.'

Harper's hands shook as she stuffed her phone into her jacket and stood up. She looked down at her uneaten cake with regret. 'I've got to go.'

'Why, what's up?'

Harper took a deep breath before letting it out with force. 'It's Abi.' *Is that poor woman ever gonna get a break?*

'She hasn't been murdered has she?' Shay asked tentatively.

Harper gave a small shake of her head. 'Why on earth would that be the first thing that comes to mind?'

''Cause that's what normally happens in the movies, isn't it? Someone doesn't want to get divorced, so they have the partner knocked off. Or frame them for something?'

'Well, it isn't the case this time. Abi's been arrested.'

'For plotting a murder?'

Harper laughed despite the seriousness of the situation. 'No, Shay. Listen, no one's been hired to murder anybody. She's been arrested for theft.'

Shay's mouth dropped open. 'What was she stealing? Food?'

'No, someone's credit card apparently. Shay, that woman wouldn't steal shit if using it as skin lotion made her immortal.'

'So what are you gonna do about it? You're a divorce solicitor, not a defence one,' Shay reminded her.

Harper knew what Shay was hinting at—that she shouldn't be too involved with her client, but what choice did she have? Leave poor Abi to stew in a cell? It wasn't as if Robyn was going to go running to her defence. 'I might not be a defence solicitor, but I know one who is.'

Shay's voice took on a serious tone. 'You're going to have to let this woman stand on her own two feet eventually. You can't always be her knight in shining armour.'

'That's all very well, but right now there isn't anyone else that can help her,' Harper said. She knew she couldn't always be there for Abi, but the woman had quickly secured a special place in her protective dome. Just when Harper thought things were going in the right direction for Abi, it was sod's law that something would pop up and spoil things. From what she could tell, Abi was a good woman with good values; a woman who loved her child and was fighting for his future, not her own—that deserved special concession in her opinion. Harper's own mother never gave a shit about her, but Abi was a woman who tormented herself for the welfare of her son, and Harper would not stand idly by while she was being kicked around.

'Do you think we'll ever get to hang out at the weekends without you running off to save lost souls?' Shay said, pulling Harper's plate across the table.

'You don't mind me going, do you?'

'Of course not, you lump of jelly,' she told Harper. 'Abi's cause is far more serious and far more important than a cake eating marathon.'

Harper pecked Shay's cheek. 'I promise I'll make up for it,' she said. 'Now enjoy that delicious, mouth-watering cake ... and no more after that one.'

As Harper left the shop, Shay called after her, 'Wouldn't dream of it. Go save the world.'

Harper scrolled through her contact list as she made her way to her car, praying Marc Smith was around. He was a smart, intelligent solicitor with a heart of gold who she'd attended university with. Even though they worked in different fields, they still maintained a close friendship. He had a conscience, *unlike some other defence solicitors out there*.

The seconds between each ring seemed like an eternity, and Harper could have cried with relief when

Marc answered and agreed to meet her at the police station within the hour. As Harper sped towards the location, a million things played through her mind. If Abi were charged, would it have an effect on her case? She didn't see why it would. She was more worried about social services becoming involved because of Jake. What stance would they take if they were notified?

Bringing her car to a halt in the police station car park, Harper hurriedly made her way inside to be informed at reception that Abi was with her solicitor. Relieved, she took a seat to wait.

'She'll be released on bail and will have to report back here in a month's time,' Marc told Harper an hour later as he exited the police cells where Abi was being held.

Harper gave him a brief hug. 'I owe you one, Marc. Thank you.'

'I'm glad I could help out. Listen, I've got to dash, but your client should be out shortly.'

Some time later, Abi sat in Harper's car as she drove her home. Finally, after twenty minutes, Abi's crying subsided, and she spoke for the first time.

'I swear to God, Harper, I did not take that woman's credit card,' Abi protested. Her eyes were maroon and bloodshot, and her skin looked terrible. It showed signs of malnutrition, something that did not sit well with Harper at all.

'I believe you, Abi,' Harper replied, placing her hand on Abi's. 'We will get to the bottom of this I promise ...'

'You know, Harper ...' Abi started, '... I don't even care anymore.'

Abi sounded disturbingly melancholy, and Harper shook her head profusely. 'No, you do. You have to. Jake needs his mummy.' She fished for her needs from her own past, 'Who else will look after him if you give up? He isn't old enough to look after himself.'

Abi buried her face in her hands. 'It just feels like every time I take one step forward I get pushed back ten. I just wish I could get out of this pit.' Her words were weighed with regret and defeat. 'It's not even like I'm a spring chicken anymore ...'

'What? Don't they say life begins at forty? Once your divorce is behind you, things will be different.' Harper smiled and playfully tapped Abi's hand. 'And look at you. Anyone with half a brain can see you have a face that would turn any woman's head.'

'You're very sweet, Harper.' Abi dropped her hands and smiled, but it was vacant.

Harper could see Abi didn't believe a word she said, and realised that Abi's immediate future looked bleak. Without her extra job at W.H. Smith, there was no way to cover her and Jake's food expenditure. Now she could only manage, barely, the rent for the small cramped flat.

They rode in silence for the next few minutes before Harper gave in to the nagging questions that needed to be answered. 'I need to ask you something, Abi. And I want you to be truthful with me.'

'Of course. Anything.'

Harper rested her chin slightly on the steering wheel. 'Have you ever had a nanny?'

Abi burst out laughing. 'A what? Do they work for free, or do you have to pay them?'

Harper frowned. 'Please, just answer me.'

'No, Harper. I've never had a nanny.' She looked at her quizzically. 'What made you think I had?'

Harper didn't answer her question; instead, she said, 'Did Robyn ever take you to see a doctor about your depression?'

Abi snorted. 'Like that was ever going to happen. She said I wasn't depressed; I was just plain lazy.'

The joke's on me it seems. What a lying bitch. And to think I fell for it. As Robyn had lied to Dylan about Abi, she wasn't even going to go there with the sex or alcohol issue. It was irrelevant now, anyway. Harper let out a breath. *And to think Dylan actually believed Robyn.*

'Do you think I should take Robyn's offer?' Abi didn't stop to draw breath. 'I don't think I have it in me to fight anymore, Harper.'

Harper glanced at her before returning her attention to the road. *Should Abi accept the offer?* The deal Robyn had put forward was lousy when her huge wage was considered. £1000 a year to raise a child? Would that even cover nappies and clothes for a growing baby? She wanted to tell Abi to find the strength from somewhere to fight on. Not to let Robyn walk away the victor. But if Abi wanted to throw in the towel, so be it.

'If that's what you want, I can inform the other party on Monday,' Harper said with her solicitor's hat on.

Harper brought the car to a standstill outside a block of flats that looked as if they'd been built in the sixties. Graffiti covered the dark brick walls, and rubbish was overflowing from the bin area. The place had a menacing feel too. Now that gave her the instant shivers. How could Robyn see the woman she once loved and a baby live in such conditions? It would have been fine if there were no other choice in the matter, but Robyn had the means to lift Abi and Jake off of the poverty line, at least until Abi got on her feet properly. Despite her earlier thoughts, Harper said, 'I think you'll be selling yourself short. I know I can get you a better deal.' Looking firmly at Abi, she added, 'But it's up to you. Have you heard back from the Child Maintenance Service?'

'Only that they are waiting for Robyn to respond. I'm sure she will drag it out as long as possible.'

'She won't be able to drag it out forever, and they will demand back payments so I wouldn't worry too much. You should get some money soon.'

'What would you do about the offer if you were me?'

Harper looked at the flats again and remembered a time when she had lived in such a place. It was something she didn't like to think of often. 'I'd fight for justice and what was rightfully mine.'

Abi lowered her voice, and Harper could hear the

shakiness in her tone as she asked, 'What about my arrest?'

A plan started to formulate in Harper's mind; fixing Abi with a thoughtful gaze, she asked, 'There're security cameras in W.H. Smith, aren't there?

Abi looked at her curiously and nodded.

She felt a sense of excitement. 'On every aisle?'

'Yes, why?

Yes! Let's hope we strike gold. 'I'll call Marc and see if he can arrange for someone to look at the footage from earlier today. There just might be enough evidence to vindicate you. As for the offer. It's time to get tough. Your level of hardship means we can bypass mediation and go straight for a financial order. I'll file it on Monday.' *Let's see what Dylan's response is to that.*

Harper's mind wandered back to Abi's theft arrest. *Would she really have put her livelihood on the line, and risked losing her job by blatantly stealing a customer's card right in front of her?* Harper didn't think so. Something just didn't sit right with her. *Who else knows Abi is desperate for money?* Harper's thoughts went around in circles, and then something Shay had said earlier that day came to mind. 'Someone who wants her out of the way or to make her look unstable.' The realisation hit her like a thunderbolt. *Jesus, Could this be the handiwork of Robyn or am I starting to get paranoid?*

Chapter Twenty-One

Without the TV blaring noise from Tiffany's reality shows, the living room was eerily quiet. Robyn sat stiffly on the sofa, her eyes roaming over the bomb site the room had become. After Abi had dropped Jake off, Robyn had gone shopping in Mothercare for additional things she thought the baby would need. Admittedly, she'd gone overboard, but only because she didn't want to come up short and find herself needing something in the middle of the night. That would mean having to phone Abi, which was the last thing she wanted to do. Little feet prodded her side causing her to turn and look down. Jake's podgy little face was in stark contrast to his skinny body. Dark curls coiled into his neck and over his forehead, and big blue eyes with long lashes that gave him the appearance of a mischievous cherub stared back at her.

'I don't know what you're smiling at, gummy?' Robyn said to the small squirming bundle on the sofa beside her. 'Is that all you're going to do all weekend— poo, piss and dribble.'

Despite the hardness in her voice, Jake kept smiling, revealing his pink gums in the process.

Robyn narrowed her eyes. 'Don't even think about getting used to coming here. This is a one-off, do you hear me?'

Jake's eyes widened, and his tiny hands grappled

in the air. Robyn instinctively held out her finger for him to grab. She was surprised by his strength.

'You've got quite a grip haven't you?' For a moment, she wondered what Jake would look like when he was older. Would he have Abi's once good looks? Her kindness and compassion? She peered closer, studying his little fingers as if seeing a human hand for the first time in her life. She watched his expression change from curiosity to joyfulness and was intrigued by the little boy's range of emotions. *No wonder your mummy loves you so much. You've got such a beautiful smile.*

For the next hour, Robyn found herself lost in his gaze. If it hadn't been for the whiff coming from his nappy, she would have stared at him all night.

'Come on then, gummy,' she said, lifting him gently and holding him against her chest. His head bobbed against hers, and she drew her head back slightly so he wouldn't hurt himself. In that instant, their eyes met close up, and she felt an immediate connection. The self-assured twinkle in his eyes enthralled her. It was as if she had known him a lifetime. Robyn buried her face in the crook of his neck and inhaled his baby powder scent.

A lump formed in her throat. Would she ever be able to forgive herself for wanting Abi to abort this amazing ray of light? How could Robyn even bear to look Jake in the eye?

What would you say if you could speak? If you knew the truth. Would you still smile at me, knowing what … what I wanted to do to you? She placed her hand on the back of Jake's head and made a promise that only God and herself could hear. It was a promise that in her heart, she knew she'd never break.

Chapter Twenty-Two

Harper stared down at the phone when it began to ring. She considered ignoring it. Her head was pounding. The case files on her desk were mounting, but all she could think about was Abi and what the poor woman must be going through. The stress of divorce was bad enough without an arrest hanging over her head. Thoughts still lingered in her mind about Robyn and her possible connection. *Would she really stoop that low?* The incessant ringing of the phone made her headache even worse. She reached down and reluctantly picked up the receiver.

'Yes?' she said in an uncharacteristically sharp tone.

'Harper, it's Marc.'

She gave a self-conscious laugh. 'Marc? Oh, I'm sorry—'

'—Bad day aye?'

Harper looked down at Abi's file on her desk. 'You could say that.'

'Maybe this news will cheer you up. The security guard from the shop took a close look at the CCTV footage, and it's as clear as day; Ms Massey didn't lift that credit card, the woman planted it on her. Anyway, he took the recording to the police, and I've just been informed they've dropped the charges. They tried to contact the woman but she'd given a false address.'

Harper leapt to her feet nearly dragging the telephone off the desk with her. She stared upwards. 'That's fantastic.' *Thank you, God.* 'Marc, I can't thank you enough for your help.'

'Only doing my job. Let's meet up for drinks soon.'

'Definitely.' Harper replaced the handset. Without a minute to lose, she dialled Abi's number. She was so elated she couldn't wipe the smile from her face.

Harper could hear the relief in Abi's voice when she shared the news. 'So there won't be any charges against me?'

'None whatsoever,' Harper said still smiling.

Silence.

'My gut is telling me Robyn had something to do with this. I mean how did that card get in my pocket? That girl must have put it there,' Abi said.

Harper kept her opinion to herself. 'Yes the CCTV showed her putting it there, but there's no proof it had anything to do with Robyn. I think we should just be grateful the truth has come to light and move on to the next step.'

Abi's voice was barely audible when she spoke. 'With the run of bad luck I seem to be having, I'm starting to think my life would have been easier if I just accepted her offer. '

'Nonsense. This is exactly what Robyn wants. To push you into a corner so you'll accept an unfair settlement. We have to fight fire with fire Abi. Are you with me?'

'Okay, whatever you say,' Abi replied wearily. 'I'd better go, I've got something on the hob.'

'Okay, I'll be in touch soon,' Harper said feeling more determined than ever. 'Take care of yourself.'

As Harper sat there contemplating the situation, the angrier she became. She wondered if Dylan knew anything about the arrest. *Maybe Robyn told her what she'd intended to do.* If that was the case it would give her more ammunition to fight with. *Boy do we need it! But I need to find out the truth?* There was only one thing to do. Call Dylan.

Chapter Twenty-Three

'Dylan, did you know?' Harper said in a raised voice down the phone.

'Know about what?' Dylan asked coolly. She was sitting at her desk in her office miles away, but she could almost feel Harper's hands lock around her neck.

'That Abi got arrested,' Harper's voice was thunderous, 'and I know your client had something to do with it. I promise you, that piece of scum you're working for is going to get what's coming to her tenfold.'

'Whoa there. You need to calm down and tell me exactly what you are talking about. Because I really don't have a clue,' Dylan said, smiling at Cathy and taking the files she had asked for.

'You really don't know? Abi was arrested for theft. Someone planted a credit card on her and accused her of stealing it.'

'And you think my client set her up? That's ridiculous.' Dylan hoped she sounded convincing. If Robyn did have her hand in this mess Dylan had obviously failed in her bid to bring Robyn and the baby closer together. She had hoped by spending time with him they would have bonded and Robyn's view on a fair settlement may have softened. *Robyn's a lot colder than I gave her credit for.* But that was beside the point. It was Dylan's job to handle the divorce—that's what she was being paid for. The last thing she needed was Robyn trying to get Abi thrown in jail. If Robyn fully trusted Dylan's abilities, she would know she didn't have to go to such drastic measures. Though she wasn't about to tell Harper any of that, of course.

'Is that all you have to say?' Harper said. 'You do know Abi could have gone to court for this, and had a conviction on her record, right? A criminal conviction!'

'If what you say is true, it has nothing to do with me, or my client,' Dylan said nonchalantly. Her flippant attitude was having its intended response. Harper was so rattled she didn't know what was going on. Now was the time for Dylan to go for the jugular. 'I think it's best for everyone if we settle this as quickly as possible. Tell your client to accept the offer now, before things get worse for her.'

'That's you all over isn't it? Strike while the iron's hot, despite who might get hurt in the process.'

Dylan had reached her breaking point. The moment of weakness at the food bank was now long forgotten. If Harper was going to brand her as a cold-hearted bitch, who was she to disappoint.

'She isn't going to get any more Harper, so—'

'—I keep telling you the offer is an insult and you know it. I just don't understand why you don't strive for justice—'

Dylan's smooth retort cut her off. '—I am not in this for justice, Harper. This is law, a practice that falls fucking far from justice. Police uphold justice. I'm a fucking solicitor, and I'm a bloody good one at that, for a reason. I don't let my heart rule my decisions, and I certainly did not become a successful solicitor to put plasters on knee scrapes. If that's your calling, you are in the wrong vocation. You should have become a doctor ... or a nun.'

'One day, Dylan,' Harper replied finally, her tone well-adjusted to indifference, 'you're going to need help, and no one will give a flying fuck, especially me.'

'It's a little too late for that, I'm afraid. Been there done that, worn the T-shirt, and you're right, no one gave a shit or came to my aid. But guess what? I'm still here, and I'm still standing despite it all. So little hero, born and bred; save your speeches for someone who gives a shit.'

This personal attack got Dylan's back up straight away. She didn't know why she let Harper get to her like this, but she did. In a way, Dylan was hurt at how Harper had misjudged her. It was one thing to have a go at her about the case, but why did she always call her character into question? Did Harper go around abusing doctors who carried out abortions, vets who put animals to sleep? These were also jobs that carried a bad rap. Though the work wasn't pleasant, what would happen if there was no one there to do them? Women would be forced to carry unwanted babies, and only God knew what fate would await them once they were born. Animals to live the rest of their lives in pain. Is that what Harper really wanted in her fantasy world?

'Let's see how this all pans out for you in court because that's where this is heading. I'm done trying to cut a deal. Let's leave it for a barrister and judge to sort out. You have a financial order winging its way to you as we speak,' Harper said.

'You know as well as I do that they have to try mediation first.'

'Not with the level of poverty Abi is in, considering how much your client earns,' Harper shot back.

'Whatever. I can't blame you for not knowing when you're in too deep. Truth be told, I do think you're good at what you do, but that ridiculous bleeding heart crap is going to get you nowhere in this business. It's really sad,' Dylan said, calmly signing a stack of letters Cathy had just finished typing for her.

'We are done discussing this case, goodbye,' Harper sneered.

'Miss you already,' Dylan said, trying to get a final rise out of Harper.

'Oh, one last thing. I'd put any idea of getting that partnership right out of your head. If this is the last case I ever practise, I will personally make sure you don't win.'

'Like I told you, nothing thrills me more than a challenge.' Dylan forced a smile and hung up the phone. Cathy stood next to her, staring.

'What is it, Cathy?' Dylan asked impatiently.

'I could be mistaken, but whoever that was, has you flustered. You still sounded normal, of course, but your hands are shaking a little,' Cathy advised. Dylan could hear the glee in Cathy's voice.

'Rubbish,' Dylan answered, but she did not dare lift her hands to disprove Cathy's observation. 'Don't you have to draft the Corey correspondence I asked you for?'

Cathy smirked but didn't bother replying. She turned on her heel and headed for her desk.

'And close the door, please,' Dylan asked evenly.

When the door closed, she looked at her long slender fingers. They exhibited a slight tremor she did not like. It was a sign of vulnerability, something that came from emotion, from the weakness of the opinions of others. She had not seen her hands do this since she was a late teen, waiting for her exam results. By this point in her life, such displays never surfaced anymore.

With her career in verbal altercation, emotional jousting and keeping cool even when the rage fumed around her, it was quite unsettling for Dylan to feel that nausea in her heart again. It was just like the nausea of a stomach, but worse. She had not felt it in years, even over a decade—a horrid cancerous condition of the esoteric heart that came from a guilty conscience or a regret of action.

Could it be that she was less impervious to caring if someone hated her than she had thought? Could it be that Harper's opinion of her mattered just a tad more to her than she wanted to admit? No, she was Dylan Blue, a she-shark not to be fucked with; not by anybody. Her hands began to steady, peeling the brunt of the small panic from her that she was becoming a weakling who cared.

Dylan sank back in her chair, and looking down she saw the folder of Massey vs. Massey. It demanded her attention for some unknown reason, but she refused to entertain the urge.

Dylan's hands had ceased their mild shaking, but that heart-nausea remained. Like a child who felt bad for upsetting its mother, she could not dismiss the recurring echo of Harper's voice.

'*One day, Dylan, you are going to need help, and no-one will give a flying fuck. Especially me.*'

Chapter Twenty-Four

'What the fuck were you thinking, Tiffany? Getting Abi arrested? Have you gone mad? You could get in big trouble for that.'

'Let them do their worst. Anyway, I didn't see you doin' anythin', and now I know why.' Tiffany flung a suitcase on the bed and began throwing her belongings haphazardly into it. 'I didn't sign up for this crap, Robyn. No fuckin' way am I having a baby in my life. I've just turned twenty-one. I've got my whole life ahead of me.'

'Look, it doesn't have to change anything between us.'

Tiffany stared at her open-mouthed. 'A baby won't change anythin'? You're livin' proof of what happens when a baby comes on the scene. Thanks, but no thanks. I think I'll pass on this one.'

Instantly Robyn regretted saying anything to Tiffany so soon. *I should have let her meet Jake first before dropping this bombshell on her. What the hell will I do if she leaves me? All of this will have been for nothing.* 'It will just be a weekend here and there.' She could hear the desperation in her own voice. 'It's no biggie. He really is a good baby. He's a good sleeper and…'

Tiffany shook her head slowly. 'All it took was one weekend, and you're gushing about it like it can walk on water.'

'His name's Jake, not it.'

Tiffany rolled her eyes. 'Whatever. Jake, "it", call him what you want. I want nothin' to do with this shit.'

'So you're saying I've got to choose between you and my son?'

Tiffany threw her hands in the air. 'He's not your fuckin' son. Your ex-bird had some random man's semen shoved up her hole. You've got as much to do with his DNA as I have with the pope.'

'Parenting isn't about DNA. It's sharing a special bond ...'

'Oh, just shut the fuck up, Robyn. You're doing my fuckin' head in. Tiffany tilted her head to the side. 'And what about Italy and your promotion? What happens with that while you run around playin' mummy?'

Robyn bowed her head. In all honesty the promotion couldn't have been further from her mind. All she could think about these past few days had been Jake. Nothing else seemed as important anymore. Robyn had a shot at being a mother to a beautiful baby boy. It was a mystery to her how it happened, but it felt as if Jake had put a magical spell on her. Robyn hadn't paid much attention to Jake when he'd been born. She had been too busy fucking Tiffany to give him a second thought. After that, Abi had been given her marching orders and Tiffany moved straight in. Thinking about it now, Robyn regretted being so hasty. She had loved every second of every minute that she had spent with Jake that weekend. So much so that Robyn had even kept back one of his babygros so she could cradle and sniff his scent whenever she was alone. Robyn rose to her feet and slid her arms around Tiffany's waist, pulling her tight against her. 'Come on, Tiff. We can work something out, can't we?' she said nibbling her ear.

'There is no "we" if you carry on with this madness.' Tiffany stopped packing and wriggled out of Robyn's embrace. Turning to face her, she said, 'Believe me, you'll soon be sick of lookin' after it. I know. I've got five younger brothers and sisters, remember. I have a much better idea of the shit that comes with kids.'

Robyn being an only child couldn't even begin to imagine the mayhem Tiffany's life must have been growing up in such a household, but Jake was one baby, not five, and Robyn's financial situation was completely different. She honestly couldn't see what the problem was. It wasn't as if she was asking Tiffany to babysit him. She was more than happy to look after him herself. All she wanted was for both Tiffany and Jake to be in her life. She didn't think that was too much to ask considering she already financed Tiffany's lifestyle.

'Tiff,' she started carefully. 'This situation is completely different. He's one baby.' *A very gorgeous one at that.* 'No offence intended, but I have the money for him to have a good life. He's not going to be dragged up on a council estate, like—'

Tiffany narrowed her eyebrows and placed her hands on her hips. '—Like what? What're you saying about my mum?'

Robyn quickly took a step towards her, closing the gap. If she was to get Tiffany on side, she was going to have to be a bit more careful with her choice of words. That was one of her many problems. When she was in a bind she always ended up digging herself even deeper into trouble. 'About your mum? Nothing. She's a great mum. I just mean we won't be cramped up in a small flat. We can travel and do lots of things, like shopping.' She smiled. Surely Tiffany couldn't refuse now. Shopping was like an addiction to her. Robyn actually thought Tiffany would sell her soul if she was offered a free reign in a shopping centre for the rest of her life.

Tiffany snorted. 'With a baby in tow?'

'Well yeah, sometimes,' Robyn said hesitantly.

Tiffany burst out laughing as she closed the case and zipped it up. 'Good luck with that one. I wish I could stick around just to see you tryin' to cope with a baby.'

'You're being so unreasonable.'

Tiffany's laughter died down. 'Says you. When you come to your senses, you know where I am. I wouldn't leave it too long, though. I might actually meet someone who will put me first.'

Tiffany grabbed her case by the handle, tugged it onto the floor and headed towards the bedroom door.

'Come on, Tiff, aren't you being a bit dramatic

here? Where're you going to go? You have nothing without me, remember.' Robyn hoped her voice relayed the threat she intended.

Tiffany stopped at the door and spun around grinning. 'That was before.'

'Before what?'

Tiffany reached into her bag and took out her lipstick. She glanced at Robyn as she ran it across her lips in a slow, exaggerated movement. 'Before you transferred all of your assets into my name. I'm actually quite well off if you think about it.'

'You wouldn't dare.'

'Wouldn't I? You just watch. You either tell your solicitor you want nothin' to do with that baby or kiss goodbye to all your money. Choice is yours. See how loved up you feel when you're broke,' Tiffany said.

Before Tiffany could open the door, Robyn stormed at her, grabbing her by the scruff of her neck and dragging her backwards. 'Where the fuck do you think you're going?' Robyn screamed through clenched teeth. 'Get in there and clean that shit off your lips, you stupid slut,' she shouted, tossing her effortlessly into the en-suite bathroom. Tiffany's body propelled forward, into the glass of the shower, smashing the screen into pieces with the velocity of her fall. For a split second, Robyn stood frozen at what she had done, but as soon as Tiffany got up unharmed, Robyn's unbridled anger returned with even greater ferocity.

Robyn stepped forward onto the shattered glass

and gripped the back of Tiffany's head, pushing her face hard into the wall. 'How many fucking times do I have to tell you?' she yelled, her mouth pressed against her ear. 'Don't. Fuck. With. Me.'

Tiffany squirmed and whimpered. 'Please, Robyn, you're hurtin' me.'

Robyn felt nothing in the heat of her rage. Tiffany cowered when Robyn spun her around. She grabbed a handful of Tiffany's hair and squeezed her hand tight into a fist. Tears poured down Tiffany's face, causing her flawless make-up to run all over her cheeks.

'Why do you have to keep pushing me? You made me do this to you. You.' Robyn screamed at the top of her voice. 'I kept warning you, but you wouldn't fucking listen would you?'

'I'm sorry, I'm sorry; I didn't mean it. I wouldn't leave you. Please let go of my hair,' she said, sobbing profusely. Robyn released her hair and stood back only to slap Tiffany across the face so hard that her eyes rolled back in her head for a brief moment before she fell to her knees.

'Please stop,' Tiffany begged, trying to push herself to her feet, before slumping back down on the floor. 'Please, Robyn. I promise I'll be good. I'll do anythin' you want.'

Robyn looked down at Tiffany, who sat rocking back and forth, her fist stuffed firmly in her mouth. The once sexy fiend wasn't so mouthy and cocky now. She looked pathetic and weak. Robyn frowned as she glanced down at her hands. *What the fuck have I done?* The anger deflated like air out of a balloon as the realisation hit her. It was too late to apologise. She would come across as being weak. If another episode like this was to be avoided, Tiffany needed to know her place. Robyn tried to keep the coldness in her voice as she spoke. 'Clean up this mess then unpack your stuff. If you know what's good for you, you won't get me angry again.'

Robyn walked out, slamming the door behind her. She exhaled a long breath as she dropped onto the bed. *Why did I let things get out of control like that? What if she goes to the police?* Fear flooded her. Her hands trembled at the thought. *No, she wouldn't be that stupid.* Not if Robyn did something extravagant for her. She knew exactly how to wrap Tiffany around her little finger. Robyn smiled to herself. *I'll buy her a car. That should do it. And now I've put her in her place, she won't have any choice about Jake being in my life.*

Robyn reached under the mattress, brought out Jake's babygro and held it to her chest. She tried to convince herself everything would go to plan once the divorce was over. *So why does everything feel like it's falling apart?*

Chapter Twenty-Five

Lloyd & Baxter was an insignificant security company compared to the other two situated in Barking, but it had been growing steadily over the past few years, especially with the current political climate calling for tighter security measures. Abi noticed that she was introduced to new colleagues almost weekly now, which she liked as there was less attention on her. Her boss had more people to manipulate and dislike now and less time to pick apart all Abi's efforts and make her feel stupid.

The month before, two new women were appointed—one as a receptionist and the other as an accountant. Contrary to what Abi imagined in her stereotypical judgement, Jennifer, the accountant, was far more amicable and down-to-earth than the receptionist, but they were both relatively easy to get along with.

Jennifer's phone rang in a long straight tone—an internal call—and Abi answered.

'Jennifer's office. She's out at the moment,' Abi said. It was Sarah, calling from reception.

'Oh, Abi, actually this is for you. There's a woman down here to see you. She says it involves your son.'

Abi's heart sank. If it pertained to her son, she always expected the worst. *But why would Tia come to my workplace? Surely she would just phone me.*

'Alright, Sarah. I'll be right down,' she replied while a streak of immense worry curled around her insides at the thought of what awaited her. *Oh sweet Jesus, what if something's happened to Tia?* She took the stairs two at a time to the ground floor offices where reception was situated on the other side of the compartment walls.

When she rounded the corner, her worry turned to utter shock.

'Robyn?' she gasped when she saw Robyn seated on the waiting area sofa as if she owned it. Abi passed a serious glance at Sarah, but the receptionist kept her conduct professional and carried on answering the switchboard. Abi's throat closed up with the vile feelings Robyn instilled in her, and she wondered what kind of foul agenda she had concocted this time with which to ruin her life.

'Abi, I need to talk to you, off the record,' Robyn said abruptly, pushing herself to her feet.

'This is hardly the time and place,' Abi protested. 'I'm at work.' The anger from the day of her arrest still resided within her. To have had her fingerprints and DNA taken like she was a criminal was something she would never forget, and she knew the woman in front of her had played a major role in it. Any last remnants of love she had felt for Robyn had well and truly disappeared.

Robyn stuffed her hands into her jacket. 'I'm quite aware of that. But this is important.'

'You told Sarah you were here about Jake.'

'I am.' Robyn shifted from foot to foot. 'There's no easy way to say this … look, I want to be a part of Jake's life.'

Abi cocked her head. Was she joking? Abi peered closer and could see by the determined look on Robyn's face that she wasn't. It was a look Abi knew well. 'Excuse me? You want what?'

'I said I want—'

Abi shook her head in disbelief. '—It was a rhetorical question, Robyn. Do you really think I'm going to let you have anything to do with my child after what you did? I just can't believe you have the frigging gall to come here.'

'What, I—'

'—Oh don't play all innocent with me. Are you saying you didn't put some blonde bimbo up to coming into my shop and accusing me of stealing her credit card?'

Robyn gave her an incredulous stare. 'On Jake's life. I swear I didn't know anything about it. When my solicitor told me, I thought she was kidding. Come on, Abi, I might be a lot of things, but doing juvenile shit like that isn't me. You know that.'

Raising a finger, Abi directed it at Robyn. 'No, that's where you're wrong. When it comes to you, I don't know anything. I thought you were a decent person once upon a time, but look how badly I got that wrong.'

'Can we discuss this outside?' Robyn said,

glancing apprehensively towards the reception desk.

'We can go to the end of the world, but nothing is going to change my mind.' Abi headed towards the exit with Robyn trailing behind her. Once outside, Abi turned to face her. 'You were trying to get what you wanted.' Abi fought back, having no idea where she found the strength to stand up to Robyn. 'Me off your back, so you're free to run around with that slut.'

'I'm swallowing my pride by being here. I made a mistake, Abi ...' Robyn's voice dropped to a whisper.

'A mistake? About what this time? Your whole fucking life is a mistake. You think you can use and abuse people like they're broken toys. But they're not. I'm not. I loved you.' Abi could feel herself tearing up, but she refused to give in to her emotions. She wouldn't give Robyn the satisfaction. 'You were my life, and you just threw it away for what?' Abi ranted without even thinking. It was as if all her concerns and complaints came pouring out, things she previously only had the courage to address in her deepest thoughts at night before she fell asleep.

Robyn bunched her short strands of hair in her hands. 'I know, I know. I was just scared and confused, that's all.'

'No, you're a coward who refused to take responsibility for the child you demanded I have. You've come here saying you want a part of his life but you haven't even arranged child maintenance. We're both living in poverty while you swan about in your flash car,' Abi retorted, her heart slamming and her hands shaking profusely. Her cheeks flushed with rage, and she didn't care who heard their fight. 'You're nothing but a fucking coward, and I'll make sure Jake knows it when he's old enough.'

Robyn set her hands on her hips, looking at the sky in disbelief. 'Why are you behaving like this? Look I promise I will send the forms back to the CMS when I get home. I just thought you'd be happy for me to start seeing him. Isn't this what you wanted?'

'What I wanted? What I fucking wanted was the love you promised me,' Abi shrieked, feeling her fear give way to an alien sensation she never knew before—confidence. She watched Robyn wince at her swift response, completely dumbstruck by her clout.

Robyn leant closer to her, now aware that passersby were watching, saying under her breath, 'What I've put you through so far is child's play. If you don't give me what I want, I promise I will drag you through every court in the country. I will make your life a living hell until I get visitation rights.'

Abi shuffled backwards. 'I wondered when you'd show your true colours. You can't help yourself can you?' With a vocal pitch, Abi added, 'I don't care what you say. You can threaten me all you want. You had your chance, and you blew it. Now it's your turn to live with the consequences.' With that, she stormed through the aluminium doors, into the building, leaving Robyn standing on the pavement stunned.

'What just happened?' Abi asked herself, but there was no answer. As vividly as she could, she replayed the whole incident in her mind, but instead of dwelling on her scores and her well-placed retorts, she kept hearing only Robyn's threats. What had she done by letting Robyn have access to Jake?

Why hadn't she realised that Robyn would never change? She was rotten through and through. *Will she really take me to court?* Abi knew Robyn had money, and a powerful father, which meant anything was possible. A myriad of emotions streamed through her in the devastating wake of Robyn's unbelievable demands.

Her whole body began to shake, and she looked at Sarah as she passed her, who stared back at her wide-eyed. Abi's feelings fought inside her to determine her next move, but the solid winner was about to bring her to her knees. Defeat came in before courage and fear, sending Abi staggering into the peaceful vacancy of the toilets, making it just in time. Her well-practiced straight face, the one she used so as not to cry in front of Tia or Harper, served her well, but when she slammed the cubicle door behind her, she could hold it no longer. Her rapidly waning body, emaciated by the stress of her downward spiralling life, shook violently as she vomited into the toilet bowl. Abi was just grateful that nobody could hear her. Her knees burnt under her weight on the cold tiles, and her fingers clenched the rim of the toilet bowl while her body convulsed until she had nothing left in her.

Her thoughts rushed, and her head spun with emotional exhaustion. For some reason, she suddenly thought of the painting in the lobby of Syner and

Associates, where she met Harper Anderson for the first time. In her despair, Abi wondered if God would pay Robyn back for all the hurt and pain she had caused her. That was not something God would do, not according to what she learnt in church, oh no. But there were other gods—gods of pain, gods of thunder, gods of love ... and gods of justice. The painting of Syn, the goddess who stood in for those unfairly treated, was all Abi saw in her head as her tears jerked her body uncontrollably.

The outer toilet door burst open, and she heard Jennifer's voice filled with urgency.

'Abi? Abi, are you alright?'

Abi didn't answer her, mostly because she was too embarrassed.

Jennifer knocked on the cubicle door. 'Abi, let me in. Let me have a look at you. I know what happened. Sarah told me your ex was here.'

'Please just leave me alone,' Abi forced out, but her voice failed her and her words bent and slurred.

'Listen, when you're ready, come to my office, alright? You're coming for a drink with me after work. Call your sister and tell her you'll be picking Jake up a little late. This nonsense will kill you if you carry on like this,' Jennifer said.

In her tone, Abi could hear tenderness and authority all at once.

'Y-y-yes. Okay. I j-just need a minute,' Abi stuttered, thoroughly ashamed of her weakness, falling apart like this and giving Robyn what she wanted.

'Okay. See you in a bit.'

Abi rested her head against the edge of the toilet, listening to Jennifer's high heeled boots click away towards the door and eventually disappear. In her mind's eye, she kept seeing the painting of the fierce goddess and wondered if it would be blasphemy to put her trust in that image, just for a while, just to perk her up somewhat so that she could have a more tangible deity to hold on to. While she engaged in her own spiritual dilemma, Abi realised that Harper's law firm had a peculiar name that made the connotation with the goddess even more uncanny—*Syner & Associates*.

Was that a sign? Was it some kind of cosmic consolation sent her way? Either way, it possessed a certain measure of magic to it that she loved. That magical property was just what she needed to keep her hope alive and to hold her heart high enough to get through this ugly mess.

Chapter Twenty-Six

Abi waited until everyone had left for the evening before she started to gather her belongings. The miserable atmosphere of the office after hours, still illuminated, but with all the stations deserted, computers off, was reminiscent of how empty and lost Abi felt inside.

The blue carpeted corridor stretched ahead of her like an insurmountable distance she needed to traverse, one she didn't have the strength for, but she knew that there was some reward at the end of that path. Jennifer would be in her office, ready to take Abi's mind off her dire situation.

She had spoken to Harper, who had reassured her that Robyn was blowing hot air about going to court to get visitation rights. Harper believed this was something they could arrange between themselves. Despite Abi's reservations, she knew Robyn had a legal right to see the child. Once Abi had calmed down, she came to terms with it. Wasn't it something she had been pushing for all along? Well, now she was getting her just desserts. She would just have to deal with it.

I just need to get the hell out of here. Above her, the white hum of the lights depressed her, and Abi swiftly moved towards Jennifer's office.

'Hello,' Jennifer said cheerfully without looking up from her laptop. 'Won't be a min, babe. I'm just finishing up here, alright?'

'Okay,' Abi answered, thankful that Jen was not an over-emotional gawker who asked a million times if she was okay.

'If you don't mind me asking, what did your ex want?'

Abi let out a heavy breath before recounting the events. Jennifer looked as shocked as Abi had been by Robyn's demands and threats.

'So what now then?' Jennifer asked once Abi stopped speaking.

Abi shrugged her shoulders. 'Dunno. My solicitor thinks she's blowing hot air with her threats, so I'll have to wait and see.'

'Yep, that just about rounds up what bullies are.' Jennifer said nonchalantly. 'All talk and no action. Right, let's get out of here, I'm dying for a drink.'

'Are you sure I'm not imposing?' Abi asked, suddenly feeling like a drag with her constant dramas. 'I mean, were you going out anyway or are you just doing this for me?'

'Oh stop it.' Jennifer smiled as she signed off and packed her empty lunch tin and travel mug into her bag. 'I was the one who made the offer, remember? Would I do that if I didn't want to take you out?'

Abi uttered a sheepish snicker, and Jennifer's green eyes flashed with amusement.

'I'm taking you to my favourite bar; they make the best cocktails ever,' Jennifer said as she tidied up her desk. 'And the porn star one will leave you floating on a cloud, babe.'

For a woman who looked like butter wouldn't melt in her mouth, Jennifer sure seemed to be the type who knew how to enjoy themselves. 'Sounds good,' Abi said, laughing at the absurd name of the drink. The closest she'd ever been to a porn star was the bootleg DVDs Robyn used to bring home and insist she watched. Not that she was a prude or anything, but porn didn't float her boat, especially the hardcore type Robyn was in to.

Half an hour later, a taxi dropped them off outside The Glass House—a popular lesbian hangout, and to Abi's utter amazement Jennifer appeared to be a regular as she nodded to several of the women loitering outside smoking. Still in shock, Abi tailed her colleague like a lost puppy. *What's Jennifer doing hanging out in a gay bar?*

'Meg. Two porn stars for me and my girl Abi here, please and thank you,' Jennifer called out over the counter at a short, middle-aged woman with deep laugh lines and a chequered hat.

'No problem, two coming your way, Jen,' she shouted back over the boisterous crowd who gathered around the bar for service.

'This place is quite busy for a weekday?' Abi said the only thing she could think to say, given this unexpected surprise.

'Yeah, but you're the most delish woman here.' A grin passed quickly across Jennifer's face.

'Oh, come off it.' Abi self-consciously brushed

her hair back. She couldn't help but think that Jennifer must have the heart of a saint to be so kind to her or … she could be telling the truth. She daren't think it was the latter. Hadn't Robyn spent the last nine months of their relationship telling her how disgusting and haggard she was? That no other woman would ever look at her except in a pitiful way.

'Seriously, you don't give yourself even half the credit you deserve.' Jennifer reached over and rested her hand on Abi's knee. 'If I'd have been there this morning, I'd have given your ex a piece of my mind. I can't believe someone would put you through the ringer like she has. If you were my girl, I'd treat you like a queen.'

Abi's face creased in confusion. She'd never thought for a second that Jennifer would be anything but straight. She didn't know why exactly, but she always imagined her going home to a man for some reason. *Don't go jumping to conclusions*, she told herself. *All she did was pay you a compliment*. Still, she had to know. 'Jennifer are you …?'

'Gay? Nah, I just come here 'cause I like the view … of course I'm bloody gay. Why do you think I brought you here?' Her voice was tinged with amusement.

Heat rose to Abi's cheeks. She knew she must be blushing furiously. Something she always did when the slightest bit embarrassed. It wasn't that she thought lesbians had a certain look. When meeting new people, she always assumed they were straight until they told her any different. Finding out about Jennifer was something she hadn't considered. 'I thought you brought me here to make me feel comfortable.'

Jennifer laughed. 'There was that as well. But I thought I should tell you about me. I wanted to before, but the time was never right.'

Abi's eyes dropped to her hands. 'There never is a right time.' Knowing wouldn't have changed anything. Since her break-up with Robyn, Abi had thought of nothing but Jake. Another relationship hadn't even entered her mind.

Jennifer tilted Abi's chin up with the tip of her finger. Their eyes locked. 'So now you know the truth…What about us, Abi?'

Abi laughed. 'What? You and me?'

Jennifer leant back, obviously hurt by Abi's response. 'Is something funny?'

'No,' Abi cried and raised her hands to her face. 'I'm not laughing at you. It's not funny as in *ha-ha*— but funny as in amusing; it's just that Robyn said no one would ever want me. That I was over the hill. But here we are.'

'Oh, I see. Take it from me Abi, you're far from over the hill.' Jennifer leant towards her, planted a soft kiss on Abi's cheek and whispered in her ear. 'You are absolutely perfect in my eyes.'

Abi's eyes darted around the room, looking everywhere but at Jennifer. *Would it be wrong to be thinking about another relationship in the middle of a divorce?* she questioned herself. Abi couldn't deny that she was attracted to Jennifer, but was it because Jennifer was being kind to her or was the chemistry between them the real thing? Either way, things were more complicated than that. Abi didn't come alone. 'You know I have a baby, Jen. He comes before anyone,' she said, half hoping it would make Jennifer back off while the other half prayed she wouldn't.

'Not a problem. I'd be a bit concerned about your parenting skills if he didn't. Anyway, I love kids. Can't say I've wanted one of my own, but having six nephews and four nieces, can you blame me?'

Abi's eyes widened. 'Oh, my God, really? That many?'

'Yep, and I love them to death, and I'm sure if you give me the chance to get to know your little boy, I'll feel the same about him as well.'

It was a wonderful revelation, after so many months of being cloistered in a loveless marriage with only motherhood as her purpose. Now she was sitting across from an attractive woman who apparently had the hots for her and as an added bonus loved children.

I feel like Cinderella, enjoying myself among the princes while the clock to my doom is ticking.

Judging her inner rant a bit melodramatic on that one, Abi gave no resistance when Jennifer placed her hands in her own.

'Abi, I know you're going through a tough time at the moment, and I'm not going to try and rush things in any way, but I want you to know I've got your back,' Jennifer said, having to elevate the volume of her voice over the shouts of a rowdy group that had just entered the bar.

'Thank you and I appreciate it, more than you'll ever know.' Abi smiled, growing more comfortable under Jennifer's intense gaze.

'How about one more drink then I'll take you home.'

Abi reluctantly nodded her head. She wanted to stay there with Jennifer. Not go back to the cold miserable place that was called home. Even for all the hell she had in her life right now, Abi felt very upbeat. Come to think of it, she couldn't remember the last time she was looking towards the future. She smiled to herself. It was true. You never knew what was around the corner in life. She had Jake, now it seemed Jennifer would complete the circle. Things were definitely looking up for her.

Chapter Twenty-Seven

'Run that by me again.' Dylan stared at the woman sat in front of her. The shock of her words hit Dylan like a slap in the face. Robyn, the hard faced woman, who only a couple of weeks ago was trying to dump her responsibilities without a second thought, was now telling her she'd had a change of heart. *It seems my plan worked after all.*

Robyn crossed her legs and leant back in her seat. 'I said I want to go into mediation with Abi. I've thought about taking her to court for visitation rights but I want to try mediation first. I need to sort out sharing custody. I'm willing to pay maintenance if she agrees.'

'Do you mind me asking why the sudden change of heart? Barely two weeks ago, you were threatening to fire me unless I got them out of your life and now—'

'—Do you have kids, Dylan?'

Yeah right. Like I have the time to be a mother. 'No.'

Robyn gave her a pitiful look. 'Then you won't understand.'

Oh, here we go with that old chestnut. No one can possibly know what true love is until you have a child. Dylan tried not to let her irritation show. 'Try me. I've never been caught in a blazing fire, but I can imagine it would hurt like hell.'

Robyn was silent for a few seconds; finally, she said, 'I can't describe it.' She shifted in her seat. 'It's the weirdest thing having someone that small and vulnerable dependent on you for their survival.'

Dylan stifled a yawn. 'Sounds amazing.' *If I ever want that I'll get something that doesn't grow into an arsehole, like a hamster or snail.*

'It is. I want to be a part of his life. I'm sure I can work things through with Abi, given time.'

'And your, ahem, girlfriend? She's onboard with this new lifestyle change?'

Robyn looked indignant. 'Of course, she is. She wants what I want.'

Dylan couldn't wait to see how Harper was going to handle this request. After recent events, would she advise Abi to tell Robyn to stick her mediation up her arse? If the boot was on the other foot, that's exactly what she would say.

Dylan only hoped Robyn's change of heart would not have a negative bearing on her partnership offer. *If things end amicably and Robyn's happy, I don't see any reason why it should.*

'Okay,' Dylan said, going ahead with the new game plan. 'You're right mediation is definitely the better option. But I'll tell you now, it's going to be a bit difficult. The financial order Abi has applied for cites poverty as a reason to not go to mediation.'

Robyn frowned. 'So I'll have to go to court?'

'At the moment yes.' When Robyn opened her mouth to protest, Dylan held up her hand to silence her. 'But, if you really don't want to go down that route…' Dylan didn't know how Robyn was going to take her suggestion, after all when Robyn's previous solicitor gave her the same advice, she was fired.

'Go on,' Robyn urged.

'I suggest you start paying child maintenance immediately, that way I can refute the poverty claim and suggest mediation.'

To her immediate surprise Robyn smiled.

'Okay.'

'Okay. Well good. Right then, moving on to the next issue. We need to talk about Abi's divorce petition. I doubt her solicitor will advise her to agree to mediation unless you withdraw your petition and agree to hers. At the moment with two petitions we're looking at going to court.'

Robyn's body visibly tensed. 'What! Where she accuses me of cheating?'

Dylan cocked her head and held her gaze daring Robyn to lie straight to her face. 'Are you sure it's not true?'

'Well, um, I…' Robyn's gaze fell to her hands. Seconds later her head shot back up. 'Alright, alright, let her have it her way, if it's gonna let me see Jake,' she said with finality.

'Okay. If you're really sure about this, I'll get in touch with Abi's solicitor and see if we can come to some sort of agreement over mediation. As I said though, I suggest you make a child maintenance payment immediately if you want to avoid court.'

'I'll do it as soon as I leave here,' Robyn said standing.

Dylan stood and held out her hand, feeling relieved things were finally coming together. The sooner she closed Robyn's case the happier she'd be. Dylan didn't like her. In reality she hadn't from the start. She couldn't quite put her finger on it, but there was something dark and dangerous about her. Robyn wasn't the sort of person Dylan would like to have in her life on a permanent basis. *I don't understand how any woman would.*

'I'll let you know Abi's decision,' Dylan said.

'Great. And, Dylan, thanks for all your help,' Robyn said warmly.

Dylan lowered herself onto her seat. *I hope she's no good at understanding body language.*

'The pleasure's all mine.'

Dylan waited until Robyn was long gone before she picked up the phone and punched in Harper's number. She wasn't expecting a warm welcome; in fact, she would be surprised if Harper picked up at all once she realised it was her calling. *Why did I have to be into someone so idealistic?* She knew that Harper had every reason to feel antagonistic towards Robyn, but what the hell had she done? Her job and that was it. Dylan wasn't the one who was putting Abi through the mill. She hadn't even met the woman. So why was she being punished for it. *Because Harper thinks you have the morals of an alley cat, that's why.*

After several rings, Harper answered. The

reception Dylan got was as frosty as she'd expected. 'I thought you'd like to know Robyn Massey wants to enter mediation with your client.'

'Is that right?'

Dylan couldn't read the tone of her voice. She took the pen from her desk and tapped it repeatedly against her knee. 'Yes, and I suggest you advise your client to try and work things out this way.'

'Was this your suggestion 'cause you're scared of losing?'

Dylan laughed, but there wasn't any humour in it. 'I told you, Harper. I do what's best for my client. My client has had a change of heart about the baby. I only do as I'm asked, nothing more, nothing less.'

'I'll let my client know.'

How the hell am I going to melt this iceberg? 'You do that.'

'I will.'

Dylan sighed in frustration. Harper wasn't letting her in. 'So I guess I'll see you around?'

'I suppose you will.'

'Harper?' she said gently.

'What?'

Dylan's heart pounded. The seconds ticked away and she felt helpless. Was this really going to be the end before it even got started? Seconds later, Dylan's tongue was still tied. The moment was lost. She had played things the wrong way, and it had backfired on her.

Finally, Dylan said, 'It was fun.'

'If you say so,' Harper said abruptly.

The connection went dead. *Fucking great. Now what? Do I just let her go? Or try and make her understand that I'm not the bitch she thinks I am.* Dylan threw the pen on the desk and reached for the phone again, but stopped midway. She didn't have much hope that Harper would listen to her explanation of how things had turned out. She was as stubborn as Dylan in that respect. As for giving up on her. Never! Dylan never stopped until she got what she wanted, and what she wanted more than anything was Harper. It was just a matter of figuring out how to get past her defences and straight to her heart.

Chapter Twenty-Eight

Who said miracles didn't happen? Abi had ridden the bus to Harper's office checking and re-checking the statement from her bank. For once in a very long time her account was in the black. Robyn had finally coughed up money for maintenance—£1400 had been transferred to her account earlier that day. Not that it didn't mean Abi wasn't still angry at Robyn, because she was. Just not as much as before. Finding the money in her account had definitely been part of the catalyst.

Abi entered Harper's outer office, pushing the door open with a zest of energy that had been missing for a long time. Maybe it had something to do the McDonald's breakfast she'd treated herself to an hour earlier. If Robyn continued to play ball there would be plenty more treats ahead, though mostly for Jake.

'Hey, Abi, you're looking well,' Shay said, glancing up at her from her desk.

'I feel it. It's been a long time since I've felt so good.'

Shay smiled kindly. 'Good. I'm pleased for you. Go in. Harper's expecting you.'

'Thanks,' Abi said walking past Shay's desk and into Harper's office.

Harper was talking on the phone, but acknowledged her with a smile and a small wave of her hand. She gestured for Abi to take a seat.

Abi slid on to the seat opposite her and once again looked down at the piece of paper in her hand. *Maybe I should frame it.* The giddiness inside was making it near enough impossible for her to keep still in her seat. She wanted to jump in the air and scream with joy. She had money, which meant control over her life. *Finally.*

Abi looked up when she heard the phone being replaced on its cradle.

'Abi I've got a new update—'

'—So have I.'

Harper clasped her hands together in front of her. 'Okay you go first.'

Abi held up the bank statement like it was the first prize in a competition. 'Robyn paid me maintenance today.'

Harper peered at the paper with squinted eyes. 'She did?'

'Yep. Fourteen hundred quid.' Abi wrapped her arms around herself tightly as if trying to contain the happiness inside. 'Oh, Harper. I can do so much for Jake with this. I can get him new clothes. Some decent food. I can even buy him a new cot. The one he has is second hand from a charity shop.'

Harper smiled, but there was a troubled look in her eyes. 'That's brilliant, Abi. I'm really pleased for you.'

'So what's your update?' Abi asked still wrapped up in a bubble of euphoria. It felt like she was on a winning streak and nothing was going to bring her down.

'Robyn wants mediation, Abi.'

Abi's eyes widened. 'She wants what?' She felt the balloon slowly deflate as the seconds ticked by.

'Mediation. To discuss access to Jake and financial arrangements. She wants to avoid going to court.'

'Why the sudden change? When I last spoke to her she was furious and said she was taking me to court.'

Harper shrugged her shoulders. 'I told you it was hot air. It makes more sense to work out a proper custody arrangement for Jake between the two of you.'

Abi stood abruptly, the adrenalin rush no longer from ecstasy but from fear. Just when it seemed she had managed to mount one obstacle there was an even bigger one ahead. 'Well I don't want it.' Abi strode over to the window and looked down at the traffic below. 'Not after all the crap she's put me through. She doesn't deserve it.'

'I think you should consider it, Abi. Going to court will be stressful and expensive. Mediation could speed things up considerably—'

Abi turned her head away from the window and held Harper's gaze. '—What if I don't want her around my son?' *Or me for that matter?* Abi's heart sunk. She knew if Robyn gained any sort of custody of Jake, it would mean she'd be in her life forever. While it hadn't bothered her before and she would have welcomed it only a week ago, things had changed and it was all down to Robyn and her outrageous behaviour.

Harper pushed herself to her feet and walked over to Abi. Her voice held authority yet was full of reason at the same time. 'Look, I know first-hand how much Robyn's hurt you. But even if it does go to court I'm certain she'll get visitation rights at the very least. If you go to mediation it will be on your terms.'

Abi could see Harper's point but by agreeing Abi thought it was letting Robyn off lightly. *How long do I really want this to go on for?* she asked herself. Instead of using all of her energy fighting Robyn she could use it to nurture Jake. Her mind buzzed with the pros and cons. By the end of it the pros outweighed the cons. 'You really think this is a good move, despite everything?'

'Yes, Abi, I really do. If I didn't, there's no way I'd advise you to take her up on the offer. And remember, if you don't agree on the financial aspects, we still have the financial order pending.'

Abi turned back to the window. It was true the way things were going there'd never be a light at the end of the tunnel. Besides, Robyn had always insisted she'd make a good mother. So why not give her the chance?

Abi ran a hand through her hair and sighed. 'Okay, I'll do it, but if she messes me about I'm pulling out straight away.'

'That's your prerogative. My advice is to go into mediation with a clean slate. I know it won't be easy but try and put the past behind you. You need to be thinking with a clear mind. Make a list of your objectives and stick to them. Don't let yourself become derailed by anything she says.'

Abi looked at Harper and smiled. It was the pep talk she needed. It was as if Harper was sending her off to do battle with the dreaded enemy. In a way she was. Who would have thought that you could hate someone you used to love so much. You only had to look at divorce statistics to realise her case was nothing new.

Chapter Twenty-Nine

Harper was exhausted, worn out. She couldn't remember the last time she was so happy to be home after a long workday. For once, Harper had reshuffled her appointments so that she didn't have to go into work early the next morning—a lay in was just what she needed. Not only did she need a physical rest, but a mental one too. The Massey case had consumed so much of her mind lately.

Harper switched on her sound system and chose a Native Indian flute CD she always played when she wanted to centre herself. Placing the disc carefully in the tray, the luminescent blue numbers registered on the display. She bought the album long before the iPod was around, and it reminded her of a simpler time when money was tight. It felt like a million years ago, but the memories were happy ones, for the most part.

Harper was glad for those hardships, it pushed her to where she was now. There was a star in the night's sky she picked when she was seventeen—a beacon that could never wash away, or be taken by the wind. Every few months, she would look up at that star, and ponder on how her life had become better or worse since the last time they 'spoke'. That way, Harper made sure that she never took anything for granted, or lost sight of what she had achieved. Like an old mariner, she navigated her happiness, measuring it and reporting to that star of hers.

On her dining room table, she selected a chocolate French fancy from its box and plonked down on one of the chairs. She sighed out loud as the cake melted in her mouth.   Amidst the soft background music and mild thunder outside her window, relaxation crept over her. A loud ringtone snapped her right out of it.

'Leave me alone,' Harper grumbled as she withdrew the mobile from her pocket. She peered down at it. The display said 'Private Number', the kind she never answered.

Eventually the phone stopped and chimed the message tone to remind her that she had a missed call. Harper only scoffed, kicking off her shoes and having another French fancy.

Again the ringtone shattered the peace of her tranquil home.

'I said go away?' She flung the mobile phone onto the sofa, as if distancing herself from it would mercifully dampen her hearing ability and rid her of the annoying call. In the wake of the second call, not even the sound of the soothing flute was relaxing her anymore. Her quiet night had now been defiled once and for all, and she got up to switch her phone off.

But as Harper's nail pressed down on the red button, the phone rang once more, evoking a sudden thought—what if Abi trying to get through to her?

'Hello?' Harper said.

'Harper? Harper, are you there?' a familiar voice

cracked over the line. It was a voice synonymous with anger and pain from Harper's past, a voice she hoped never to hear again.

'Yes,' Harper replied without emotion. 'How did you get my number?'

'You've got your details on the internet. It wasn't that hard to track you down.'

'And why would you, of all people, want to track me down?' Her fingers clenched the phone.

'Because I need some help,' her mother said. 'Your dad's dead; he's gone.'

Harper said nothing. Truth be told, she didn't know how to respond. Inside, despite an acknowledgement that death brought sadness, she lacked any emotion at all.

The thunder rumbled a bit louder outside as if it announced the melancholy conversation, but Harper hardly heard it. All she heard was her mother's voice, explaining with great effort how Harper's father had fallen from a high rise building where he was working and met his death instantly. *Drunk no doubt.*

'So at least he didn't suffer,' the hated voice added, but Harper heard only that her stepfather was dead, and as she tried to find a way to feel, she realised that all she experienced was relief.

Lucky him. 'Sorry to hear that,' Harper mumbled, hardly trying to sound convincing. 'But he wasn't my father. He was your husband, and that's all he was to me. Like you aren't my mother.'

'How can you say such a thing? I've never stopped thinking about you. I'm proud you've made such a success of your life ... I'm very proud of how you turned out,' her mother choked.

'How did I turn out? I am exactly the same person you kicked out of your house. I'm a successful solicitor with a good income and a nice home ... not the "piece of shit that would amount to nothing" as your husband so eloquently put it.'

Harper's stomach churned and her heart ached with the injustice of what they did to her at such a young age, when she needed them most—when her own mother had stood there and let her alcoholic, drug abusing stepfather throw her out of his house ''Cause he was done raising another man's bastard child'. That fateful day defined her purpose in life. She learnt that all things came to pass as they were supposed to, no matter how close it brought one to a brutal crash of faith. At the time it made no sense, and she was left to fend for herself, fresh out of secondary school with no family to give her that much needed foothold.

'Harper, why can't you ever let go of things? I thought you'd have outgrown clinging onto the past by now.'

'Clinging onto the past? What? Am I supposed to just forget how my own mother treated me? How you stood by and watched me become homeless?' Harper said, trying to calm her tumultuous heart. 'What the hell did I do wrong? I wasn't evil. I wasn't a criminal. I was your daughter. Your own flesh and blood. But no, that was not enough for you.'

Harper wanted to sound angry, but all she uttered was hurt; years of pain that made her voice bend uncontrollably as the tears burnt into her lids. As much as she tried to fight it, the tears rolled down her cheeks from the onslaught of the unfair treatment she believed she had successfully abandoned long ago.

'You turned out alright didn't you? What life would you have had if you stayed here? Up the duff and on the social that's where. You should be thanking me. Not holding a grudge.'

There was a brief silence before her mother spoke again. 'Look, Harper, I need some money. He left nothing. Can you help me out?'

Harper gave a short bitter laugh. 'Are you for real? I could have been dead for all you knew, yet you didn't give a shit then but now you're broke, you somehow made the effort to find me.'

'There's so much you don't understand, Harper. I did what I did for you. You've got to believe me.'

Boom! There it was. The emotional blackmail Harper knew so well. She was wondering how long it would be before she started her crap.

'How much do you need?' Harper said, controlling her voice as best she could, failing miserably at sounding composed.

'As much as you can spare. Things have been a bit tough lately. What with benefit cuts and everything.'

Harper didn't have the energy for this. If giving her money would make her go away she would give it

to her with pleasure. 'I'll sort it out for you tomorrow.'
Now please go away.

Her mother's voice softened. 'I knew you
wouldn't let me down. So are you gonna come to the
funeral?'

'What's the point? He didn't want to see me
when he was alive, why the bloody hell should I pay
him that courtesy?'

'If you knew what I've been through ... what I
tried to save you from ...'

Harper ignored the sobs on the end of the line.
The tears were ten years too late. 'I'm going now. I'll
post you a cheque tomorrow.' Harper disconnected
the call without another word.

Hearing her mother's voice reignited old
thoughts and fears she had swept conveniently under
the carpet. But now, confronted with a situation where
she had to address her own emotional abuse, she could
not help but travel back to her sixteenth year and the
unpleasant storm that ushered her into her coming of
age.

Turmoil and moroseness signified her childhood,
but in her late teens it all just snowballed into a giant
fuck-up of pure hypocrisy and judgement that
culminated in her discharge from her family for good.

With her nose in her cup, sipping at the liquid
madness of the strong black nerve rush, Harper
allowed herself to drift back to that terrible time, now
so blissfully far behind in her trail that it detached itself
as someone else's life. These days, she was content.

Happy? Not yet. Contentment was the precursor to happiness, once the bridge of success had been traversed. That bridge was the path which she was still navigating between two river banks—one of becoming the best at what she did with her exceptional track record as a solicitor, and the other of keeping her soul intact doing so. It was a fine cord, and Harper's trapeze act was thus far quite balanced.

Her goal had been to liberate others' repressed rights by becoming a solicitor, but she went one further and crowned it with a humanitarian approach. This was certainly not the norm in the cold and unfair world of law, but that was precisely what Harper wanted to change. Money was never the reason she chose that profession.

Justice was.

With all the injustice she had suffered throughout her life, she elected to fight the similar scourges with their own methods. In courts where innocent people, good-hearted people, got judicially sodomised by those who had more money, Harper Anderson was the spanner in their spokes ... and she loved it.

Chapter Thirty

Dylan thought she'd handled Robyn Massey's case quite well, even if she did say so herself. Okay, so she hadn't brought the case to a complete close yet, but that was through no fault of her own. If she were being honest, she was strangely pleased that Robyn had blind-sided her and opted for mediation. Unlike all of her other cases where she hadn't given a damn about those involved, this one was different. Maybe some of Harper's caring nature had managed to rub off on her. Whatever the case, she was relieved it would be resolved fairly. Her dad, on the other hand, had a different perspective. Sitting in the lavishly decorated living room of her parents' home, Gregory stared at her with a look of disappointment.

'All I asked you to do was win the case, was it really that difficult?'

'You asked me to avoid court, which I've done. If you knew Robyn Massey, you'd know what a stubborn piece of work she is.' Dylan turned to her mother, who was sat looking her usual prim and proper self—make-up applied with precision and her short bob, flawless. 'Mum, you're a baby person, explain to him about broodiness.'

Her mother sipped her tea from the china tea cup, the large diamond ring on her wedding finger glinting in the sun's rays. 'Don't get me involved. This is between the two of you.'

Thanks a bundle.

There was a gentle knock on the door before Rosa, her parents' housekeeper came into view. 'Mr Maynard, a Mr Massey is here to see you.'

From the look on Gregory's face, Dylan could see this was an unexpected visit.

He sighed as he cast a look towards Dylan. 'Bring him through.'

Dylan began to rise but stopped midway when her dad raised his hand.

'No, young lady. You're staying here. This is your doing. You explain to him what's going on with his daughter's case.'

Crap! Dylan glanced at her mother for some sort of reassurance, but she placed her tea cup down and stood, managing to avoid eye contact.

'I'll be in the kitchen if I'm needed,' her mother said, hurrying from the room.

What had she expected from her? Dylan's mother hated conflict. Whether it was with Gregory or Dylan, she always managed to slip away and hide herself until whatever was brewing blew over. In a way, this had caused Dylan to lose some respect for her. She was like a Stepford wife. Great on the outside, but empty on the inside. They had never had the sort of mother-daughter relationship she'd seen so many of her friends have with their mum's. It was her dad who Dylan had always been closer to. The one who had guided her and shaped the attitude she carried with her today. Now that she had done wrong in his eyes, he was throwing her to the wolves. *So much for family loyalty.*

Dylan clasped her hands tightly together, feeling as if she were in a lion's den waiting to be mauled. For the first time ever, she began to doubt herself. Had she let the case slip out of her hands because of her feelings for Harper? Dylan would be the first to admit that she hadn't been her usual pit-bull self when it came to handling the negotiations, but things could have turned out a lot worse. At least Robyn wanted something to do with the child now, which had been Dylan's intention.

Her head snapped up as she heard footsteps nearing. Dylan took a deep breath. If Massey had come round to give her dad a bollocking, she would give him a piece of her mind. She was going to stand firmly behind her decisions. *I am not my mother!* Dylan would fight fire with fire if she had to. She rose to her feet as the living room door opened and Massey bounded in. For a large portly man, he moved with the agility of a younger person. Dylan was taken aback when she saw the beaming smile on his face.

'Gregory my man ...' Max Massey extended his arm and shook Gregory's hand profusely. 'I knew you were the right man to come to.'

Gregory grinned, but Dylan could see confusion in his eyes. 'This is Dylan,' he said, outstretching his arm to her. 'She's handling your daughter's case.'

Dylan straightened her shoulders and walked to

her father's side.

Max gripped her slender hand with his large one. 'Dylan, my daughter has nothing but praise for you.'

Dylan's eyebrows rose involuntary. 'She does?'

'Yes. If it weren't for you guiding Robyn through this mess, I wouldn't have met my grandson. To be honest, I had my doubts about how this would all turn out. Knowing how stubborn my daughter can be. I'm amazed you managed to get her into mediation. This couldn't have turned out any better. Her whole attitude has changed.'

Dylan held his gaze and said with an air of confidence, 'She's been a pleasure to work for Mr Massey.'

Gregory's face resumed it's normal expression. 'She certainly has,' he said squeezing Dylan's shoulder affectionately.

Max turned his attention back to Gregory. 'I thought I'd pop by to discuss that business I mentioned, Gregory.'

Dylan returned to her seat and grabbed her jacket. 'In that case, I think I'll make a move.' She hurried to the door before her dad could talk her into staying. 'See you tomorrow.'

Outside, Dylan took a backward glance at the house. *Well, I'll be damned. What a turn up for the books.*

She almost laughed out loud at the oddness of the situation. *Our client's happy with mediation, who would've thought it?* Normally they wanted her to perform miracles and make their spouses disappear as fast as possible, not make them spend even more time with the person they now hated. It felt good to have both parties trying to move to a more amicable agreement. Buoyed by this new feeling of one hundred per cent happiness, Dylan realised there was only one person she wanted to share it with. Whether Harper felt the same way was another matter. *I suppose there's only one way to find out.*

Chapter Thirty-One

Harper paced her living room without any direction. All she knew was that she was furious. Her tears eventually ceased from the emotional numbness that came over her, and a welcome emptiness filled her. There was no grief, no longing of what could have been between her and her stepfather. One less odious voice was worth the lack of sympathy she felt. Only now, confronted by her past, did she realise the level of bitterness she still harboured.

To her relief, she wasn't going to spend the night crying or even moping around morose. She felt alright, actually. Her fury subsided the more the news of Ted's death sunk in. It took Harper all of fifteen minutes to recover from the phone call. Soon she was lying on the sofa in the faint light that peeked from the kitchen, with her music to keep her company.

Her doorbell rang, but she pretended not to hear it, no matter how clear it was. *Perhaps*, she thought, *whoever buzzed it would give up and leave*. On the third buzz, she moaned under her breath, dragged herself wearily off the sofa and walked slowly to the front door.

'Is she serious?' she whispered when she saw Dylan through the peephole. Harper was pissed off all over again. How was it that people like her mother and Dylan, bad people in her opinion, had such thick skins? They thought they could treat her like shit and expect her to just forget it all when it suited them? Annoyed, not only for Dylan's audacity, but also because her peaceful night alone had just disappeared down the drain for the second time, she opened the door. Harper made no secret of the fact that she was not in the mood for company.

'Hey, gorgeous.' Dylan smiled slyly. 'Look what I brought! I had a very happy client.'

Dylan lifted a bottle of Dom Pérignon champagne in the air and wiggled it like the first prize at a talent contest as she brushed past Dylan.

'Come in, why don't you?' Harper kicked the door shut with her foot. 'I hope you're in a hurry,' she told Dylan. Her disposition was so out of character that even the cutthroat visitor with the ironclad confidence looked as if she felt unwelcome.

'What's up with you? I thought you'd be happy about the latest development in the Massey case,' Dylan said, making her way into the kitchen. 'It's a win-win situation, don't you agree?' Dylan pulled opened several cupboard doors as she spoke.

'The glasses are in the cupboard above the sink,' Harper muttered, dragging her feet as she went back to the sofa and reclined. 'Have one glass, then go.'

'That's a bit rude isn't it?' Dylan said.

'Dylan,' Harper said wearily, 'I've had my fill of drama today. I don't get overtime for this shit. I thought I made it clear that we would only see each other in a professional capacity.' Harper's cattiness got its second wind.

'Like I told you before, I leave my professional life at the office. Maybe you should do the same.' Dylan held out her palms in front of her. 'Look, I didn't come here to fight,' Dylan replied from the kitchen as the glasses clinked daintily in her hand. 'We're different people when we're off the clock, aren't we?'

'Really?' Harper almost shouted. Her exasperation was overwhelming, and even the smooth talking Dylan seemed uncertain of her attitude. 'As far as I know, people's jobs shouldn't influence their personal lives selectively. You might be fucking two-faced to serve whatever end you need to achieve, but my personality and loyalty are pretty damn consistent. That way, people will always know that they can trust me.'

'Christ, what the hell's got into you? Are you enjoying that bitch suit you're trying on for size? Do you like how snugly it fits your personality? Because it does. It becomes you perfectly to be a cynical cow,' Dylan said, putting a glass of champagne down in front of Harper, who didn't make an effort to engage her.

Harper knew her anger and frustration wasn't about Dylan or the Massey case. It was about her mother. The woman that had abandoned her. But she didn't care. She needed to vent on someone. Dylan claimed not to be fazed by anything, so Harper assumed she could take it. 'I love how you think you can leave your wickedness at your office, where you facilitate the destruction of people's lives; their real lives that, unlike you, they can't shed whenever they feel like it.'

'You're in denial, sweetheart, and you feel that realisation clamping onto your logic daily, and you can't stand it,' Dylan argued, knocking back her drink in one before pouring another. 'You chose this career because you're a good fighter. Just. Like. Me.'

'I'm nothing like you,' Harper protested, sitting up suddenly to face Dylan.

'Okay whatever you say. Now drink,' Dylan told her, and shoved the glass toward her. 'I'm not leaving until this bottle is empty.'

'Is that so?' Harper asked with a tone brimming with sarcasm. She grabbed the bottle and headed for the kitchen, intent on emptying it into the sink.

Dylan chased after her, 'Oh no you don't!'

'I will if it's the only way to speed up your departure. Don't tell me it would be rude of me to kick you out of my flat? We are both aware you wouldn't know the difference between rudeness and decency, so I'm in good company,' Harper ranted as she stumbled towards the sink.

Dylan wrestled the bottle from Harper's grasp and set it down on the worktop. 'Harper,' Dylan said, turning Harper to face her, 'I'm not leaving until you tell me what's really going on with you. I'm worried about you.' Caressing Harper's hair gently, with her free hand Dylan tenderly took her defensive hand by the wrist and slowly lowered it, locking her fingers in Harper's.

Harper couldn't fight back. She simply didn't want to. Staring wordlessly at Dylan, her heart pounded. Dylan pulled her closer. An unexpected warmth surged through her. The air around them grew heavy as Dylan held her so tight; she could feel Dylan's body mould into her own. Then Dylan kissed her. Her warm tongue snaked its way easily into Harper's mouth, slowly caressing every part of it. The deeper Dylan pushed, the faster Harper's pulse accelerated. Harper didn't want it to ever end, because if it did, it would give her time to think about what she knew would inevitably happen. Then what? Would Dylan simply move on to her next conquest? At that moment in time, Harper didn't care about the future anymore. Her mind was still in turmoil from her mother's call. She wanted, no *needed* something, anything, to banish the past from her thoughts. Thankfully Dylan was doing just the job as her hands pressed, stroked and cupped parts of Harper's body that made her knees tremble. Harper's fingers moved swiftly along Dylan's shirt, unbuttoning it with lightning speed before tugging it off. Dylan responded in kind and quickly slid Harper's T-shirt over her head, before pulling her back into an embrace. A delicious shudder heated Harper's body at the feel of Dylan's smooth soft skin against hers. Any doubts were quickly banished. All Harper could think about now was getting Dylan into bed as fast as possible. Between long drawn out kisses, she led the way as they stumbled down the hall, fumbling with the buttons on their trousers. Harper wanted to capture every last second of this moment. To imprint it on her memory forever. They entered the bedroom and Harper fell onto the bed while Dylan remained standing, loosening her hair. The dark tresses tumbling carelessly down her shoulders.

'My God, you are so beautiful,' Harper whispered as her eyes greedily drank in Dylan's tall, lean body. With the light from behind her in the hallway, the yellow halo accentuated her perfect curvature. Dylan's small firm breasts heaved as she breathed hard, sweeping her long hair back in one swift movement.

Harper slipped out of her remaining clothes and spread her legs invitingly to accommodate Dylan's body atop hers. Harper drew Dylan's face to her, pressing her open lips on Dylan's once more, savouring the sweetness of her tongue. It was beyond strange to be kissing Dylan. To be lying naked with her, feeling Dylan's unfamiliar breasts in her mouth, hearing her groans of arousal as Harper's fingers found their way to Dylan's intimate centre. Despite the strangeness, everything seemed so right. Harper bit her lower lip as Dylan slowly made her way down her body, kissing and nipping parts of her skin as she went. Every place her mouth touched left a flame of liquid fire. Finally stopping between her legs, Harper spread them apart even further and clutched Dylan there as her tongue feather-touched her clit with tantalising persuasion. Harper's body pulsed with anticipation.

The thunder rumbled outside the window where Harper and Dylan made love until the early hours of the morning, but the storm was only just beginning. It lurked on the horizon of both women's lives while they blissfully forgot that they were bitter rivals.

Chapter Thirty-Two

Harper awoke just before 8 a.m., her arm still wrapped tightly around Dylan's waist. The cool air on her nude body was like a fresh caress, which made her shiver just a little. She could still feel Dylan's presence on her skin, and it made her smile. Though Harper knew she'd crossed the line, there wasn't one second of the previous night she'd take back. All she had to do was make sure her feelings for Dylan didn't sway her in any way when it came to finalising the Massey divorce. *As long as we both agree not to talk about the case in our personal time it should be alright.* Harper reasoned. Sweeping a strand of hair away from Dylan's face, Harper gazed at her. She couldn't believe how someone who dealt with the kind of people she did, slept so well. The same way she couldn't help being attracted to the ruthless woman, and part of her hated herself for it. Yet, at the same time, she had hoped to influence Dylan to become softer, more compassionate and to teach her that money and prestige wasn't everything, just like winning was not the definition of one's power. Harper wanted to get Dylan so close to her that she couldn't help but see that there was more to accomplishment than just devastating the opponent. Achievement could come from helping others, from obliterating unfairness and injustice as much as the ego needed to feel superior.

Harper pushed herself up onto her elbow, leant forward and planted a quick kiss on Dylan's lips. Before she could pull away, Dylan's eyes flashed open and she smiled as she pulled Harper back towards her, holding her tight in an embrace.

'I dreamt about you all night,' Dylan said.

'I hope I wasn't in a nightmare.'

'No, it was the perfect dream. I felt so happy. We were standing in front of a new building holding a pair of keys. It was the beginning of something, but you woke me up, and I never got to finish it.'

Harper leant in and nibbled on her ear. 'That positively sounds like us moving in together. Don't you think it's a little too soon for that?' she teased.

Dylan laughed, pushed Harper onto her back and straddled her. 'I might be impulsive but not that impulsive.'

'Are you saying I'm not girlfriend material? Dylan, you offend me. In my own bed as well. I'm hurt.' Though it was meant as a joke, there was a hint of truth in it. Was Harper girlfriend material? Or were they destined to be friends with benefits for the duration of their relationship, however long it was? She dearly hoped not.

There was a sensual flame in Dylan's eyes as she said, 'Hmm, I wonder how I can make it up to you.'

Harper grinned. She knew a hundred and one ways. 'Well, you remember what you did to me last night …'

Dylan slowly traced her finger along Harper's

collarbone. 'If I recall, I did quite a lot of things to you last night; you're gonna have to be more specific.'

Harper drew Dylan's head towards her and whispered in her ear.

Dylan laughed. 'Oh, that. Do you think we've got time? It takes at least an hour to warm up for it.' Suddenly looking panic-stricken, she reached for her phone on the bedside cabinet and glanced at it. '… Oh shit, is that the time? I've got to go. I've never been late for work in my life,' she said, climbing off Harper and stepping onto the floor.

Harper slapped Dylan's firm arse as she bent over to pick up her clothes. 'Chicken! Any excuse. I'm going to think it's a fluke now.'

'Oh yeah?' Dylan turned to study her for a few seconds. 'We'll see about that.' She picked up her phone again and punched in some numbers. Harper lay back with her hands behind her head as she listened in on Dylan's call to work.

'Cathy, I'm going to be a couple of hours late.' She rolled her eyes. 'Yes, I'm fine. No, a walk-in hasn't replaced me …' A few seconds later, Dylan placed the phone on the night stand and climbed back into bed. She threw the covers back.

'Fluke, aye. I'll show you a fluke,' Dylan said laughing as she pulled Harper up into her arms and kissed her hungrily.

Harper knew she had sealed her fate by opening her heart to Dylan. She only prayed that now she was in, Dylan wouldn't trample on it.

***

Sometime later, the women sat in the kitchen drinking coffee in silence. Harper was lost in thought. What should have been a feeling of exhilaration was marred by what she had to do later that day. Send money to her mother. Just thinking about the woman soured her day. Even after all of this time, the day her mother threw her out felt like yesterday. So did the feeling of rejection. She didn't hear or see Dylan move out of her seat. The first she knew of it was when Dylan's arms encircled her from behind. It was just what she needed.

Dylan kissed the top of her head, then snuggled her face into the crook of Harper's neck. 'Penny for your thoughts?'

Harper reached behind and stroked Dylan's hair. 'It's not important.'

'You thinking about the Massey case?' Dylan probed.

Harper sighed. Maybe it would do her good to talk to someone about it. She had kept it to herself for so many years. *Maybe that's why I'm still so bitter.* 'No, it's just my step-dad died.'

Dylan moved to the side of her chair and crouched down. 'Oh, no. I'm so sorry.' She reached up and kissed her cheek tenderly.

Despite the warmth Dylan's kiss elicited, Harper could hear the coldness in her own voice when she spoke of Ted. 'Don't be. I hated him. He was a bully who made my life hell.'

Dylan took her hand and held it to her cheek. 'When did you find out?'

'Last night.'

'Ah, that explains your mood yesterday.'

Harper turned to face her. When she looked into her eyes, all she saw was compassion. The one emotion Harper thought Dylan had been born without. But there it was, staring her in the face. In a twisted way, she thought that was one thing she ought to thank Ted for—showing the humane side of Dylan.

'There's no way I'm going to his funeral. But I don't know if I should go and see my mum. Despite everything she did, I still kind of feel obligated to make sure she's alright.'

'What happened between you two?'

Without hesitation, Harper relayed the sorry tale of her life at home. She didn't tell Dylan the whole story, though. She missed out the part where her stepdad put locks on the fridge and cupboard doors, so she had to root through bins at the supermarket late at night to eat. Or that she'd have to stay over at a friend's house if she wanted to have a shower and wash her hair. All of this abuse was done under the guise of discipline. Bit by bit, Harper bared her soul to the woman she had once thought of as cruel and uncaring. Dylan listened patiently, stroking her hand tenderly as the memories evoked pain in her heart. Harper could see the sadness in Dylan's eyes when she finally brought the account to an end.

'Do you think seeing her again could bring you some closure?' Dylan asked.

'I don't need closure.' Harper's voice held the venomous bite of the adder. 'I had it. Until yesterday anyway.'

'Do you want her to keep unsettling your life in intervals?'

'No.'

'Then you do need closure,' Dylan said softly.

Harper shrugged her shoulders. 'I know it sounds cold, but I don't look at her as a real mother. She chose him over me, and I don't think I can ever forgive her.'

'There's only one way to find out—go and see her. I'll even drive you there myself.'

Harper's eyes widened. 'Really? You'd come with me? Why?'

'Why not. I'd like to get to know you better.' She raised an eyebrow and a faint smile played on her lips.

Harper laughed self-consciously. 'You make it sound like we've got a future together.'

Dylan feigned shock. 'What? Do you think I'm going to let you out of my clutches now I've finally managed to knock down the wall you surround yourself with?' She kissed Harper on the lips. 'Not on your life.'

Harper giggled and rested her head on Dylan's shoulder. *How could I have ever doubted you?*

Chapter Thirty-Three

The reality of the night Dylan spent with Harper had finally managed to sink in. Intimate pictures of Harper in her arms ran through her mind. Then the image changed to Harper in the kitchen pouring her heart out to Dylan. She had been genuinely moved by Harper's story. It gave her an insight into Harper's character. *No wonder she wants to save the world. She wants to be the hero in her own dreadful story.* Dylan stood by the advice she had given her. There was no point in running. The past caught up with you eventually. Dylan had shocked herself by offering to take Harper to Dorchester to see her mother. Dylan had never been within a mile of anyone's parents before. That sort of thing spoke of commitment. So why now? What had changed? *I have, that's what.*

Having a sexual relationship with someone didn't mean she was committed. Dylan was sure she could enjoy Harper's company without any complications. They were both adults, getting their needs fulfilled from each other. There was nothing wrong with that. Few of Dylan's other conquests had made it to a second date or even overnight.

Dylan found herself whistling throughout the entire journey to work. She strode towards her office with a spring in her step.

'Good morning, Cathy,' Dylan said, smiling.

Cathy looked up at her with a frown. 'It is?'

'Of course it is. Spring is near which means it's the start of new beginnings.'

Cathy shifted uncomfortably in her seat. 'If you say so, Ms Blue.'

'I most certainly do. I'm going to make a coffee. Do you want one?'

Cathy stared at Dylan in astonishment. 'You? Making me a coffee? Have I done something wrong?'

Dylan's forehead creased in confusion. Cathy looked like a deer caught in a car's headlights. 'Done something wrong? What makes you say that?'

'Are you going to fire me?'

Dylan rolled her eyes. What was wrong with the woman? Was Dylan being polite such a rarity it caused such a drastic reaction? 'Cathy, I only asked if you wanted a coffee. Jesus, what's up with you?'

Cathy eyed Dylan suspiciously. 'Um, no I don't think I will, thanks.'

'What do you think I'm going to do?' Dylan raised her eyebrows. 'Spit in it?'

Cathy laughed, a humourless exhale. 'As if.' Her voice was a squeak.

'Suit yourself. Anyway, I think I owe you lunch for making you miss that date with your mum a few weeks ago. Take her to Tallinn on the high-street.'

Cathy's eyes widened. 'Tallinn!? That's like my month's wages,' Cathy protested.

'Ask for the manager Mario.' Dylan carried on speaking as if Cathy hadn't spoken. 'Tell him to put the bill on my tab.'

Cathy grinned, her eyes lighting up. 'Really?'

Dylan gave a nod of her head. 'Cathy, in this life, learn never to look a gift horse in the mouth. That's how opportunities are lost.' She picked up a pile of envelopes on Cathy's desk addressed to her and flicked through them. 'Order whatever you want. Enjoy yourself,' she said distractedly as she walked into her office reading her mail.

Dylan closed the door softly behind her. She glanced at the clock on her wall. Would Harper take her up on her offer to drive her to Dorchester she wondered? The thought of spending another night with Harper sent ripples of pleasure through her.

Her mobile phone rang. Without hesitation she took it out of her pocket and pressed accept. It was just the woman's voice she wanted it to be, saying the exact words she wanted to hear. Dylan's heart flipped. *Dorchester is on.*

Chapter Thirty-Four

Harper dragged the sheets off the bed and tossed them in the laundry basket. She opened the window to see that the weather was still unsettled, but at least the thunder and hard rain had stepped aside for a friendly light drizzle. But as she opened the taps and waited for her shower to warm, she was forced to deal with reality.

Her mother had called again just after Dylan left, pleading with Harper to return one last time. Harper had told her she'd think about it and cut the conversation short. Dylan was right, she had to bring some closure to that part of her life if she were ever going to let it go. *Dylan.* Thinking her name brought a flurry of butterflies to her stomach. As she stepped into the exhilarating warm water and closed her eyes, Harper thought of Abi as well, hoping her mediation with Robyn would resolve their issues. She was another person who desperately needed closure. *Touch wood everything will go to plan and Abi can move on with her life.*

Her mother's beckoning kept pressing in her mind as she lathered her body, and with every stroke of soap over her skin, Harper came nearer to making up her mind. Therapeutic for a bit of pondering, her circular motions were like the repetition of a mantra, bringing her closer to clarity. Was she obliged to give her mother another chance, no matter what amount of shit still floated in the sewage that was her past?

She stepped out of the shower and towelled off.

If I go back, even for a day, should I be looking at forming a new relationship with my mother? She tormented herself with assumptions she could not entertain after so many years. *Oh, God, why do I have to be so weak when it comes to my mum?* The thought of her mother being all alone tore at her heart strings. In that split second, she decided to go back, and if Dylan's offer was still open, she'd take her back to Dorchester with her. It was one journey Harper felt she couldn't make alone. It surprised her, after all this time, that when thinking of home she was reduced to feeling as scared and vulnerable as she had done when she was sixteen. No matter how many times she gave herself a good talking to, the child in her still remained intact. Harper needed to be more like Dylan. A woman as strong as her wouldn't hold onto memories that should have been left exactly where they belonged—in the past.

It's not like I haven't tried.

For a second, Harper wondered what it would be like to be Dylan. To be fearless. To have no doubts or regrets. To face life head on. *Terrifying.* No, Harper would never be like that, nor would she want to be. She might be soft and emotional, but she could look herself in the mirror with the knowledge she had done her best to make someone's life better. *Could Dylan say the same thing?* Thinking of Dylan reminded Harper that she'd better check that Dylan was available to go with her.

A quick call to Dylan confirmed she could make space in her work schedule to drive Harper home. When Harper finished dressing and applying her make-up, she went online and booked their accommodation. There was no way she was staying in her mother's house, her childhood pen. After Harper made the reservation, she left for work, hoping for an easy day ahead. With these new developments, and personal stuff to deal with, Harper needed to put in for a day's leave to sort out her family duties. It felt strange even to think about family, something that had for so long been absent from her life.

Chapter Thirty-Five

Robyn was fast regretting letting Tiffany know she was going to her first mediation session with Abi that day. Though Tiffany hadn't said anything out loud, her withdrawal and mood swings spoke volumes. What else could Robyn have done? Lied to her? No, there was no need for that. Tiffany had to know her place, and there was only one way of letting her know where that was—by Robyn doing exactly as she pleased, regardless of Tiffany's feelings.

'So you're goin' through with this "mediation" then?' Tiffany asked from where she sat on the sofa. The area around her was in its usual state: magazines strewn on the leather sofa, dirty plates and cups on the coffee table. Today, Robyn closed her eyes to it and let it pass. She couldn't afford to leave the house wound up. She had to be calm and serene.

'Yes, I'm going through with it,' Robyn said defiantly. 'You got a problem with that?' Robyn glanced towards her, hoping the look in her eyes portrayed what she was thinking. If Tiffany did have a problem with it, Robyn would have to deal with her in the only language she understood.

Tiffany smiled. 'Nope, no problem at all.'

'Good. I might even take Jake to the park afterwards.' Robyn crossed the living room floor and stopped in front of Tiffany. 'You can come if you want.'

Tiffany picked up her magazine and flicked through it. 'I can't. I promised I'd do some stuff for my mum. Next time. Definitely.'

'Good.' As Robyn bent down to kiss her, she noticed Tiffany flinch. It made her both empowered and also a little guilty. Robyn had to keep reminding herself that it was Tiffany's fault she had lost her temper. If Tiffany hadn't antagonised her, that fight could have been prevented. *Well, hopefully she's learnt her lesson now.*

'I'll see you later, then,' Robyn said, grabbing her keys off the coffee table.

'You sure will,' Tiffany said.

Robyn wanted to skip out of the house. To sing from the rooftops. She was happy, and she wanted everyone to know. It had only been two weeks since she'd seen Jake, but it felt like a lifetime. She recalled her dad's face when he met Jake for the first time. He'd been over the moon to finally have a grandson. He wasn't bothered that they weren't related by blood. Neither was she anymore. The fact that she was going to have a hand in raising him with her values was more than enough to convince her she would be a real parent.

Thankfully, her dad shared her views. She was a daddy's girl. Whatever made her happy, made him happy.

Robyn made the half an hour drive to the location where she would meet up with Abi. She had let Abi choose the time. If it gave her a sense of control, all the better. All Robyn wanted now was to have equal custody rights.

Robyn arrived at the allocated meeting place, and was pleasantly surprised to see Abi pushing Jake in his pram as she turned into the car park. She parked in the first available spot and jumped out of the car.

'Abi, Abi,' she called out after her.

Abi turned. Shielding her eyes with her hand, she looked in Robyn's direction. Robyn locked the car and jogged over to her. Without so much as a glance at Abi, Robyn walked straight around the buggy and took Jake out.

'Hey, gummy, how you doing?'

Jake wriggled in her hands, giggling as she made funny faces. Finally propping him on her hip, she turned her attention to Abi.

'He looks like he's grown a bit since I saw him.'

Abi smiled politely but said nothing.

'Hey, I was thinking—after the meeting, do you fancy going to the park?'

Robyn watched as doubt crept over Abi's features. 'Or we could get some ice cream if you like.'

'I don't—'

'—Why don't you wait and see how you feel when we come out of the meeting?' Robyn said, knowing Abi wouldn't be able to say no once she saw how willing Robyn was to bring things to a satisfactory end.

Robyn was right, two and a half hours after their first meeting, they strolled side by side down a leafy path in Hyde Park. Overhead, birds twittered in the branches of the old oak trees.

'This is great isn't it?' Robyn said, inhaling deeply. She genuinely felt on top of the world. The meeting couldn't have gone any better if she'd scripted it herself.

'This could have all been avoided if you'd just—' Abi said.

'—I thought we agreed in mediation to let go of the past and concentrate on the future.'

'Okay, okay. Sorry I said anything.'

'Good. So you're a hundred per cent happy with all the arrangements?'

'Yes, do you mind if we sit for a minute, I'm a bit tired?'

'Sure,' Robyn said, gesturing to a bench nearby. 'It will give me time to play with gummy, won't it?' she said to Jake, who looked up at her with a beaming smile. Robyn bent down and planted a kiss on his lips. He smiled in delight and her heart soared. *He really is priceless. What's £2000 a month and a ten grand lump sum, when I get to see him three days a week?* Robyn thought she'd got off lightly, considering how much she really had in savings. Luckily, Robyn had purchased her house before they met, so it couldn't be included in the settlement.

Abi dug into her bag and withdrew some baby wipes. She reached into the buggy to wipe his face. Robyn grabbed her hand before she reached him. 'I'll do it,' she said, taking the wipe from her and meticulously cleaning his little face.

'Do you ever think about us?' Robyn said out of the blue. The familiarity of Abi was making her nostalgic for a time that she'd thought was the worst period of her life. *If only I'd have known back then that it would be like this, I would never have left.*

Abi turned to her and Robyn leant back slightly, feeling uncomfortable under her gaze.

'No, not anymore,' Abi finally said. 'Like you, I've moved on.'

'Meaning?'

'Meaning …' Abi smiled, and Robyn noticed she had a faraway look in her eyes. 'I've met someone.'

For some unknown reason, Robyn's world shook at its foundation. *She's met someone?* A stab of jealousy tore at her heart. She had always assumed Abi would remain single now she had a child. When did she get the chance to go gallivanting, looking for women?

'I hope that doesn't mean Jake's neglected,' Robyn said with a tinge of possessiveness.

'Jake will always come first, no matter what.'

'Good.' Robyn's jubilant mood vanished rapidly. Hearing Abi's news was the last thing she wanted. Grim thoughts crowded her mind. Someone else was going to be sharing Abi's bed, spending time with Jake, having a family Robyn now so desperately wanted. The knowledge was more than she could bear. She shook off her dark train of thought. 'I'd better be off,' she said, standing abruptly.

'Okay,' Abi said, rising to her feet.

'No, you stay and let Jake have some fresh air.'

'Any chance you could drop us home? It will be a nightmare trying to get back by train. The buggy's a pain to manoeuvre.'

Robyn leant over the buggy and kissed Jake. 'See you soon, gummy.' She straightened up and looked Abi in the eye. 'You want a lift home, call your fucking girlfriend. I'm not a taxi service.' She turned abruptly and headed towards the car park. Adrenaline firing every nerve caused her to jog the rest of the way.

Robyn was going to have to rethink her decision about mediation. She wasn't going to fund Abi's lifestyle with her new bitch. Not with her money. *No way, no fucking way!*

Chapter Thirty-Six

'Are you sure you don't want me to come with you?' Dylan asked Harper when they were finally settled in their hotel room.

Harper stood by the large window overlooking the bustling street below. 'Positive.'

'At least let me give you a lift.'

She shook her head. 'You've had a long drive. Relax. Order room service.'

Dylan pushed herself to her feet and walked over to join Harper. 'Okay. I'll have a bottle of champs on ice for when you get back. I brought some oils and candles for a late night soak.'

Harper stepped into Dylan's open arms. 'You're a right charmer, aren't you?'

Dylan wiggled her brows. 'I aim to please.' Her arms encircled Harper, one hand in the small of her back.

It was impossible to steady her erratic pulse anytime she was close to Dylan. The effect Dylan had on her was like nothing she'd experienced before. Like being wrapped in a silken cocoon of euphoria.

Harper's lips brushed against Dylan's as she spoke. 'I'd better go.'

'Okay. Call me if you need anything, and I mean anything. Even if you need to vent.'

'Will do,' Harper said, giving Dylan a long-lasting

kiss.

Harper caught a cab outside the hotel to take her to the pub where she'd arranged to meet her mother. Up until that moment, Harper hadn't given much thought to what she'd say or how she'd feel when she saw her. Now the time was almost upon her, it was unavoidable. Should she shake her hand or, like normal daughters would, embrace her? *We've hardly got a normal mother-daughter relationship though.* Bringing Dylan along was a great idea, she was an emotional safety net Harper direly needed. The past couple of weeks had flown by and they had seen each other, discretely, nearly every day. All in all, everything was well in their little paradise, apart from the fact that Dylan shied away when ever Harper spoke of the future. It wasn't as if Harper wanted to snare Dylan. She just wanted to know where she stood. For now she would let things lie as they were, but she couldn't avoid it forever.

An odd mixture of feelings swirled within her as the cab crept forward in the dense traffic. As the buildings passed her moving car, some still standing exactly as they had years ago, some demolished and replaced by new structures, she felt a sweet nostalgia for the familiarity of Dorchester. It was good to be back as an older, wiser woman, and to know that she had a nice, secure life to return to whenever she wished. It was as she drew closer to the pub that Harper thought more and more about her flat in London which served as an anchor, as a beacon for her whilst she went deeper into the doldrums of her childhood. It was as if her current life was an older sibling holding her hand so that her old life's ocean current would not sweep her off into the dangerous deep.

Her thoughts turned to Ted, she was relieved his funeral had already taken place. Briefly, she heard his condescending remarks about her sexuality and choice of friends echo through her tainted memories, those few shards that somehow survived the virtually successful obliteration of everything that she had experienced as a young girl.

The cab pulled up outside The Inn pub. Harper paid the fare and stepped out into the cool afternoon breeze. Her elongated reflection in the car window looked powerful and very well groomed, her hair pulled back in a ponytail was the perfect style to accentuate her high cheekbones and striking grey-green eyes. In a black leather jacket and designer jeans, she strode gracefully toward the entrance. Harper slung her tan leather bag's belt across her chest, and let it flop about her right hip as she cast her eyes up at the sky.

Overhead, the flattened clouds floated in like the baby waves of the tide that crept over the wet sand, until the whole sky was covered by a dark grey dome of fleece. Harper pushed the door open. Inside, the bar was relatively busy with couples having lunch. MTV played on a large TV screen.

As Harper scanned the room for her mum, her

stomach churned with anxiety. She seriously contemplated calling Dylan to pick her up so she could get the hell out of Dorchester and this whole situation, but the familiar sound of her mother's voice behind her prevented that from happening.

'Harper?' June said. 'You came!' She slammed two hands over her mouth in astonished emotion and pinched her eyes shut.

Harper was at a loss what to do. She stepped forward, her hand hovering awkwardly above June's shoulder. 'Please don't cry.'

'I'm sorry,' June said, blinking back the tears welling in her eyes. 'I just can't believe you're here.'

Neither can I. 'Do you want to sit down or go for a walk?' Harper asked, inspecting her mother's features. She looked tired, crushed and … defeated. Life had certainly taken its toll.

June touched her stomach. 'Best we stay here, if you don't mind.'

'Of course not. You grab some seats, and I'll get us a drink.'

'Okay, thank you,' June said, her eyes still glued to Harper's face in disbelief.

Harper turned and walked towards the bar, glancing back briefly to see her mum shuffling towards the nearest table. Though she was only in her sixties, she had the gait of someone much older. Her mother looked so helpless. Harper swallowed down a lump forming in her throat. *Don't start getting sentimental*, she warned herself.

A redheaded woman wiping the bar looked up as Harper approached. Her eyes widened.

'Oh, my God—oh, my God, Harper is that you?'

Harper's hand flew to her mouth. She'd been so caught up with her mother, she'd failed to realise the woman standing behind the bar was her old school mate. 'Beanie?'

'The one and only,' she said running around the bar. Swooping Harper into her arms, she hugged her. Harper squeezed her back tightly. 'It's so good to see you, Beanie.'

'I know, it's been an age.'

Harper drew back slightly. 'Let me have a look at you. You haven't changed a bit.'

'Yeah, course I haven't. I look like shit.' She tapped her stomach. 'Having four kids will do that to ya.'

'Four! Weren't you the one who swore blind she'd never have kids?'

Beanie laughed. 'Yeah, I know, but if you saw my hubby, you'd understand why.'

Harper joined in with her laughter.

'So what brings you back here?' Beanie asked.

Harper glanced over her shoulder in her mother's direction. 'My mum. Ted died.'

'Yeah, I heard. No great loss to humanity though is it? Everyone tried to get your mum away from him, but she'd never leave, no matter how many times he put her in hospital with broken bones.'

Harper stood there, blank, shocked and badly

shaken. 'What?'

Beanie's cheeks turned scarlet. 'Oh. Didn't you know?'

Harper felt bile rise to the top of her throat. 'He was hitting my mum?'

Beanie nodded. 'For years.'

Harper glanced towards her mother, sat leaning on a table. *Is that why her spirit was broken?*

Harper let out a long, audible breath. 'I didn't know,' she said more to herself than Beanie.

'Can we get some service here, like today?' An irate customer called out from behind them.

Beanie cast the man an evil glare. 'Keep your bloody hair on,' she said before turning back to Harper. 'How long you back for?'

'Just today.'

'Too bad. Make sure you give me your number before you leave.'

'I will do.'

Beanie leant in for another hug. 'What you both drinking?'

'Tea please.'

Beanie grinned. 'Not like the old days then? I'll bring them over in a sec.'

'Thanks,' Harper said, turning and slowly walking over to her mother. So many thoughts and questions ran through her mind at breakneck speed. Ted had put her mother in hospital. When did the beatings start? Yes, Harper knew Ted had been a bastard and was mentally abusive, but that was as far as it went.

Obviously, she was very wrong. Was it happening while she was at home? *Surely I would have known. There would have been signs.* She racked her brains, trying to recall any incidents. There were a few times her mum had bruises, but she'd told Harper she had banged into something. Harper was a young teenager who thought her mum was just clumsy. Why would she think any different?

Harper pulled a chair out across from her mother and sank onto it. *Should I tell her I know about Ted hitting her?*

'How have you been, Harper?'

A flood of emotion overcame her. When Harper spoke, she hoped her voice wouldn't crack. All she kept seeing in her mind's eye were images of that big brute laying into her mother. 'I've been good.' It was all she could think of to say. She really wanted to talk about Ted's actions and, more importantly, why her mother hadn't told her about it.

'Are you happy?'

For a moment, Harper gave a genuine smile as she thought of Dylan waiting for her back at the hotel. 'Yes,' she said truthfully.

A look of relief crossed her mother's features. 'Good. That makes everything alright.'

'What about you? How've you been?'

'Can't complain. I want to hear about you, Harper. Any kids?'

Harper shook her head and smiled. 'No pets either. I just don't have the time.'

Beanie appeared at the table and discreetly placed down the tea cups, said hello to June, then quietly withdrew.

June looked at her with a cloud of concern. 'I hope you're eating properly.'

'Of course,' Harper said, thinking of the late night takeaways she ate on a regular basis. 'You look tired.' Harper stopped short of calling her mum. Not being able to utter the word that was loaded with so much meaning.

June picked the cup up with a trembling hand and blew on the hot liquid before taking a sip. 'Nothing new. I don't sleep much with the pain ...' She stopped abruptly as if she'd said too much.

'You're in pain?'

'Oh, it's nothing,' June said, brushing it aside with a wave of her hand. 'The odd pain here or there. It's to be expected at my age.'

Harper had to say something about what Beanie had told her. It was killing her to remain silent. As much as she didn't want to put her mother on the spot, if they were going to move forward, bringing everything out into the open was a necessity.

'Mum.' She forced the word out. 'About Ted ...' she said slowly.

June's face clouded with uneasiness before she lowered her gaze to the table. 'I know what you're going to say. No doubt Beanie's already told you.'

'Well, you wouldn't have, would you?'

June's face dropped. 'No. Because it would have

made things worse … for both of us.' June's words stumbled out in a flurry. 'I had to make you go, Harper. He threatened to burn the house down with you in it.'

'Why didn't you leave?'

'Believe me, he would have hunted me down wherever I went. I made my own bed.'

June slowly opened her jacket and glanced around. Tentatively she pulled up her jumper to reveal a mass of thick white scars covering her stomach.

June's face was deathly pale. Her voice drifted into a hushed whisper. 'He threatened to do this to you and more. I wasn't going to let you suffer the same fate as me.'

Fury almost choked Harper. What kind of an animal would do such a thing to the woman he claimed to love? She was glad she didn't know where he was buried. If she did, she would have spat on his grave.

Chapter Thirty-Seven

Jennifer opened her front door wider so Abi could enter. 'Come in, babe, this is a nice surprise.' Her words dragged behind one another.

'You said to drop in when I was in the area, so here we are.'

Straightaway, Abi knew there was something off with Jennifer. When she entered her flat, the stench of weed confirmed it. She was stoned. Abi didn't even know Jennifer smoked, let alone smoked weed. Abi took Jake from the buggy and stepped inside the flat.

'And you must be little Jake,' Jennifer said, taking Jake from Abi's arms before she could protest. Jennifer threw Jake in the air as she led the way down the narrow hallway. 'Hope you don't mind sitting in the bedroom, I'm having some down time today,' she said, giggling in unison with Jake, who was having a whale of a time with his air antics.

'No, not at all,' Abi said, keeping her eyes firmly on Jennifer's hand, ready to jump in to save Jake from a nasty fall if necessary. She needn't have worried as Jennifer sat him safely against the pillows on her unmade bed.

The sweet scent of marijuana permeated through the air, intoxicating her senses. 'Do you mind opening the window? It's really smoky,' she said, seeing Jennifer through a light haze.

'I take it you don't smoke?'

'No.' Abi glanced at Jake and thought about his little lungs being exposed to the toxins in the air. 'Look, I can see I've come at a bad time.' She crossed the room and gathered Jake in her arms. 'We'll do this another time,' she said, hurrying out of the room.

'Oh, come on, don't go. We can sit in the living room if you like.'

Abi opened the front door then turned to face her. 'No, seriously. You're relaxing. And Jake will need feeding soon.' She kissed the top of his head, and her heart sunk when she realised he stunk of weed. What if someone smelt him? She was a fool for entering the flat in the first place. She should have turned around as soon as she realised there was dope there. Abi placed Jake back in his buggy and strapped him in. By this time, Jennifer was standing in the open doorway. Her face was a sea of confusion. 'Abi, I hope me having a puff hasn't put a spanner in the works.'

Abi straightened up. 'Don't be silly. It's just bad timing, that's all.' She wasn't that bothered by Jennifer smoking weed in her own home, she just didn't want it around Jake. 'I'll see you at work.'

Jennifer held out her arm. 'Kiss?'

Abi's eyes dropped to Jennifer's lips. *Oh what the hell.* She took a step forward and leant in to kiss her. Jennifer pulled her in tight, and before she knew it, her tongue had entered her mouth. The slow sensual kiss had her melting in Jennifer's arms within seconds. The sound of a door in the block of flats being slammed shut brought it to an abrupt end.

'I'll see you soon?' Jennifer said.

Abi nodded and in a daze stepped away, wrestling with the buggy to turn it around before heading towards the lift. She licked her lips and smiled to herself. *When was the last time I felt like that?*

Abi was still grinning when she arrived home and had barely got Jake out of his pram when the doorbell rang. In her happy glow, she opened the door without thinking who it might be.

'Robyn!' Abi looked at the large teddy Robyn held in her hand.

'I thought Jake would like this,' she said, putting it down on the floor.

'You should have let me know you were coming.'

'Why, is your girlfriend in there?' Robyn jerked her head forward.

'No, but I'm giving Jake a bath and putting him down for a nap.'

'Let me give him a quick cuddle, and I'll be off,' Robyn said, holding her hands out.

Without thinking, Abi handed Jake to her. It was too late by the time she realised her mistake. Abi cringed when Robyn sniffed Jake's head, then his clothes. Her eyes shimmered with the intensity of her anger as she took an abrupt step towards Abi and sniffed her hair. 'Have you been smoking drugs around him?' Anger flashed in her eyes.

'It's not what you think.'

'What the fuck do I think? I'm not stupid. He

fucking stinks of weed. And so do you.'

Abi reached out and grabbed Jake from her hands. 'I haven't been smoking anything. I walked into a room—'

'—Pull the other one.' Robyn gave a disdainful snort. 'I knew you'd be an unfit mother. I knew it.'

Abi drew in a shaky breath. 'What the hell does that mean?'

'That Jake deserves better, that's what. If you think I'm going to let him grow up with you, you've got another think coming.'

Fear ripped through her so fast her knees buckled. 'What you on about?'

Anger marked Robyn's every word. 'Fuck mediation. It's over. I'm going for full custody of Jake. When the judge hears about the drug infested environment you live in, they'll be more than happy to award it to me.'

'You wouldn't be so cruel, Robyn.'

'Wouldn't I. You just watch me. Then you and your girlfriend can smoke until your fucking lungs rot.'

Robyn spun on her heel and started for the stairs.

'Please, Robyn. Don't start any more trouble. Please,' Abi begged.

'Instead of standing there whining, I'd spend as much time with Jake as you can for now. 'Cause you ain't gonna have him much longer.'

Abi's entire world fell around her feet at Robyn's parting words. She knew Robyn wouldn't stop until she got what she wanted. Robyn was going to win. She always did.

Chapter Thirty-Eight

Five hours later, Harper returned to the hotel. The afternoon had been both emotional and mentally exhausting. When she thought of what Ted had put her mother through, she cursed the day they ever met. If he wasn't dead already, she would have liked to kill him herself. Nothing would have given her greater pleasure than to see the man suffer. *I hope the fucker is rotting in hell.*

Not surprisingly, Dylan was working on her laptop when Harper walked into their room.

Dylan looked up at her in surprise. 'That was quick.'

Harper laughed. She knew how easy it was to get so lost in work that you didn't realise time was flying by. 'Dylan, I've been gone for hours.'

'You have?' she glanced at her phone. 'Is that the time already?'

'I take it you haven't eaten either?'

Dylan grinned sheepishly. 'If you consider two oatmeal biscuits with copious amounts of coffee eating, then yes I have.'

Harper shook her head. 'You're terrible. I'll order room service if you don't mind. I just wanna chill out.'

'Sounds good to me. So …' Dylan closed the lid on her laptop. 'Tell me how it went.'

Harper pulled off her boots and sat on the edge

of the bed. She exhaled a pent up breath in a long sigh, then told Dylan about the conversation she'd had with her mum, repeating details of Ted's abuse word for word. Her mum having to beg for money for basic needs. The other women he flaunted in her face. The drinking, the beatings, the whole lot.

'That is absolutely horrific,' Dylan said, an hour later, after listening to Harper's woeful tale about her mother's life for the past fifteen years.

'I told you he was a good for nothing bastard.' Harper took a bite of the gourmet burger room service had delivered moments ago. As promised, on the cabinet a bottle of champagne stood in a silver bucket of ice. For now though, Harper was occasionally sipping from a glass of coke.

'Why didn't your mum go to the police? Women's aid? Why would she stick around with such a monster?'

'She was scared he would go after her … and me.' Knowing what Ted was capable of now, there was no doubt that he would have followed through with his threat. The image of her mum's stomach flashed up in her mind, and she quickly squeezed her eyes tight in the hope of banishing it. Harper couldn't bear to think what she had suffered at his hands. But she couldn't turn the clock back and undo all that had been done. All she could do now was make the future a better one for her mum, by offering her help so she never had to ask anyone for anything ever again.

'So all this time you were hating your mum for making you leave, and she actually did it to save you.'

'Would seem that way.' Harper dipped a French fry in ketchup and fed it to Dylan.

'Are you trying to make me fat?'

Harper grinned. 'Nope, I love you just the way you are.'

Dylan raised her eyebrows. Only then did Harper realise what she'd said. *Love. How the hell did I let that slip out?* 'You know what I mean,' she said quickly, swallowing a large gulp of coke.

Dylan's eyes widened as she stared at Harper. 'Yes. I think I do.'

Harper finished the rest of her burger in silence. Dylan picked and prodded at the chicken salad she had before her. As she watched her, Harper couldn't help but wonder if Dylan realised that she really was falling in love with her. If she did, she didn't seem too bothered about it. In fact, she was quite blasé.

'So what was the last word when you left your mum?' Dylan said, breaking the silence.

'I'm going to be there for her from now on.'

Dylan smiled. 'That's good.'

'We've got a lot of catching up to do. I'd like you to meet her.'

'Maybe,' Dylan said, throwing down her napkin and moving around the table to her. 'Talking of catching up … I do believe you and I have a date in the bathroom with a bottle of champagne and candles.'

Harper shook out her hair. 'I wouldn't miss this date for the world,' she said, taking Dylan's outstretched hand.

Harper hadn't missed Dylan's lack of commitment to meet her mother. Either Dylan wasn't interested in meeting her mum, or she wasn't looking for a committed relationship. Only time would tell which one was true.

Chapter Thirty-Nine

Tia opened her front door whilst speaking on the phone. Her eyes widened when she saw it was Abi. 'Abi? Was I meant to look after Jake today?' Tia said pressing her phone against her chest.

Abi shook her head. 'I … I need to … I need—'

'—Hold on for a second.' Tia put the phone to her ear. 'Fin, I'll call you back in a minute,' she said before disconnecting the call. Beckoning Abi into her house, she eyed her with apprehension. 'Are you alright? You look a bit—'

'—I'm fine. Just tired. Can you watch Jake for me?'

Tia reached out and squeezed Abi's arm. 'Of course, but only for a few hours, I've got an important meeting at six.'

'That's long enough,' Abi assured her.

Abi crouched down in front of Jake asleep in his buggy. She had to make this goodbye a quick one. Swallowing down the lump forming in her throat she said, 'I love you little man.' She kissed his forehead, keeping her lips pressed there for a few seconds. 'Forever.'

Abi stood, rummaged in her bag and brought out a pen and as scrap of paper. 'I'm gonna go home and try and get a proper sleep.' She scribbled on the paper. 'I'll leave you Robyn's number in case I can't pick him up later.'

Tia's phone started to ring. 'Okay, if you must,' she said distractedly. 'Look, I've got to get this. I'll get Jake out of his buggy after this call. Go home. We'll speak later.'

Abi stepped forward and pulled Tia into a hug. 'I love you, Tia. Thank you for everything.'

'Yes, you too, now go,' she said, extracting herself from Abi's embrace and ushering her out the door. Abi heard Tia speaking on the phone as the door slowly closed behind her.

Abi was relieved Tia was otherwise distracted. If she hadn't been, there would have been a flood of questions. She may have even tried to persuade her to rest in her spare room. That would have made her plan even more difficult than it already was. She had to strike while she had the courage to do so. *Just one more thing to do, then I'll be free.* At the end of the road Abi stopped in front of a post box. She reached into her bag and withdrew a white envelope addressed to Robyn's solicitor. She pushed it through the hole. *I can't be strong anymore.* Maybe Robyn's assessment of her was right. She was an unfit mother. Otherwise how could Abi even contemplate what she was about to do?

Arriving home, Abi shrugged off her jacket and went straight to Jake's room. The smell of baby powder was overwhelming. It made her sad to think that she'd never hold him close to her again, or hear his laughter. What was the point of going on? She was going to lose him either way. Dead or alive. Reaching into the cot, she picked up Jake's favourite teddy bear. Then she removed a photo of him from its frame and took both items with her to the bathroom. The weakness she had fought so hard to keep under control seeped through her as she opened the wall cabinet. A small pill bottle stood on the shelf, whose contents would finally put an end to the misery her life had become. With trembling fingers she picked up the bottle and emptied the small white pills onto her open palm. Putting every last one of them in her mouth she bent over and drank from the tap until her mouth was empty. *No amount of punishment can hurt you when your body has no heart left. You can't feel pain when you're dead.*

Walking calmly to her bedroom she drew the curtains and laid sideways on her bed. Her mind was still on Jake and the effect her actions would have on him. *Robyn will make sure he has a good life, I'm sure of it.*

With Jake's picture pressed against her face and his bear against her heart, Abi closed her eyes and waited for darkness to embrace her.

Chapter Forty

Dylan drove her Mercedes into the private garage beneath the block of glass fronted apartments. She glanced at Harper and laughed at her expression.

'You live here?' Harper asked.

Dylan nodded. 'For the past three years.'

Harper let out a low whistle. 'I thought only billionaires lived in places like this.'

Dylan brought the car to a stop in her reserved bay. 'Not quite,' she said as they exited the car. She had to admit the building was an impressive sight. Overlooking the River Thames, her apartment had some of the best views of London. The night view of the London Eye and Houses of Parliament was spectacular. They rode up in the lift to the top floor in silence. Dylan was tired and feeling like a fish out of water. The past few weeks had been something she'd never experienced before. She was actually feeling close to Harper, enough to let down her guard. Though Dylan had to admit, Harper's own honesty had a lot to do with it. *Maybe she's a little too honest.* Harper's use of the word love at the hotel had unsettled her a little. Was it just a figure of speech or was there an element of truth to it? Dylan wasn't sure which she preferred. Nothing like this had ever happened before. Her usual game plan was to get her needs fulfilled then move on to the next willing player.

This was the first time she had been up close and personal with a woman she'd slept with.

Dylan led the way along the plush carpeted hallway. She unlocked her door and pushed it open, motioning for Harper to enter first.

'My God, how the other half live,' Harper said laughing. 'How on earth do you keep this place so clean?'

Dylan scanned the open planned place and saw it through Harper's eyes. The dark hardwood floors complimented the white walls, on which colourful artwork hung, giving the room a warm homely feeling. The kitchen, all sleek black granite worktops and chrome accessories, was a place Dylan barely spent any time at all. If she wasn't getting her morning coffee or wine from the fridge it was a place she tended to avoid, preferring to eat out or order in.

'I love it,' Harper said crossing the room to look at the photographs on the wall.

Dylan walked over to join her. 'Coffee?' she said trying to distract her. There was one picture she didn't want her to see. It was too late. By the look of surprise on Harper's face she had already spotted it.

Harper turned to Dylan with a puzzled expression. 'Isn't that your boss?' Harper said pointing to the picture of Dylan and Gregory together.

'Yes,' Dylan admitted reluctantly. No one outside of their immediate family and close friends was aware they were related. That's why Dylan used her mother's maiden name. She didn't want people thinking she'd got where she was because of her father.

'Wow. He must be some boss if you've got a picture of him on your wall.'

'Harper, he's my dad.'

'What?! No way.'

'I'm afraid so.'

'That explains everything ...' Harper's hand flew to cover her mouth. 'Sorry I didn't mean ... I mean ... just wow. It must have been tough being his daughter if his reputation's anything to go by.'

Dylan shrugged off her jacket and walked into the kitchen. Flipping on the kettle, she took out two mugs before glancing over her shoulder. 'You know what they say, the apple doesn't fall far from the tree.'

'I would've believed that before I got to know you. But not now,' Harper said softly.

'Harper,' Dylan started. She needed to knock off Harper's rose tinted glasses before she got too carried away. 'I'm still the same person I was a few weeks ago. I haven't changed. Just because we've slept together doesn't mean I've turned into an angel.'

Harper's face creased in confusion.

Shit. Why did I have to say all that crap? The truth was Dylan had changed, whether she liked it or not. Before Harper had a chance to backtrack Dylan's mobile phone shattered the tense atmosphere.

Perfect timing. Not. Dylan grabbed her phone from her jacket and looked down at the caller ID expecting someone from work. Instead, 'Ice queen' flashed up. The name she'd given Robyn.

'I won't be a minute,' Dylan said trying to avoid looking into Harper's pained eyes. She answered the phone as she walked into her bedroom and closed the door behind her.

'Robyn,' she said trying her best to sound inviting.

'Mediation isn't working. I want this over and done with. Only this time, no stalling. I want full custody of Jake.'

Dylan tried to hide the surprise in her voice. 'Full custody?'

'That's right. The bitch has got a new girlfriend and they're taking drugs around my son.'

Her son? Hearing the vermin in Robyn's voice Dylan had no doubt whatsoever Robyn's anger was due to the fact that Abi had a new girlfriend. The green-eyed monster was raising its head and she wanted Abi to pay.

'I can't talk now. It's best you come and see me in my office.'

'Today?'

Dylan rested her head against the door. Did this mean she was going to have to go into battle with Harper again? No, that would bring the end to their relationship. *Relationship? Is that what we're in?* Instead of feeling fear, she felt ... giddy. Harper meant more to her than she'd realised. First things first. She had to get Robyn out of her hair. 'Meet me in my office in an hour,' she told Robyn before disconnecting the call. Dylan found Harper hovering near the front door when she exited her room.

'I'm going to make a move,' Harper said.

'Harper, I think we need to talk—'

'—No you were right. Nothing's changed. I guess I'll see you round.'

'What I should have said was…' Before Dylan could finish her sentence, Harper was out the door and Dylan was left staring at it, her mouth agape.

I love you too.

Chapter Forty-One

Two voices echoed sharply as Abi slowly emerged from her deep sleep.

'Can you hear me?' a middle aged woman with hair pulled tightly into a bun on top of her head, peered closely at her. Behind her stood another younger woman dressed in jeans and a jacket, talking to a doctor, but Abi couldn't figure out what she was saying.

'Where am I?' Abi asked the nurse, her head pounding and her chest aching.

'At St Thomas' Hospital.'

'What have I done?' Abi shrieked, suddenly panic stricken.

'I was hoping you could tell us, love,' the nurse replied. Her face was fraught with concern.

Abi looked around for Jake and suddenly remembered she'd told Tia to call Robyn if she didn't pick him up.

'Jake!' She sat up and swung her legs onto the floor, ignoring the cold under her feet. Abi had to get to Tia before she called Robyn. 'What's the time?' she gasped, her hands shaking in panic.

'Four o'clock.'

Abi's stomach churned and pulled into a tight ball. There was still time. 'On Monday?' she said aloud. That meant she'd only been out for a couple of hours.

'On Tuesday, love,' the nurse replied.

The nurse's words sounded in slow motion, sealing Abi's fears in the vacuum that sucked in her sense of reality. 'Oh no, it can't be,' Abi said, her voice quivering audibly and her eyes stretched in absolute frantic dread.

The nurse grabbed her by her flailing arms as Abi struggled wildly to get up and run.

'Take it easy,' the nursed warned, 'Your stomach's been pumped and you need to conserve your energy.'

Abi began sobbing, her arms growing limp in the nurse's hands. 'But you don't unders-tand ... I-I have to get to my son.'

'Your sister will be back in a minute. She's only gone to warm your son's bottle.' The nurse reassured her as she released her arms.

'My sister? Tia. Jake,' Abi uttered through her whimpering and shaky voice. 'They're both here. Robyn hasn't got him?'

The nurse gave Abi a puzzled look. 'I don't know who Robyn is but yes, your sister has your son. She was the one who found you at home.'

Oh God no. Poor Tia. The thought of Tia finding her was enough to send Abi back into her panic stricken whining.

'Come on now, you've given your sister quite a shock as it is. Don't let her see you in this state, think of your son.'

That was the point, she had been thinking about

her son. That's what had tipped her over the edge. Abi jerked forward when she heard the familiar sound of Jake cry. Tia held him on her hip bouncing him up and down as she tried to soothe him. Abi could see the tears in her eyes as she neared.

Taking the nurses advice, Abi swung her legs back onto the bed and sat up. 'Tia,' she began. 'I don't know what to say.'

Tia handed Jake to her and pulled Abi into her arms. 'There's nothing to say,' she said reassuringly. 'If I hadn't been so wrapped—'

'—It's not your fault, you hear? This is my doing. I let myself get into this position, but no more. If Robyn thinks she can throw her weight around and take my son away from me, she'd better be prepared for war.' Abi could hear her voice growing stronger. 'I want you to call my solicitor and let her know what's happened.' She gazed down at Jake. 'I'm gonna fight for you, Jake. I'm not going to be a victim anymore, I promise you that.'

Chapter Forty-Two

Shay eyed Harper with amusement. 'I hate it when I can't read your mood.'

Harper laughed. 'You can't read it because I'm at peace,' she lied, fanning her hands out on her desk. So Dylan got cold feet. So what? It wasn't the end of the world and Dylan wasn't the only fish in the sea. If she'd have known from the beginning that Gregory was her dad she would have kept a wide berth. How could he not have passed his ruthlessness down to his daughter? *And I thought I had it bad.* The time they had spent together over the last few weeks had been nice. M*uch, much more than nice.* But the short lived experience was over now and she had to do what she normally did. Brush herself down and start all over again. Not that it would be easy. Far from it. It was hard to fall for someone and be rejected, *but hey ho, that's life.* Who was she kidding? How was she going to stop thinking about her a zillion times a day?

'What's on my agenda today?' Harper asked Shay who was sitting across from her.

'You've just spent the night with the hottest woman in London—bar yourself of course—and you're at peace. Either she was a major let down, which I doubt, or you've had a falling out already.'

Harper eyed Shay with a raised eyebrow. The woman never missed a thing. Harper laughed.

'Nothing happened, Shay, we're just friends. Now can we get back to work issues, please?' As much as she loved Shay, she wasn't about to out herself. Sleeping with Dylan was unethical and shouting about it from the rooftops was the last thing she was going to do. As far as Shay knew, there was an attraction and that's how far it went. The less she knew about it the less chance of Shay getting dragged into a messy affair if anyone ever found out.

Shay studied her for a moment. 'Why don't you give Stella a call?'

Harper rested her chin on her open palm. 'And why would I do that?'

'Dunno. You look a bit lost.'

'How did you get to know me so well, Shay?'

'Because not only do we work together, we happen to be friends and you can't help confiding in me.' She grinned and adjusted her glasses.

'Hmm, I don't know if that's a good thing or not.'

Shay stood. 'You know it is,' she said with a smile. 'I'd better get back to work.'

'Me too.' Harper sighed wistfully, she thought she'd found a confidant in Dylan as well. *Turns out I didn't after all.*

It took Harper several seconds to find her phone at the bottom of her bag when she heard it ringing. The minute the call was connected the hairs on the back of her neck rose. An unfamiliar voice was informing her about a suicide attempt. At first she thought the caller had dialled the wrong number. It wasn't until she heard Abi's name that an adrenaline rush propelled her to her feet.

'Is she going to be alright?' Harper asked, dreading to hear the answer.

'Yes,' came the reply. 'I'm sorry I should have introduced myself. I'm Tia, Abi's sister.'

'Which hospital is she in?'

'St Thomas'. Abi asked if she could see you urgently. She thinks she might have messed up her divorce case.'

'Tell her not to worry about anything. I'll be there as soon as I can.' Harper was already on her way out the door as she spoke.

Shay looked up at her from her desk as she hurried by. 'Something's come up. I've got to go.'

'Oh?' Shay looked up at her quizzically.

'I won't be back today, I'll see you tomorrow.' Harper decided against telling Shay the news for her own good. Harper knew it would remind Shay of a time when she herself had been in the grip of darkness and despair. No, she wouldn't do that to her friend.

Twenty minutes later a taxi dropped Harper in front of the hospital. The initial adrenaline rush from Tia telling her the news had dissipated. Now her mind was full of worry. What could Abi have done to spoil her chances of getting a fair divorce settlement? When she hadn't heard from her she assumed the mediation went well and they were moving forward. So it was with great surprise that things had turned sour so quickly. *Unless it has nothing to do with the divorce and there's something else bothering her.* She wouldn't have to wait long to find out what. Harper hurried towards the reception.

It took several minutes for Harper to be given the name of the ward Abi was on. Soon after she was walking along a narrow passage, peeking in each cubical to find Abi. Harper passed several nurses stood chatting behind the nurse's station. Straight ahead she caught sight of Abi, sat up in bed, holding a sleeping baby. Looking at the loving way Abi held her son, it was hard to believe that she could have attempted to take her own life and leave him behind.

Abi glanced up as Harper neared. Harper noted the trembling of Abi's bottom lip and soon tears welled up in her eyes. 'You came.'

'Of course I did.' Harper leant over and kissed Abi's cheek, then turned her attention to the baby. 'He's beautiful, Abi,' Harper said stroking his face.

Abi smiled. 'Thanks. You haven't met my sister, have you?'

'No, not in person. We spoke on the phone.' Harper turned to face the blonde haired woman and held out her hand which Tia took in a firm grip.

'Thanks for coming,' Tia mouthed.

Harper smiled and looked around for an empty seat.

Tia rose to her feet. 'Why don't I take him to the café so you two can talk,' Tia said holding out her arms for Jake.

'Thanks.' Abi kissed Jake's forehead before handing him over.

'See you in a bit,' Tia said before disappearing behind the drawn curtain.

Harper sat down in the vacant chair and pulled it closer to the bed. She rested, what she hoped was a reassuring hand, on Abi's arm. 'Do you want to talk?'

'You must think I'm a pathetic and horrible mum.'

'I would never judge you, ever,' Harper said softly.

It was several minutes before Abi spoke, when she did her voice shook with emotion. 'I just couldn't take it anymore. Robyn threatened to apply for full custody of Jake,' she said wiping away a tear that had spilt from her eyes. Her voice rang with panic. 'The thought of Robyn taking Jake away from me…' She shook her head. 'I just lost it and well …' She lowered her chin to her chest. 'You know the rest.'

Harper cocked her head. 'I thought during mediation you were sorting out visiting rights, what turned it in to a custody battle?'

Abi looked uneasy. 'It's my own stupid fault. I went to see …' She hesitated for a moment. 'A friend. She was smoking weed. I know I shouldn't have gone into her flat—'

'—You don't have to explain your actions, Abi. Carry on, what happened?'

'Robyn came round unexpectedly and could smell weed on Jake. She accused me of taking drugs. I've never taken drugs in my life. I swear.'

Harper squeezed her arm. 'I doubt a judge would take your son away from you if you have no history of drug abuse. She'd have to provide evidence. Robyn saying Jake smelt like weed really wouldn't cut it. It seems she was trying to frighten you.'

Abi snorted. 'It worked.'

Harper wasn't too bothered about the accusation. It was Robyn's word against hers. 'If she carries on with her nonsense I'll arrange for you to take a drug test,' she said with an air of confidence. 'That will soon put her back in her box when it's negative.'

Abi twisted the thin blue sheet around her fingers. 'There's something else.'

Feeling uncharacteristically alarmed, Harper steeled herself. The look of fear in Abi's eyes told her it was going to be something she didn't want to hear.

'I sent a letter to Robyn's solicitor telling her what a shit mum I am and that Jake deserves to be with Robyn. I didn't see the point in there being any confusion about who Jake should live with if I wasn't going to be around anymore.'

Oh shit. That is bad. Could she ask Dylan to 'lose' the letter? Harper couldn't bring herself to do it. It was unprofessional and unethical. *There must be another way. How can I prove that it's Robyn's actions that have pushed Abi over the edge?* Her only chance was to find some sort of evidence that Robyn was abusive.

Harper stood and paced the small cubicle wondering what she was going to do. An idea sprang to mind. 'Abi, you said before that Robyn sent you emails, abusive emails, before she kicked you out. Did you use an email program or a web based service?'

'I used the program Outlook. Why?'

'Do you still have the laptop?'

'No, well yes, but not at home. It's at Robyn's house. Because she bought it, she said it was hers. But anyway, she deleted my whole inbox before I left.'

Damn. That put a stop to that idea straight away. Harper's eyebrows furrowed. 'Maybe there's a way of retrieving them.'

'Really?'

'It's a possibility.' Harper tapped her foot on the floor. 'And there's definitely no way you can get the laptop?'

Abi's eyes remained fixed on Harper's when she said, 'Is it illegal to enter someone's house if I still have a key?'

Chapter Forty-Three

'Dylan, have you got time to speak?' Harper said down the phone to Dylan.

'Of course I have. You sound upset. Take a deep breath and tell me what's wrong?'

'Were you aware that Robyn has withdrawn from mediation and wants full custody of Abi's son?

'Well, yes. I had a meeting with Robyn. She said—'

'—Why the hell wouldn't you have told me?' Harper said. 'Abi's in hospital. She nearly died because of you and your fucking client.'

Dylan's jaw dropped and she slowly rose to her feet. Cathy appeared in the doorway holding her mail. She indicated for her to leave it on her desk then waved her away. 'What happened?'

'Oh so you didn't know your client withdrawing from mediation was going to send Abi over the edge?'

'That's awful,' Dylan said in a low tone, her eyes falling to the floor and looking for a suitable emotion in her scarce reserve of feelings. The one that came to the fore was not one she was familiar with— contrition. 'Harper, I swear to you—'

'—Your word ain't worth shit to me. I know you'll probably use this information against my client but do you know what. I don't care. You need to know the harm your actions cause to innocent people.'

'If you just listen for one min—'

'—Why should I? Your client has totally worn Abi down to the bone with all this shit.'

'Harper,' Dylan addressed her firmly, 'I'm starting to get really pissed off with your accusations. Don't lay the blame at my feet. I'm not the one responsible for this mess. If you want to have a go at someone, call Robyn Massey, not me.'

Dylan pressed the end call button with force. *Oh I hate these bloody mobile phones.* She dropped the phone on her desk with a clang. Dylan wished Harper had called her on her work phone so she could have slammed the phone back onto its cradle. It was so much more satisfying than hitting a button. If Harper had actually listened instead of jumping down Dylan's throat she would have known the outcome of her meeting with Robyn. That Dylan had advised Robyn that going for full custody was a waste of time and money. But no, she wouldn't hear her out. Harper was so self-righteous sometimes it drove her mad.

In the haze of her annoyance Dylan picked up her mail and flipped through it. She looked down at a crumpled envelope that someone had tried to straighten out. Tearing it open she took a step away from her desk and eyed it cautiously. It was a handwritten letter from Abi.

As she read the letter something terrible dawned on her.

What was to stop Abi from going through with it next time Robyn pulled one of her stunts? Did she really want Abi's blood on her hands? If Harper disliked her now, she would hate her for an eternity. Dylan stood motionless for a few seconds.

Suddenly she became animated again and made her way to Gregory's office for what she knew would be the death blow to her partnership. If she was going to lose Harper, there was no use in keeping the very job that had caused her loss.

Minutes later she entered Gregory's office. He looked up in pleasant surprise. 'I thought you'd be busy on the Massey case.'

'That's what I need to talk to you about.'

'Sit.' He gestured to the empty seat opposite him.

'Dad...'

He raised his eyebrows and gave her a look of disapproval.

Dylan sighed. 'Sorry, Gregory. There's a bit of a problem.'

'I thought we didn't have problems, Dylan, only solutions.'

'There's only one solution. I can't work on the Massey case anymore. I have to leave the company.'

'Leave? Why?'

'Because...' *Oh God this is so embarrassing.* She felt the heat rushing to her cheeks. 'Because I slept with the solicitor whose dealing with Robyn's wife's case.'

There was a long silence. Dylan didn't realise she was holding her breath until she was forced to exhale through her mouth. Where she had expected to see shock on his face there was only a look of indifference.

'And?' he finally said.

'And...it's unethical.' *Bloody hell, I'm even starting to sound like Harper. What's next?*

'Unethical? Did you have sex in public?'

Dylan dropped her gaze to the floor. She really didn't want to be talking about her sex life with her father, whether it was relevant or not. 'Of course we didn't.'

'So no one else knows?'

'That's not the point.' Her voice lowered to barely a whisper. 'I have feelings for her.'

Gregory made a face. 'Feelings?'

'Yes feelings, you know, that thing when you love someone.'

Gregory burst out laughing. 'You have a one night stand and you think you're in love. Come on, Dylan, I expected more of you.'

'It wasn't a one night stand.' She stood up abruptly. 'And another thing. Abi Massey is in hospital. She tried to kill herself because of the stress of this case.'

Gregory made a church steeple with his fingertips as he paused to consider her. 'Tried and failed.'

'That's beside the point. I don't want her death on my conscience if she tries it again. I can't be involved in the destruction of people's lives anymore. Not for any amount of money.'

Gregory's voice was cold as he stood up and walked behind his chair. He gripped the edge of the seat with both hands. 'And you want to give up your chance of partnership and career here because of a weak willed woman trying to top herself. It might not be this case, if she's so inclined, anything could push her over the edge.'

Dylan stifled a scream, electing to keep her temper under control. 'This is a human being we're talking about "Dad". A real person whose life is going down the drain because of the likes of us,' she said. 'You know I used to think there was something wrong with people who didn't see the world like us. It's taken this to realise, it's not them, we're the ones that are damaged. We're vultures, picking away at the dignity of victims until they've got nothing left.'

His voice softened. For a split second they were father and daughter. Not boss and employee. He threw her an embarrassed look. 'I get it. You're having your woman monthly thingy. Believe me I understand. Why don't you take a few days off? When your hormones are back to normal come back to work, and end this goddamn case.' He finished with a sharp edge to his tone.

Dylan's jaw tensed. Gregory was starting to piss her off with his refusal to take her seriously. That was one of the things that irked her about him. Her dad always thought he knew Dylan better than she did herself. 'I'm not having any "thingy" as you put it. And I'm not going to change my mind,' she said adamantly.

Gregory shook his head, a benign smile on his face. 'Leopards don't change their spots, Dylan, you should know that.'

If he was expecting his analysis of her to be met with a whoop of joy he was sadly mistaken. 'That's where you're wrong, and I'll prove it.' Dylan hoped she'd said enough to make him realise that she was done screwing people's lives up. The thing was, it wasn't her dad that she had to try and convince—it was Harper.

Chapter Forty-Four

Dylan was apprehensive. It wasn't an emotion that sat well with her. Abi's letter was securely in the back of her jeans. She still didn't know what she was going to do about it.

After the discussion with her dad, she finally saw him for what he really was—a cold, uncaring, calculating bastard. Had he shown one ounce of humanity she could have forgiven his interest to move on with the case. But to dismiss the woman's troubles as if she'd told him Abi had stubbed a toe was unforgivable. Dylan knew she could be single minded but her dad's behaviour was downright nasty.

Dylan stopped her car outside Harper's flat. *What the hell am I doing here? I'm the last person Harper will want to see right now.* Despite this, Dylan found herself walking towards her flat and up the flight of stairs. She hesitated before knocking. *Can I hear a baby crying?* She pressed her ear against the door. She wasn't hearing things. It was a baby.

Intrigued, she pressed the door bell and waited. A minute went by before Harper answered. The look on her face said it all. She hated her.

'What?'

'Can I come in?'

'I really don't think that's a good idea. I'm busy.'

'So I can hear.' Dylan glanced over Harper's

shoulder. 'You didn't tell me you had a baby. Were you saving that one until you had me hooked?' she teased.

Harper's face remained expressionless. *Okay so humour isn't going to do it.*

Dylan's finger tapped nervously against her thigh. Harper was the only woman she knew who could make her feel on edge. She had a knack of making Dylan think she was in the wrong, even when she wasn't. 'If you won't talk to me inside, we'll talk here.' When Harper made no move to slam the door in her face she continued. 'How's Abi?'

'Like you care.'

Dylan let out a heavy sigh. She wanted to step forward and shake some sense into her, maybe even yell at her, *I AM NOT RESPONSIBLE FOR ABI TRYING TO TAKE HER OWN LIFE.* Knowing that wouldn't go down too well she just said, 'Give me a break, Harper. How can you think for a minute this sort of news wouldn't have shocked me?'

'I'm sure it's not the first time your actions have had such dire consequences.'

Dylan stepped back as if Harper had struck her. She might as well have. It was as if someone had punched her in the stomach. 'That's a bit below the belt.'

A blonde woman came into view carrying a baby, stopping behind Harper. She glanced at them both before saying to Harper, 'Do you mind if I heat him a bottle.'

'No of course not.'

The woman started to turn around. Dylan eyed her suspiciously. Had Harper moved on so quickly? It hadn't been more than twenty four hours since they'd been wrapped in each other's arms, surely it meant more to Harper than a meaningless shag. 'Aren't you going to introduce us?' Dylan said.

The woman shifted the baby onto her opposite hip and held out her hand and introduced herself. 'Tia. And this little fellow's my sister's son Jake.'

Dylan swallowed hard as it dawned on her who the woman was. She looked frantically towards Harper. Harper glared back at her with narrowed eyes.

'And you are?' Tia asked.

Words failed her. 'Dy—

'—She's an old friend of mine,' Harper interjected quickly.

'Nice to meet you,' Tia said before heading back down the hallway.

Dylan felt a lump form in her throat. Even in these circumstances when Harper must have thought she was a despicable person, she still protected her. 'You didn't have to do that you know.'

Confusion clouded Harper's eyes. 'Do what?'

'Not tell her who I was. I'm a big girl you know. I don't need protecting.'

'Don't I know it? Look if you came to find out about Abi, she's gonna be fine, okay?'

'Harper.' Dylan took a step closer and reached for her. Dylan would have given anything to hold her in her arms for even a second. To rewind the clock back to that morning in her apartment. Only this time, she wouldn't rebuff Harper when she noted how much Dylan had changed. She would agree and tell her it was because of her—Harper Anderson, the kind, gorgeous woman that she had fallen in love with.

Harper shuffled back, her expression pained. 'Please don't make things harder than they already are.'

'But—'

'—I can't do this. I'm sorry.' Harper gave a small shake of her head and started to close the door.

'Wait,' Dylan pulled Abi's letter from her pocket. She couldn't believe what she was about to do. 'I think somebody sent this to me by mistake.'

Dylan handed Harper the paper. Without waiting for her to read it, Dylan turned and walked towards the stairs.

'Why would you do this?' Harper called out after her. Some of the coldness in her voice had gone.

Dylan glanced over her shoulder. 'I've got nothing to lose. I'm no longer Robyn's solicitor. Despite what you think, I'm not your enemy, Harper. I never have been.'

Dylan was never one to admit defeat. But in this instance, she knew a losing battle when she saw one. She had no choice but to let Harper go. Maybe one day in the future, when the memories of the Massey case were well and truly behind them, they could hook up again and try and rebuild that bridge that had been well and truly burnt.

Chapter Forty-Five

Abi's main concern at that very moment was not about getting into Robyn's house and retrieving her computer. It was the worry that one of the neighbourhood watch team might spot her staking out the house and call the police. After her previous experience, the last thing she wanted was to be brought to their attention again. She'd only been discharged from the hospital the day before and she could do without any more drama. Abi poked her head around the trunk of the large oak tree she was hiding behind. She'd been waiting outside her old residence for the past hour. Robyn normally left for work at eight but her car was still in the drive. Abi was in the process of deciding whether to leave it for another day. No sooner had the thought crossed her mind, she heard the chatter of Robyn and another woman. Two car doors slammed shut followed by the revving of Robyn's car. Heart pounding, Abi pressed her back against the tree, attempting to make herself invisible. What seemed like a good idea hours ago, now seemed ridiculous. What if Robyn came back and caught her. There was no doubt in her mind if that happened, Robyn would get her thrown in jail without a second thought.

Robyn's black Lexus reversed out of the drive and sped off down the road. She waited a few minutes before breaking her cover, walking quickly across the road, her head turning in every direction, checking to see if anyone was watching. Abi was in a nervous frenzy as she hurried up the pathway towards the place she once called home.

Memories of her life with Robyn flooded her. The beginning had been good, too good she realised with dismay. The saying that 'if something's too good to be true it normally is' came to mind as she strode up to the front door. For a split second she wondered if she'd been too hasty with her assumptions. What if Robyn had changed the locks? Then what? She'd be back to square one. She needn't have worried as the lock opened easily as she turned the key.

Stepping inside quickly, Abi shut the door behind her. The place looked exactly the same as when she'd been living there. Oak wooden floors. Large Buddha figurines placed strategically either side of the wide entrance hall. Abi inhaled deeply. Even her favourite scent of vanilla incense remained. Deciding now wasn't the time to get nostalgic, she ran up the stairs to Robyn's office, the floor creaking beneath her. Though she knew there was no one in the house to hear, she trod a bit lighter.

'Right, now where are you computer?' she muttered aloud. Abi headed straight for the filing cabinet where she had last seen Robyn put it. She pulled at the drawer. Locked. That was to be expected. The cabinet held some of Robyn's confidential papers from work. Abi also knew Robyn was a creature of habit. Her hands fumbled underneath the desk. *Voila*. A small key was taped there which she knew would give her the access she needed.

Abi pulled the drawer open, scarcely believing her luck. There, under a pile of papers, laid her Apple Macbook. The very one Robyn had given her for her birthday. *Now I'm taking back what's rightfully mine!* She removed the computer and replaced the papers in an orderly fashion, certain it wouldn't give away her presence. As she shut the drawer, a file tab named 'divorce' caught her eye. Intrigued she pulled it out and flipped through it scanning the sheets of paper with her mouth agape. A statement showing a transfer of £500,000 to Miss Tiffany Adams lay on top of the pile. She flicked through the rest. Stocks and shares were now in this woman's name. The name sounded familiar. Where had she heard it before? It suddenly dawned on her—W. H. Smith. *She planted that credit card on me. So Robyn did have something to do with it!*

Abi continued to read through the papers, the fury inside her mounting with each page. *So all the financial information I had about her was only the tip of the iceberg.* Abi was amazed at the amount of money Robyn had. During their marriage Robyn dealt with all the finances, another form of control no doubt. Yes, she knew Robyn was wealthy. *But not that wealthy*! Abi needed to sit down before her legs gave way beneath her. Robyn had so much, yet had fought her every inch of the way for a measly two grand a month.

Abi doubted there was any chance of making a

claim on the funds now they were in someone else's name, but she thought it might give them some leeway if Robyn knew they had proof of her dodgy dealings. It had to be illegal, surely.

Abi took her phone from her pocket and lay the sheets of paper on the desk. She snapped picture after picture of Robyn's lies and deceit. It needn't have even gone this far. If Robyn would have stepped up to the plate at the beginning things would have been so different. Abi didn't care about Robyn's affair anymore. Nor was she worried about the idle threats of applying for full custody. As Harper had once told her, it was time to fight fire with fire.

Chapter Forty-Six

'Take a deep breath and start again,' Harper said, as Abi did as she advised and inhaled deeply before releasing an unsteady breath. Abi had rushed through her office door barely five minutes earlier. Her hair was windswept and her forehead perspired with a thin film of sweat.

'Okay, okay. I got it. I got the laptop.'

'You did?'

'Yep,' Abi said proudly as she withdrew it and plonked it down on Harper's desk. 'It was in the exact place she put it before she kicked me out.'

'So she hadn't changed the locks then?' Harper hadn't said anything at the time, but she had wondered if Abi would actually be able to access the premises. That was the first thing spouses normally did to stop the ex-partner from coming back and removing possessions.

'No, thankfully she thinks I'm too meek to go rooting round her place.'

Harper flipped through the contacts on her phone. 'I'm gonna give my friend a call. He knows all about restoring deleted files. If he can retrieve what she sent you it will be dynamite.'

'Fingers crossed,' Abi gulped at the glass of water Harper had pushed in front of her. 'There's something else.' Abi withdrew her phone and pulled up the pictures of the statements she'd photographed. 'She's been transferring her assets to her girlfriend, well I assume it's her girlfriend anyway. Looks like it's the same woman who said I stole her credit card.'

So I was right. Harper shook her head in dismay. 'I'm speechless. I really am.'

'So was I, but it doesn't matter anymore. Their plan backfired. But at least I have proof now, here look.'

Harper took the phone from her and looked at the images. 'Disposed of her assets has she. A judge would look extremely unfavourably upon this. And look at the amounts. Jesus, she's trusting isn't she?'

'You think?'

Harper raised her eyebrows. 'Would you transfer this much money to someone you didn't trust?' Harper asked, surprise in her voice. Not that she should have been. People could be very unscrupulous when it came to money and things they considered 'theirs'. Hiding money by transferring it to family or friends wasn't as uncommon as people thought.

'No but then I'm not a sneaky rat like Robyn. It's a Robyn special. She does something to get into your bad books, then buys you off by making some kind of grandiose gesture. Well, whatever she did to piss this woman off must have been major.'

Harper shook her head in dismay. Hearing about Robyn's less than desirable attributes, she couldn't help but wonder what had attracted Abi to Robyn in the first place. They seemed like chalk and cheese. Abi was kind, thoughtful and by the looks of it very loving. Whereas Robyn seemed to be cold and without a beating heart. Could it be the money that attracted women to her? She doubted that had been the case for Abi. From what she knew of her she was too idealistic to be that shallow. All the same, if the money was there she was entitled to it and Harper wouldn't be doing her job if she didn't ask Abi her intentions. 'Do you want to go after the money?'

Abi shook her head vehemently. 'It would cause more stress than it's worth.'

'Imagine what you could do with it, Abi.'

Her voice was intense as she spoke. 'Money's not worth my sanity. It would be nice, but I'll manage somehow. I've got to.'

Given Abi's fragile state of mind Harper didn't push it. The longer the divorce proceedings dragged on the more likely Abi would buckle under the pressure again. It was up to Harper to make the process as painless as possible.

'I still can't believe Robyn's solicitor didn't receive that letter. What a blessing in disguise. I would never have written it if I was in my right mind.'

'Hmm. You might have sent it to the wrong address, these things happen.' Harper decided against telling Abi the truth. What purpose would it serve? If word ever got out Dylan would be in serious trouble and so would she for ripping the document up.

'That's true. No doubt Robyn's solicitor will soon be back on track trying to pound me into the ground.'

'Actually, she's removed herself from the case.'

'Has she? Is that normal?'

She considered the question for a moment. 'It does happen. I don't know why it's happened in this case though.' Harper still couldn't believe it herself. Dylan transferring the case to someone else was the last thing she could have imagined. Okay, so it may have been a bit tense between them but they were both professionals. *I wonder what she told her dad?*

'Maybe she found her conscience,' Abi said breaking into her thoughts.

Harper snorted. *Dylan with a conscience? Not likely.* 'Dylan? I doubt that very much,' she said without thinking.

Abi covered her mouth with her hand and stifled a yawn. To Harper she looked exhausted. Her eyes were puffier than usual and her skin looked an off grey. It was strange, Harper pondered, how new love could make you radiant but the loss of it turned you into a shadow of your former self.

'Do you know this solicitor then?' Abi asked.

'Yes, sort of.'

Harper glanced at her watch as a distraction to side step the topic. Since Dylan's last visit she didn't know what to make of her anymore. Every time she thought she'd nailed her, Dylan changed course and did the total opposite of what she was expecting. It was like being on a rollercoaster without any brakes.

Harper looked from Abi to the laptop. 'Right.' Harper picked up the computer and slid it into her drawer. 'I'll get my guy to go through this later and see what he can retrieve. In the meantime sit tight. I'll wait to make contact with Robyn's new solicitor, in case the emails can give me some leeway.'

'Excellent.' Abi rose to her feet. 'I forgot to say thank you for having Tia and Jake round yours the other night. It really helped Tia having a distraction. What I did shook her up pretty bad.'

'I can imagine. She loves you very much. You have a beautiful family around you, Abi. Remember that.'

Abi stopped by the door before leaving. 'Oh I will. Not everyone gets a second chance.' She smiled. 'I guess I'm one of the lucky ones.'

Harper returned to her seat and leant forward on her desk, placing her hands on the side of her head. She hated to admit it to herself but she had acted rather hastily in her reaction to Abi's suicide attempt. Of course Dylan was right. It wasn't her fault. Deep down Harper never thought it was. Her anger had been misdirected for all the wrong reasons. Dylan had rebuffed her and it hurt like hell, more than she had been willing to admit. So she had done the only thing she could. Retaliate under another guise. Calling her up like that was about her making Dylan feel like shit. There was no other explanation. She wasn't proud of it. It was totally out of her character. *Love makes you do crazy things* … She closed her eyes. *Like risk losing your licence, swallowing your pride … oh, Dylan, is that what you wanted me to know? And I was too stubborn and blind to see.*

Over the next hour Harper's mood swung between anger, hurt, love and hate. She paced the floor of her office, unable to stop the images of Dylan flooding her mind. Her laughter, smile and yes her compassion of all things. Dylan had been there for her when Harper needed her most. So why when things were going so well did Dylan reject her? Push her away as if she meant nothing to her? Harper abruptly stood up. *I'm gonna drive myself insane going round and round in circles.* There was no point trying to come up with the answer herself. She had wasted valuable time sitting there procrastinating. Instead of shying away from the situation she should have confronted Dylan on the spot and asked her where the relationship was going. Being a straightforward sort of person, Harper had no doubt Dylan would have told her the truth. Even if the truth hurt, she had to hear it from Dylan's own mouth. This didn't have to be the end of everything, it could be the beginning of something beautiful. Or it could be the final nail in the coffin. It was only a matter of time before she found out which.

Chapter Forty-Seven

Dylan had spent the past few hours fidgeting and tidying things that didn't need tidying. *Welcome to the world of unemployment. Boring, boring, boring.* She had never felt so restless. Normally her life was full of activity, but today, she couldn't motivate herself to step outside the confines of her home. *Maybe I'm depressed.* She shot the thought down immediately, knowing what was wrong with her. She was love sick. Visions of Harper standing near the wall looking at her photos assaulted her thoughts. Up until that point everything had been great. *Funny how your life can go down the pan in a matter of minutes.* Had her life really unravelled to the point where she had no job or the woman she loved in a matter of days? *Unbelievable.* Her dad had been calling incessantly, asking when she was returning to work. It amazed Dylan that he didn't get it. He knew her inside out, so it should have come as no surprise to him that when she made a decision, she stuck to it. Returning to work for him was a definite no-no.

Dylan made her way to the kitchen. What she needed was a caffeine kick. She flipped on the kettle, took a mug from the cupboard then opened the fridge. *Oh no.* she'd run out of milk. Now she would have to leave her apartment. Changing out of her jogging bottoms and vest into jeans and a jumper, she grabbed her car keys and headed for the door.

Ten minutes later she was in Tesco trailing around the wine aisle, the lack of milk promptly put out of her mind. As she reached up to grab a bottle from the top shelf, she heard a familiar voice calling her.

'Ms Blue.'

Dylan turned to come face to face with Cathy. She forced a smile. Dylan had never seen Cathy outside the office before and the situation felt odd. She suddenly realised how stupid it was to have a woman near her age address her as Ms.

'Cathy, how are you?' Dylan said, continuing to smile through her discomfort.

'Alright.'

The two women stared at each other in an uncomfortable silence.

'I'm just getting some milk for coffee.'

Cathy eyed her basket with raised eyebrows. 'Yeah I can see that.'

Dylan looked down and felt her cheeks flush. 'Oh, I mean—'

'—I never thought I'd say this to you, but I'm proud of what you did.'

Dylan frowned. 'What I did?'

'Leaving your job the way you did. Everyone's talking about it.'

'But how did you know?'

'Your mad ex-client came in ranting and raving at Mr Maynard for you abandoning her. Serves her bloody well right if you ask me. What a bitch. She's nearly as bad as—' She stopped abruptly and turned away.

Dylan grinned. 'It's okay, Cathy, you can say it. As bad as me?'

Cathy shrugged. 'Well you did ask.'

'You're right.'

'So what are you gonna do now then? You're not coming back are you?'

'No, I don't want to be on that side of the fence anymore,' she was amazed to hear herself say.

'If I could, I'd leave tomorrow. That place sucks the life out of ya. I feel like I've sold my soul to the Devil. That place is pure evil. And as for Mr Maynard—'

'—It's best you stop there, Cathy. I know he's a bastard but he's still my dad.'

'He's your ... oh my God.'

'Yes. Imagine how I feel?' Dylan said. Why had she been so blind to how toxic the company was? She'd been so caught up with winning and earning a high wage that she couldn't see the wood for the trees. It had taken meeting Harper to lift the veil from her eyes. Dylan was getting ready to say goodbye when a thought entered her mind. Cathy wanted out of the cess pit. She was an excellent assistant, thoroughly dependable and Dylan worked well with her. Dylan was unemployed. Although she had enough money to live comfortably without ever working again thanks to a hefty inheritance left to her by her grandmother, Dylan liked having a job to go to. But one that didn't include hurting people.

Without giving it a second thought she said, 'How would you like to come and work for me?'

'For you. Like me and you?'

Dylan rolled her eyes. 'Yes, Cathy, me and you.'

Cathy's voice was tinged with ice. 'Depends. Will it be the new you or the old you?'

God was I really that bad a boss? Thinking about the way Dylan drove Cathy mad with her demands, Dylan conceded she might have been. 'The new me. I promise,' Dylan said. The new Dylan wouldn't be a walk over for a boss, but a fairer more considerate one.

Cathy laughed without humour. 'Good. Because if I'm honest, I didn't like the old you.'

'And if I'm honest, neither did I,' Dylan informed her wearily.

Cathy's face suddenly lit up with a genuine smile. Dylan was ashamed to admit it was the first time she'd seen Cathy without a scowl on her face.

'Cool, so you'll be in touch,' Cathy said. It wasn't a question, more like a statement. 'You know where to find me, but please don't leave it too long. I don't know how much longer I can handle that place.'

Dylan reached out and squeezed her forearm. 'Don't worry it'll be soon.'

'Cool. See ya then,' Cathy said brightly and turned to go, then glanced over her shoulder. 'Will I have to call you Ms Blue?'

Dylan rolled her eyes. 'Most certainly not!'

The drive home was done in a daze. As Dylan

caught the lift from the parking garage her mind was full of wonder. Could she do it, run her own company? Of course she could. The one thing Dylan couldn't do was represent the kind of people she had done whilst working at her father's firm. *Harper wouldn't like that.* The thought came out of the blue. What did it matter what Harper thought? It wasn't as if she was going to see her again any time soon.

The lift came to a stop and Dylan stepped out. The bottle of wine bouncing off her leg as she strode down the hall. As she rounded the corner she stopped abruptly, her heart leapt in her chest. Harper was sitting on the floor outside her apartment. Her head was down, looking at her phone. Knowing Harper hadn't seen her, Dylan thought about doubling back. Then realised how stupid it was. Where was she going to go exactly? She was home.

Dylan straightened her shoulders and continued walking. As she neared, Harper looked up. 'Hi,' she said using the wall to help her to her feet.

'Hi, yourself,' Dylan said, unlocking the front door and pushing it open. She stepped inside and glanced over her shoulder with an expectant look. 'Are you going to stand out there all night?'

Harper cocked her head. 'It's considered rude to enter someone's home without being invited in.'

Dylan laughed humourlessly. 'Are you joking? When has being rude bothered you before?'

Harper stuffed her hands into the pockets of her sheepskin jacket. 'Listen, I'm gonna lay my cards on the table alright. Once I've finished you can tell me to piss off, but at least we'll both know where we stand.'

'Go on then. I'm all ears,' Dylan said gesturing for Harper to follow her to the kitchen. Dylan placed the bottle in the fridge then turned to Harper. 'Have you come to blame me for—'

'—Will you just shut up for one minute. This isn't easy you know.'

Dylan folded her arms across her chest. *Just say it and put me out of my misery. You want nothing to do with me and you don't want me to darken your doorstep again, blah blah blah.* She couldn't understand why Harper didn't just call her instead of having to do it face to face. It was humiliating to say the least.

When Dylan remained silent, Harper rolled her eyes. 'You're not making this easy for me.' Harper's gaze dropped to the ground as she shifted her weight from foot to foot. Eventually she looked up. Her eyes narrowed as if she was about to deal a deadly blow. Dylan dropped her arms to her side and tightened her fists. *Here it comes.*

'Look I came to say sorry—'

'—Oh whatever, look ...' she started before Harper's words finally sunk in. Her face creased in confusion. 'Did I just hear you apologise?' she asked in astonishment. *Well, I didn't see that one coming.*

Harper gave a deep sigh. 'Yes, Dylan, I apologised.'

'For?'

Harper held Dylan's gaze with eyes that a woman could easily drown in.

'For blaming you for Abi's predicament. For saying all those horrible things to you. I was a bitch. You didn't deserve it.'

'So why say it?'

'Because...because I was angry with you.'

Dylan brushed the comment away with a careless hand. 'Tell me something new.'

'No really. I'm not saying my attitude towards you wasn't appropriate sometimes.' She smiled sheepishly. 'But not last time. It was cruel of me, but I wanted to punish you.'

'Well you did. In more ways than one.'

'Dylan, I'm sorry I hurt you.' Harper walked around the table and stopped in front of her. She combed her fingers through her hair and gave a small shake of her head. 'My emotions just get the better of me sometimes. It's just been so frustrating seeing you, wanting you and knowing that you didn't feel the same way.'

'Are you crazy?'

Harper's voice was low and soft. 'Yes. Crazy in love with you. There I've said it. I'm sorry if it's not what you want to hear, that you don't think of me as girlfriend material ...'

'Shut up and come here.' Dylan pulled Harper against her and wrapped her arms around her waist. Looking deep into her eyes she said, 'Harper Anderson, do you have any idea how much I love you?' She pressed her lips against Harper's. 'I knew you were trouble from the minute I laid eyes on you.'

Harper drew back slightly. 'Me?' she said with mock seriousness.

'Yes you. You've changed my world for the better, Harper.'

'That's exactly what love's supposed to do.' She wrapped her arms around Dylan's neck and leant in to kiss her. 'I'm looking forward to making it even better.'

Dylan parted her lips and welcomed Harper's inquisitive tongue. Her dad had always discouraged her from believing in fairy tale endings but Dylan was living proof they did exist. She was living one right now.

Chapter Forty-Eight

Things could not have got any worse even if lightning was to come down and strike her in the head. Robyn slammed her front door behind her. The anger inside her was all consuming. Who the fuck did that solicitor bitch think she was walking away from her case? Did she know who she was fucking with?

Robyn poked her head round the living room door and was surprised not to see Tiffany sat on her lazy arse. That woman had to go. Good looks and sex on tap was not enough anymore. She'd had her fill of women. If she never saw one again it wouldn't be too soon. *Fucking hell, even my own solicitor fucked me over, how bad can it get?*

Robyn thundered towards the kitchen, her impatience growing when she saw it was empty. She walked over to the fridge and slammed it shut with force when she saw it was bare. *That bitch was meant to do my shopping today.*

'Tiffany,' she yelled at the top of her voice. 'Tiffany, get down here right now. I said right now.'

Robyn listened for her footsteps. Hearing none she moved quickly to mount the stairs. 'I swear if you're fucking sleeping…' She reached the bedroom door and pushed it open. 'Did you…' her words trailed off. The bed was still made and Tiffany was nowhere to be seen. Frantically she checked the bathroom, her office and the two spare rooms. No sign of her.

Where the hell can she be?

Robyn dialled Tiffany's number on her phone. The line went dead. She redialled and was met with the same dead line. Had Tiffany forgotten to pay her bill? That was the only explanation. She would have serious words with her about financial responsibilities when she got home. Still annoyed, Robyn went back to her bedroom to change out of her suit into something more comfortable. At first she didn't notice there was more space in the wardrobe than usual. It was only when she hung up her jacket and didn't have to push the other clothes aside that she realised the amount of empty space there was. Frantically she checked the chest of drawers. It was the same. Only her clothes remained. 'No, no, no, no, no,' she screamed as she ran into the bathroom and opened the cabinet door. Every single trace of Tiffany was gone. It was as if she was never there. 'That bitch has done a runner,' Robyn said, her hands shook as she sat on the edge of the bath. She needed to calm down and get her thoughts together. *Come on think.* She pressed her palms against her eyes. *Where would she go?* Robyn sprang to her feet. 'Fuck, the bitch has got my money!'

She pulled out her phone in sheer panic. Her solicitor would advise her what to do. Barely able to get her thoughts straight, Robyn's clammy hand held onto her phone like it was her last lifeline. She felt some comfort hearing Debbie Brown's voice.

'Debbie, it's Robyn Massey.' She didn't bother exchanging pleasantries. 'That … Tiffany has done a runner. All of my stuff's still in her name. Help me out here. What do I do?'

The reply that came back caused Robyn to lose her balance and she sunk to her knees. Debbie's words rang loud and clear in her mind.

'There's nothing you can do. Your assets are legally hers. My best advice? Find her. Sooner rather than later.'

Adrenaline soon propelled Robyn to her feet. She had better get round to Tiffany's mum's place before she went on a spending spree.

An hour later, Robyn returned home without Tiffany and without her assets. Whether Tiffany's mum had been lying about not seeing her, Robyn didn't know, but whatever the case, Tiffany was gone. So it seemed was her money and stocks. *I am royally fucked!* She couldn't help but wonder if it was Tiffany's plan all along to fleece her. How could she have been so stupid thinking she could trust her? But Robyn had and that action had come back to bite her on the arse, hard. What was she going to tell her dad? He was already pissed off with her for stopping mediation and putting access to Jake at jeopardy. When she had told him about her plans to get custody of Jake he had threatened to cut her out of his will. Followed by saying 'A bird in the hand is worth two in the bush'. She supposed he was right. If she failed in her bid she could lose access to Jake altogether. There was no way she could risk losing her inheritance. Especially now.

Robyn walked over to the drinks cabinet and took out a bottle of brandy, pouring herself a large measure. The alcohol left a blazing trail of heat down her throat as she knocked it back in one go.

'You win, Tiff,' she said pouring herself another drink. She held it in the air in mock celebration. 'You always told me not to underestimate you. I should have listened.'

Robyn sat down in a reflective mood. *I should have listened to a lot of things.* Her mood mellowed into one of bitter acceptance. She had lost big time. She could just imagine Tiffany going through her money like water. Robyn seriously doubted there'd be any left by the end of a year. The shares themselves were worth more than she cared to remember. She forced her thoughts elsewhere. What was done was done. There was no point crying over spilt milk. She could make that money back in a few years. But if she ever caught sight of Tiffany again she would strangle her with her bare hands. For now Robyn had to concentrate on the future. She was on her own in this big empty house. It scared the living daylights out of her. She forced herself to take deep breaths. *How could this have happened to me? Why didn't I just stay with Abi?* The thought crossed her mind in a flash. Could she really go back to Abi? Robyn smiled warming to the idea of a readymade family. She figured she deserved to come out on top after all the shit Abi and Tiffany had put her through these last few months. Once she offered

Abi an olive branch Robyn was sure she would welcome her with open arms. Abi had loved her once so there wasn't any reason she couldn't do it again.

Chapter Forty-Nine

Abi bounced Jake up and down on her knee trying to think of a polite way to reply to Jennifer's question. *Is there any future for us?* As much as she liked her, Abi knew in her heart that there wasn't. She had been flattered by Jennifer's attention and did find her attractive but there wasn't any spark. Not one ounce of chemistry. It was a shame and a blessing at the same time. Yes, she would have liked some companionship. As much as Abi hated to admit it, she still hadn't got over Robyn despite her awful treatment of her. That wasn't to say that she would ever dream of rekindling their relationship. Abi would rather walk on hot coals before she did that. But she knew she had to give herself time to heal. To mend her broken heart. Such a feat was going to take longer than a few weeks or even months. When Abi loved she loved deeply so it wasn't a matter of just getting over her and moving onto the next one. Besides, she had Jake to think about. Especially his little lungs. Though it never interfered with her decision to not take things any further with Jennifer, she really didn't think it would be appropriate to be hanging out with someone who took drugs of any kind. It wasn't the example she wanted to set for her son.

As if reading her mind Jennifer said, 'Is this about me smoking weed? 'Cause if it is, I can tell you now

I'm not a junkie.'

'Don't be silly, I didn't think you were. And no it's nothing to do with the weed.' She squeezed Jake in her arms. 'I just wanna enjoy my son. It wouldn't be fair on you or anybody for me to try and commit to something. I don't think my heart is big enough for two at the moment.'

'I told you, I don't mind coming second. We could have something good, Abi, you me and Jake. I can look after you.'

Abi inwardly flinched. It was déjà vu. *That's exactly what Robyn said to me.* No, she wouldn't be travelling down that road again. She would look after herself. She didn't need to lean on anybody anymore—not even Tia.

'I appreciate that, Jen, but really I'm not ready.'

'When then?'

'I really don't know. Maybe never if how I'm feeling is anything to go by.'

'You're gonna go back to your ex aren't you?' Jennifer asked in an accusatory tone.

'What? No of course not...' Abi was saved by the bell ringing. 'I'd better get that, it might be my sister,' Abi said. She hoped it was. That way Jennifer would get the hint and leave. Abi didn't like where their conversation was going. With Jake planted firmly on her hip she hurried from the living room to the front door. The smile on her face faded when she saw who it was.

'You! What the hell do you want?'

Tiffany took a step back. 'Please calm down—'

'How the hell have you got the gall—'

'—Please hear me out. I don't have much time. I've gotta plane to catch. I just came by to give you this,' she said taking an envelope out of her pocket.

Abi looked at it suspiciously. 'What's this? Another trick? Are there drugs in there?'

'No, it's my way of saying sorry. Robyn told me so many lies about you. I thought you were a right cow, but I know the truth now.' She took off her sunglasses to reveal a black eye.

Abi's hand flew to her mouth. 'Oh my God, Robyn did that to you?'

Tiffany nodded. Her eyes glistened with tears. Despite her feelings of anger, Abi felt a pang of sympathy for the woman. She was so young. So naïve. How could Robyn have done such a thing?

'Anyway, I really am sorry about what I did to you.' Tiffany looked at Jake with sorrow in her eyes. 'I hope you both have a good life,' she said stuffing the envelope into Abi's hand.

'Wait until after the divorce to cash it, in case someone goes snoopin' in your bank account.'

Before Abi could ask her what she was talking about, Tiffany turned and ran for the stairs. Abi adjusted Jake on her hip and ripped the envelope open. Her jaw dropped. 'What the …' She squeezed her eyes shut, waited a few seconds, then opened them again. *No, I'm not dreaming.* In her hand was a cheque for £500,000.

'Hey, Abi, you're phones ringing.'

In a daze, Abi turned and Jennifer walked towards her, holding Abi's phone.

As Jennifer neared she said, 'Look, I'm gonna make a move. Let me know if you change your mind. See you at work.'

Abi was still at a loss for words. She nodded mutely as Jennifer brushed past her. The ringing of her phone brought her back down to earth with a thud. *£500,000. How can this be happening?* 'Hello?' she said answering the phone.

It was Harper.

'Are you okay, Abi?' There was concern in her voice.

'More than okay.'

'Well I've got good news. My guy managed to retrieve all of the emails Robyn sent you—'

'—It's okay, Harper. I don't think we are going to need them anymore. I just want this over and done with.'

'Are you sure?' Harper sounded doubtful. 'We can—'

'—Believe me, Harper, once I tell you what just happened, you'll know I couldn't be surer.' Abi breathed in a sigh of relief, knowing she would never have to ask Robyn for anything again, for herself or Jake. Abi was finally free and she vowed never to put herself in such a vulnerable position again, *for anyone.*

Chapter Fifty

Dylan jerked up into a sitting position. The water from the bath seeped over the edge onto the tiled floor. 'You have got to be kidding me.'

Harper smiled and blew a handful of bubbles in the air. 'Nope. Five hundred grand to the penny. The best thing is. It's legal. The money lawfully belongs to Robyn's girlfriend, sorry ex-girlfriend, and she can do whatever she wants with it.'

It almost seemed surreal that things would have turned out the way they had. At the beginning of the case she would never have thought there could be a happy ending. But there was. Harper had found love with a woman she could not have imagined only months earlier. So much had changed in her life in such a short amount of time. Her mother, Dylan, even the actions of Tiffany had proved to her that there was goodness in people if you just gave them a chance. Maybe somewhere along the line there was even hope for Robyn.

'I take it you're not going to declare Abi's sudden wealth?' Dylan asked cocking her head to the side.

'As far as I'm concerned it's hearsay. You know Abi's word isn't to be trusted. Robyn wrote that on paper in black and white. So I can't help but assume Abi's lying about her big windfall as well.'

Dylan pulled Harper up by her arms to meet her

half way. Soap suds slowly slid down their bodies.

'And you call me sneaky?' Dylan said.

'I think I called you a lot more than that.'

Dylan laughed. 'Yeah, that's true.' She gave a small shake of her head. 'Robyn must be spitting feathers right about now.'

'Serves her right, that'll teach her to think she's above the law.' Harper dabbed her finger on Dylan's nose leaving behind a small mound of fluffy white bubbles. 'At least now the case will be straightforward. She's agreed to the terms of the mediation. So hopefully no more threats about custody. Boy am I glad. This case is enough to put me off marriage for life.'

'I hope not,' Dylan said, taking Harper's hand in her own.

Harper's eyes dropped to Dylan's mouth. She would do just about anything to guarantee a lifetime of kissing her lips. 'Okay, maybe not.'

'I'm glad to hear it.'

'So that's Abi's life sorted. What about you? You got anything in the pipeline?' Harper asked.

'Actually I have…'

Harper reached under the water and slid her leg up Dylan's thigh.

Dylan let out a playful squeal and clamped her hand over Harper's to stop her going any further. 'No, not that.' Dylan grinned 'You really are insatiable aren't you?'

Harper pouted. It was true. She was. Usually she

could take or leave sex. But being around Dylan, she felt like she was on heat. 'It's your fault. You shouldn't be so sexy.'

Dylan brought Harper's hand to her face and gently kissed each of her finger tips. The warmth that spread through Harper's body had nothing to do with the temperature of the water.

'Back to your question. I'm thinking of starting my own practice.'

Harper's eyes widened. 'Really?' she asked trying to keep the surprise out of her voice. She was obviously a crap actress. Dylan sensed her doubt a mile off.

'You sound surprised.'

'To be honest, I wasn't convinced you wouldn't end up back working for your dad.'

Dylan didn't miss a beat. 'No way. I want to be a part of something that I'm proud of. Which brings me to you. I want us to be partners.'

'I thought we'd agreed to that already,' Harper teased.

'I meant—'

'—I was kidding. I know what you meant.' She stroked Dylan's cheek. 'Can I think about it? It's quite a big decision to make.'

Dylan's face dropped. 'Sure.'

Harper felt a sense of sadness when she saw the disappointment in Dylan's eyes. Harper was not an impulsive person by nature. Everything in her life was structured and well thought out. Could she really resign and take a step into the unknown with Dylan. It didn't take long for her heart to make the decision for her. Harper reached for the bottle of champagne by the side of the bath and refilled their glasses. She held hers mid-air. 'I'd like to propose a toast.'

'To?' Dylan replied half-heartedly.

Harper smiled. 'To our partnership of course.'

Dylan stared at her in disbelief. 'Are you having me on?'

'Nope.' Harper clinked Dylan's glass. 'Here's to us and a long and happy future.

Dylan leant forward and pressed her lips against Harper's. 'I'll drink to that.'

Chapter Fifty-One

Six months later

'I can't believe this is real,' Abi said, spinning in circles in the spacious living room of her new three bedroom house.

'Believe it, you deserve it,' Harper said watching her with a sense of pride. Over the last few months Abi had gone from strength to strength. After the divorce was finalised she seemed to have a new lease of life, especially after she told Robyn where to go when she'd tried to worm her way back in. Robyn had taken it quite literally and moved to Italy for a work promotion, only visiting Jake once a month. If Abi was upset about it she never said anything. She hardly mentioned Robyn at all. They all seemed to have landed on their feet. Blue and Anderson's solicitors was finally up and running. The added bonus for Harper was Shay making the move to their company as well. It would have been hard to leave her behind. Dylan had brought in her secretary, Cathy and the four of them had fallen into step behind each other easily.

Harper liked working with Dylan. She was constantly surprised by her dedication to help those that were in need. Dylan had finally restored her relationship with her father after a few weeks of no contact. He had told Harper when they met, that he was proud of his daughter and the good she was doing. Harper believed it to be a genuine statement.

'Right! Glasses, or cups at the ready, please,' Dylan said, smiling at Harper before popping the cork on the champagne bottle. She poured the fizzy liquid into four plastic cups, while Tia served young Jake with some apple juice for the occasion. Harper walked to Dylan's side and slid her arm around her waist as Dylan toasted, 'May we all, from the moment we entered this doorway ... enjoy only love, happiness and prosperity.'

The women cheered in agreement. Harper leant closer and whispered in Dylan's ear, 'I love you.'

'Love you too,' Dylan replied. Harper's heart skipped a beat as it always did when Dylan said those three little words.

The sound of a van pulling up outside caused them to turn their attention to the front door. 'I think the removal people are here.' Abi walked a little closer to the window. 'Oh no it's not.' She corrected herself. 'It's a delivery van.'

All eyes watched as the burly man moved to the back of his van and took out a large parcel. Seconds later he called through the open door, 'Anyone home?'

'In here,' the women called back in unison. The four of them looked at each other and laughed at the synchronicity.

The man appeared at the living room, breathless as he struggled to get the large flat parcel inside. 'Where'd you want it?' he said, as he dragged it into the middle of the room.

Abi's face creased in confusion. 'I don't know what it is,' Abi started.

'Just against the wall please,' Harper said to him, before turning to Abi. 'It's a housewarming gift for you.'

A wide smile spread over Abi's mouth. 'For me?'

Harper signed the delivery note and the man made a quick exit.

'Go on, open it,' Harper encouraged.

Abi walked over to the package and gently tore the wrapping from the massive frame. She gasped when the painting revealed itself. Her eyes filled with tears as she beheld the magnificent old painting of the Norse goddess with her stern eyes and majestic hair.

'Syn! You gave me Syn? Oh my God, Harper,' she shrieked ecstatically. Abi flung her arms around Harper and gave her a long endearing hug. 'Wow!'

They both looked at the regal oil painting.

'She'll be here to watch over you. Just as she has been all this time.' Harper glanced down at the engagement ring on her wedding finger and smiled. *Just like she has over me.*

Made in the USA
Columbia, SC
27 June 2017